SCENES FROM THE
SECOND STOREY

Published by Morrígan Books
Östra Promenaden 43
602 29 Norrköping
Sweden
www.morriganbooks.com

Editors: Amanda Pillar & Pete Kempshall

ISBN: 978-91-86865-00-9

Cover art by Reece Notley © 2010

First Published September 2010

SCENES FROM THE SECOND STOREY

EDITED BY AMANDA PILLAR & PETE KEMPSHALL

MORRIGAN BOOKS

AVAILABLE TITLES FROM MORRIGAN BOOKS:

IRON KHAN
BY LIZ WILLIAMS

HOW TO MAKE MONSTERS
BY GARY MCMAHON

VOICES
EDITED BY MARK S. DENIZ & AMANDA PILLAR

GRANTS PASS
EDITED BY JENNIFER BROZEK & AMANDA PILLAR

DEAD SOULS
EDITED BY MARK S. DENIZ

THE PHANTOM QUEEN AWAKES
EDITED BY MARK S. DENIZ & AMANDA PILLAR

REQUIEMS FOR THE DEPARTED
EDITED BY GERARD BRENNAN & MIKE STONE

DEDICATIONS

MARK S. DENIZ

The God Machine — for seventeen years of inspiration.

AMANDA PILLAR

Thank you to all those amazingly creative individuals who produce works of art on a daily basis for my, and other peoples', enjoyment.

PETE KEMPSHALL

To Mum and Kim for ensuring I had the right tools, to Lauren and Sean for making me proud every day and to Caroline for fifteen years of good reasons.

AMANDA & PETE WOULD LIKE TO THANK:

Ruth Shelton, Sharon Ring, Ian Mond and Adam Williams for their proof-reading and help. And, of course, Reece Notley for her brilliant cover.

FOREWORD

So where did it all begin? Definitely not in any traditional way you may have heard before, that's for sure...

It was the summer of '93, and I was a mere twenty-two years old, walking home from a shopping trip when I spied a cassette case on the ground. It was battered, a BASF cassette in a Sony case (don't you hate things like that?) with no writing anywhere on either the former or the latter. I had my Walkman with me — incidentally, I was listening to a New Order compilation I had made for myself — and I switched tapes, curious.

The anticipation turned to disappointment as I heard Kurt Cobain's familiar voice singing the chorus to 'Smells Like Teen Spirit', and even though I suspected *Nevermind*, I hoped it was a compilation. As I wound through the tracks, murdering the batteries in the Walkman, I was disappointed to find one side of the cassette was, indeed, Nirvana's cult classic. I already owned *Nevermind*, so it seemed there was no new music for me.

Yet there was still hope, for side B beckoned. And side B was...well, nothing I had heard before. There was a gravelly voice opening up the track, with something about us seeing life as an inexhaustible well ('Dream Machine'), before a song of such sheer power and intensity that I was smitten, right then and there.

But, and the big but, was that I had absolutely no idea who the band was. I walked home, going through the first five tracks; they were unmistakably the same artist. I had to hear the rest. I made the decision to take the tape to the two specialist record shops in the town to find out who the band was — I had to find out.

After dropping off my shopping, I began the twenty minute or so walk back into town, annoyed that my batteries died about halfway there, during a very powerful line about some things always being there if you dream ('Seven').

The first shop had absolutely no idea about who it was, even after asking the co-owner from the back, who was, to many of us in the town, a guru for quality music. This meant putting my faith in the 'lesser' specialist, who had only been in the town a few months. He put the tape in the stereo, pressed play and nodded along to the tune — but was this in acceptance of the quality or an indication that he knew who it was? I had to know.

"Yep, it's The Garden Machine," he said and I was at once relieved and disappointed. Relieved that I'd finally found out the band's name and disappointed at how terrible it was. I asked if he could get hold of the album and he said he would try and order it. I didn't like the 'try' in the answer and so went back to the real specialists and informed them who it was. They hadn't heard of the band, but said they'd look into ordering their albums.

So three weeks (and many rewinds and plays) later, I received a phone call from the second record store, saying they had my vinyl copy of The God Machine's *Scenes from the Second Storey*. Did the owner just say 'The God Machine'? That was a much better name.

I re-arranged my day and went to the store to pick up the LP, immediately buying a plastic sleeve for it and spending a few minutes just reading the title and the names of the tracks, tracks that I'd played extensively in the three weeks leading up to this. And, of course, none of the titles were the same as those I had given each song.

Before returning home with my prize, I popped into the other shop, apologised for giving them the wrong name and thanked them for having a look for me. They were fine about it, in fact, said it was strange as only just last week somebody had come in and asked them to order a copy of *Scenes from the Second Storey* by The God Machine. Owner of the cassette? Your guess is as good as mine.

SIDE B

Seventeen years on and not only does the album still resonate with me, inspire me and amaze me, but I dare to suggest that it is even better than it was then. The *I* that listened to the album as a twenty-two year old was only hearing a minute essence of what was contained within; even now I am at a loss to describe just how good the album is, in entirety and when thinking about each individual song.

The album has a darkness, a melancholy, which, clichéd as it seems, requires a bit of living to appreciate; there needs to have been some form of tragedy in life to fully get the album. Keats had it right when he talked about the understanding of both joy and sorrow. You could never really appreciate either without experiencing both. We need comparisons, we need references.

After many years of listening to the album, immersing myself in it time and time again, I decided I wanted to do a literary cover version — the ultimate homage. My musical skills, somewhat better than the singing of a dying cat, were certainly not adequate for this task. No, what I wanted was to write a collection of thirteen stories, each one an interpretation of a song from the album, attempting to do them justice with my own words, my own ideas.

More years passed with the collection yet to become a reality, but my experiences continued on in Keats' fashion. I immersed myself in publishing and editing, became accustomed to seeing how other writers worked; how their ideas emerged from the nascent to the tangible. I felt that my cover anthology might benefit more from other peoples' perspectives and I started to contact the writers whose work I admired, asking them about the possibility of writing a short story based on the song lyrics and music from the *Scenes* album.

While my love for this band is deep-seated, it came as no surprise to find that most of the authors I contacted were unfamiliar with either the band or the album, yet they were interested in the project. I had already worked closely with many Australian writers, so most of those I contacted in the beginning were Australians. I filled a book with thirteen authors very quickly. However, I did have writers I wanted to work with from other countries as well, and that led to the decision to publish two books, both of which I would edit and both of which would be a homage to both the album and a complement to each other.

Of course, now my book was no longer a mere idea, Murphy had to raise his head — a massive workload at Morrigan Books meant that editing two books was practically impossible. I asked my in-house editor, Amanda Pillar, to work with Morrigan Books' contributor Pete Kempshall, to edit the Australian version. I then contacted my long time proof-reader/editor/friend, Greg Ballam, to work on the international version with me.

Whichever of the versions you have in your hand (I sincerely wish that you have both), I hope you enjoy the stories within — excellent stories all — crafted by writers with a real eye (and ear, it seems), for the story inside a story.

Perhaps after submerging yourself in the quality to be had within the pages, you will consider it time to listen to one of the best, most inspiring albums of all time.

Mark S. Deniz
July 2010

CONTENTS

DREAM MACHINE

DAVID CONYERS

In time, Adamson was made whole again.

For an eternity he had existed only as dissected body parts, quantum parcels of flesh that endured every imaginable pain. Some were fried in oil. Others were frozen, then shattered with a hammer or electrocuted with currents of varying intensity. A few were chewed in the mouths of demons that would never swallow. Testicles were squeezed in pliers until they bled and bruised. Iron nails were hammered into fingers. Maggots fed upon lips. Ears were serrated on cheese graters.

Adamson felt it all.

Only his eyes and mouth were left intact. Fish hooks held taut by wire suspended these organs inside the frame of a metal box. The box sat upon a conveyor belt which trundled through every level of Hell, visiting each portion of his tortured flesh on a circular route, ensuring that no stimuli associated with his pain were missed. His eyes watched. His mouth screamed.

It hurt just as much when they put him back together again.

They first rebuilt his head. Impish, ashen-skinned creatures collected and catalogued his returned parts and sewed them together with the care of delicate tailors. When his skull was made whole with binding rivets, and the flesh on his face was properly layered — now resembling a completed jigsaw puzzle — he was suspended from a mesh of wires, pulleys, hooks and pins, a frame upon which to build the rest of him. It was then that Adamson received his first visitor.

Hell's Overlord burnt with the blinding light of a furnace. His skin reflected the embers of fire. His every footstep scorched black the hot stone floor. Imps too slow to scamper from his path were trampled before they ignited.

"How long do you think it's been?" the Overlord's voice crackled. His breath was like petrol fumes riding the air on a hot Earth summer day.

Now that Adamson had a throat again, he swallowed. A conservative guess was best. Hard-learned experience taught that boasting only worsened one's situation in Hell. "Ten thousand...maybe twelve thousand years?"

The Overlord's blistering grin was thin. "Seventy-six years, Mr. Adamson. It feels a lot longer in Hell, doesn't it?" He leant close, his breath burning Adamson's flesh.

Adamson didn't care about the scorching heat as he knew burning, understood that kind of pain. "Why are you putting me back together?"

"You stopped screaming, Mr. Adamson. For five years, not a peep out of you."

Adamson nodded, realising only now that he had been silent for a very long time. There wasn't a pain he could now imagine that he hadn't already endured and grown used to. "So what's next?"

The Overlord brightened like a flaring sun. "We'll talk about that later, when you are complete."

X

Adamson's flesh was fused with metal. When he had a torso, when bones included everything down to his lumbar vertebrae, and his arteries were networked sufficiently so his heart could pump once more, he finally accepted that his body would never again be completely human. Metal rods and bolts became the foundation upon which his muscles, sinews, fat and skin were rebuilt. In time, his upper torso resembled a rusted suit of medieval armour. Its metal pinched, rubbed, blistered, stabbed, serrated and cut at his flesh, but he expected that. In his experience, no action was ever taken in Hell that was absent of pain.

One hundred and eight days later, Adamson was finished.

With his new fingers, Adamson explored his outer skin. String, rubber bands, piano wire and the pincers of decapitated bull ant heads held his flesh together. He discovered a helmet that folded as segments into the back of his armour, ready to flip up and over to conceal his head completely.

"You'll want clothes," said an imp, and the creatures began their fastidious work, sewing aprons of leather into a melange of pants and boots. Like his armour, they were integrated with his flesh.

Six days later, Hell's Overlord visited to admire his minions' work.

"You are ready now."

"Ready for what?"

"Your training, Mr. Adamson."

A hand like the sun reached behind Adamson, grabbed the segmented helmet and snapped it shut over Adamson's head. For the first time in seventy-six years, the world became dark and silent.

X

Adamson snatched back the helmet and was surprised by the stillness of the world where he found himself.

The constant crackling and screams, of blistering winds, of manic laughter, it was all gone. This new dimension was controlled by darkness, so different to the brilliant, searing light that had blinded him every day. His skin was cold here as if Arctic winds blew upon it. Water dripped far away, heard from many places. There were whispers of voices asking half-formed questions, begging for ill-defined assistance. Adamson strained to understand what they were saying, but there were too many, and they were more elusive than the pained screams that he had become familiar with.

He waited for his eyes to adjust to the near dark...and discovered dank stone corridors without windows or end; a labyrinthine crypt.

"What is this place?"

No one answered him.

In Hell, there was always someone or something that would torment. Here no one seemed to listen. He was just one more whisperer, talking to himself.

Adamson stumbled through the darkness, feeling every nail and broken shard of glass sewn into his flesh, cutting with every flex of his muscles. Thousands upon thousands of endless corridors echoed with more than just the sounds of his footsteps. If he were to move a little faster, he felt he might catch up with another lost traveller, someone he expected to hear just around the next turn. But he never saw another soul.

There were always stairs leading up or down, and even sideways, and pits that fell to lower floors, or openings in the ceiling to higher levels. There were no windows. There were no doors. Light shone but it had no origin. Shadows moved and Adamson suspected rodents, though he never saw one.

In time he discovered the paintings.

There were scenes of so many subjects, most from a high perspective as if seen from a floor one level up. All were painted in dark, light-absorbing colours. Some were of men and women, or monsters, posing artistically even though they appeared to be long dead. Others were of nothing in particular; a stream, a corner in a room, the surface of a kettle, the fur of an unidentified animal — yet all promised to reveal a sinister truth that existed just beyond the edges of the frame. They had a sense of gravity about them, as if they were the easiest things to fall into. Each was framed in old wood, cracked and mouldy, and most hung crooked. Adamson tried to pull some down, but none could be removed from where they hung, as if they were fused with the wall as completely as he was fused into his new body.

Later, he discovered paintings with subject matters that felt more complete. The first depicted a lounge with many couches on which lay various people, each in a state of drug-induced bliss. Drips fed them. Medical staff wandered amongst them, observing with detached interest.

Another painting was of a school playground. Kids were playing, dancing. They too looked happy. Adamson didn't like this painting, not until he spotted a shadow creeping into the scene that might have been cast by an intruding camera.

The painting next to it had no people, but it suggested something unpleasant was about to occur, and Adamson could only admire the artist's subtle brilliance. It was of a lighthouse and a small cottage with a hole in its roof. Between the two buildings was a beaten-up truck. It only required someone suffering to feel complete, and Adamson felt that someone would walk into the scene at any moment.

After ten thousand or more paintings, Adamson passed a scene that made him look twice, even though it was more mundane than others he had seen. Perhaps it was the subject matter that stopped him, but he doubted it. For a second, he felt intense heat burning his back as his shadow gained definition, but only for a moment.

He thought upon Hell's Overlord who had put him here, and realised this was not a coincidence.

He looked at the painting again, wondering why he must stop now. The depicted scene was a corridor, of wooden walls, floor and ceiling, damp and cracked and old. The light wasn't right, as if the dull luminosity in Adamson's world had crept into the picture. The corridor seemed to be out of proportion, as if the left wall was far longer than the right. At its end, there was a single olive-green door with a faded yellow star positioned in its centre. There was a key in the lock. It was like all the other paintings, nothing different about it in its unsettling blandness and obscurity.

Adamson strained his serrated ears. He heard noise wafting from the room, of a woman humming a muffled song. Suddenly, he understood where the whispered noises he heard everywhere originated, but the more he tried to distinguish individual words coming from the scene, the more elusive they became.

He touched the painting, but he didn't fall into it as he had expected to.

Adamson remembered how he had been transported to this world, through the closure of his helmet. Perhaps that was the key to entering the paintings. He unfolded it quickly, shrouding himself in darkness.

<h1 style="text-align:center">X</h1>

He hastily removed his metal mask. The corridor was stretching now that he was inside, lengthening as he walked towards the olive-green door with its star shining for him. His hands seemed to stretch away from his body when he reached out, like they had become spaghetti. His head felt light, as if he were spinning and the world was rotating counter to his turns.

He grabbed the door handle, rattled it.

The singing abruptly ceased.

Adamson twisted the key, flung open the door.

He saw a hotel room, dirty and hot. The single window looked out across a dusty street in some forgotten desert town. An attractive woman lay upon the bed, wearing only knickers and a tight-fitting singlet that came down to her bellybutton. Considering his hideous appearance, she should have been terrified of him, but she wasn't, as if she'd encountered his kind too often in the past. Confidently, she pointed a revolver with stylised demons etched into its metal. Adamson didn't even have time to blink as he was shot through the chest.

The pain was indescribable, even for a man who believed he had sampled every torment imaginable. His chest became cold, like there were needles swimming through his flesh, but it was an agony far worse than that.

He fell to the floor.

The woman stepped over him, spat on him. She looked inconvenienced and angered by his sudden appearance in her private moment. "Tell the Overlord that he'll have to send better than you if he wants me dead."

She raised the weapon to shoot him again.

"Tell him that scum..."

He snapped his mask over his face and the world went dark again.

X

Adamson opened his helmet with trepidation. To his relief, he had returned to the same dank corridor. He was lying before the same painting, only this time it depicted an open door and the woman standing in it, silhouetted in its frame. She held her demon revolver, but she no longer appeared threatening; she looked dead to him now.

Time inside the painting had come to a standstill.

But time had not stopped for Adamson.

The pain still wracked him. Cold spread quickly through

7

his body like cracks forming on the surface of a frozen lake, ready to shatter. He could barely move. It was impossible to stand, so he dragged himself down the dank corridors, searching for...what? He did not know.

He felt that he should die, but didn't. He had forgotten that in Hell, death was never an end. He realised that perhaps this was still Hell, only another level of which he'd been previously unaware.

He passed more paintings, while bleeding an endless supply of his boiling blood wherever he dragged his corpse-like hulk.

Eventually he found a scene depicting a surgery.

He snapped shut his helmet.

X

Adamson's visor was opened for him.

He was strapped by leather belts to an operating table. Thick, green, dirty paste in clear translucent bottles dripped into tubes that in turn fed his veins. Surgeons in green smocks walked with bare feet over a muddy floor littered with broken glass, rusted nails and black oily serpents. Faces barely concealed behind their surgical masks had lost their symmetry, as if their flesh had melted and warped, their eyes had enlarged or shrunk, and mouths split from ear to ear. The walls were the fabric of tents, held aloft by wooden struts and splashed with blood. Adamson could hear rotating blades moving in the unseen skies above, and a distant soldier telling his underlings to "Shoot the fucking Vietcong chink in the head", then gunshots.

"That's a demon bullet you've got in you, soldier," said the lead surgeon, acknowledging Adamson. He plunged a serrated knife into Adamson's chest and began to saw.

Adamson felt the pain of the cut, but it was nothing compared to the ice spreading through his body. "Am I going to die?"

Thick, black oil dribbled from behind the surgeon's mask as he laughed. "You'd be so lucky." He stabbed again, spraying an attending nurse with Adamson's steaming blood, disintegrating her skin where it touched her. She seemed not to care, licking the corruption away with her barbed tongue.

"Where am I?"

"Does it matter? It's all the same in this place, just variations on a theme."

"I don't understand."

"You talk a lot for a soldier who's supposed to be under."

"But I'm not under."

"Are you sure? All your vitals say that you are."

"But I'm not. I'm talking to you."

"You are under. I'm the doctor. So shut up."

He cut again.

Adamson let them work, pretending to be unconscious while listening to distant, irregular gunfire and explosions.

He was not alone inside the field hospital. Other men and women strapped on other tables were cut apart and put back together again by more demonic surgeons. Most of them screamed; he figured them to be Hell's rookies. Not Adamson though, he was done screaming. He'd screamed enough for a thousand lifetimes.

When they pulled the bullet from Adamson it clawed and bit at his flesh, desperate to remain inside him. The surgeon had the creature clamped between the barbs of rusted prongs that were icing where they held the monstrosity. He threw it squirming into a metal dish where he splashed it with a beaker overflowing with caustic, bubbling liquid. The bullet wailed mournfully as it dissolved, but it didn't disappear completely. Like Adamson, it couldn't die.

With the bullet removed, the icy pain vanished, and they

sewed him back together.

"You're done, soldier."

The lead surgeon snapped shut Adamson's helmet.

X

Complete again, Adamson returned to the painting of the woman. During the time he had been away, she hadn't moved or changed at all. She remained silhouetted in her door, trapped.

If he returned to the scene, he thought, she wouldn't have seen him leave, and would shoot him again. He was not yet ready to face her, but that didn't mean he didn't want to, when he was prepared. Time, for once, was on his side.

Adamson considered his options. If the surgeons in one painting could rebuild him, surely a warrior in another could train him.

Adamson explored. So many levels, so many paintings; eventually he found what he was searching for — a monastery set high on snow-capped mountains overlooking a vast, lifeless tundra. He was drawn by the halberds, scimitars, shields and maces that littered its entrance.

Adamson had found what he needed.

X

Covered in snow, Adamson stepped through the monastery's golden gates, forged from wailing mouths that bit at him when he pushed his hand against their metal. Dark storm clouds rumbled over the mountains, forking lightning.

Inside the courtyard he encountered a warrior nun, perfectly still in deep mediation upon the cold grey slabs of stone flooring. Her features were all wrong to his eyes, everything in alignment with the vertical. Two eyes sat above each other, the mouth rotated so the slit pointed towards the nostrils, also arranged vertically. Her elbows branched into two forearms, her wrists into four hands, and then into forty fingers. Her legs were similarly augmented, like broccoli.

To her left and right, were two long walls of millions of chaotically arranged metal blades.

When she sensed his presence she stood silently and took up a sabre, which until that moment had remained concealed beneath her red satin robes. She advanced, swinging and swishing the blade in a complex motion while her body moved through the steps of a practised martial routine. She demonstrated her moves five more times, each occurrence with the same honed perfection. Then she passed the sabre to Adamson.

He attempted to repeat her moves, which he discovered were complicated and precise. Every time he made a mistake she demonstrated the entire routine again. He paid attention because he had learned long ago to be patient through any adversity Hell could throw at him. After his first six attempts she stepped backwards, indicating that he must stand midway between the two walls of blades. A cluster of hands indicated that he should prepare to practise her teaching again.

Adamson moved to begin but her raised finger stopped him. She stepped back, away from the space between the walls.

With no other option, Adamson complied. He was prepared for a single knife to attack him, but not the entire wall of blades rushing around him, cutting, swishing, stabbing at every space in between — except the places where he should be in order to master the exercise.

He was cut to pieces many, many times.

He didn't need the field hospital here: dissected, his body parts crawled together until they were whole again. All the while, the warrior nun remained still and silent, except to occasionally instruct him when he became stuck. Her patience was infinite.

After many months of intense learning, eventually Adamson could perform his teacher's more basic manoeuvres without a single scratch. On that day, she awarded him a weapon, her sabre, and sent him on his way.

X

He returned into the painting of the woman. She hadn't moved since he had left her, and she finished the sentence she had started back then "...like you don't..."

He swung his sabre with lightning speed. She wasn't prepared for his newfound skill — his weapon separating her head from her body before she could squeeze the trigger of her weapon for a second time.

X

"You are learning, Mr. Adamson," said Hell's Overlord, speaking from the canvas of a painting through which he had chosen to communicate with him. It was burning to cinders while they spoke. "I'm impressed."

"Who was she?"

"Does it matter?"

Despite the constrictions of his armour, Adamson shrugged. In the scheme of all things cosmic and godlike, people's lives really were inconsequential, but he wanted to know anyway. He wanted it to be personal.

For some reason, the Overlord answered him. "Her name was Molly. She betrayed an agent of mine operating in Australia called Synder. I had to teach her a lesson. Molly's with me now, thanks to you, being dissected and distributed to my torture factories as we speak."

"They are just meaningless names."

"Exactly."

"You waste my time, telling me nothing." He'd wanted emotion. He'd wanted to understand why she deserved the Overlord's pain, what she had done that had been so awful.

The painting burnt to black dust. Adamson walked to the next frame where he knew the Overlord would be waiting for him, burning into its canvas.

"You're turning into a smartass, Mr. Adamson. I don't like it when my subjects think they know better than me."

Adamson shrugged again. It was true he felt confident. The application of his newly perfected skills had resulted in a successful mission, giving him a new sense of accomplishment and power. He felt he had won the right to bask in his moment of glory. "I'm your assassin, correct? Hell's Assassin on Earth."

"If the name pleases you, take it."

Adamson grinned for the first time in an eternity.

"Do you know why you came into my care, Mr. Adamson? Do you remember?"

Feeling unsettled and not sure why, Adamson tried to recall why he had been sent to Hell. Dismembered and tortured for so long, he had forgotten that he'd once been a man on Earth. He tried to recall those memories, but they remained elusive.

"No, Mr. Adamson?"

"It's been so long."

"Then let me show you again, shall I? Why don't you stare into your dream machine?"

Hell's Overlord vanished from the painting, but he did not appear in another as Adamson expected.

So Adamson waited. Patience was his greatest virtue. Patience was the only way to survive Hell.

In time he heard a machine, gurgling, burping, farting and hissing.

Adamson walked towards the noise and turned a corner,

seeing the machine — a conglomerate of a hundred pale human bodies knitted together into one organism — appearing from nowhere and looking completely out of place in the dark, dank corridors. Human arms, legs, buttocks, feet, hands, breasts, sexual organs, backs, abdomens and necks twisted in and out of each other as one great machine. Heads were not visible, tucked inside.

A fat belly in its centrepiece danced with a scene projected onto it like a motion-picture film, of a man and a woman huddled together in a snow-covered park. The man wore a trenchcoat and a fedora, the woman her best velvet Sunday dress. They both looked cheap, poor, like they lived on the street, and they shivered against the cold.

Beneath the scene, human knuckles with letters and numbers carved into their flesh represented the keys on a typewriter. The words PRESS ENTER TO PLAY flashed beneath the still image.

Adamson spied a knuckle with the word ENTER, so he pressed it.

CENTRAL PARK, NEW YORK, WINTER 1933

Adamson tried to remember when he had last been in New York. Now that Hell's Overlord had prompted him to think about his human past, the date held meaning for him. It was the time of the Depression. The man in the scene had no work. He was always hungry. He had forgotten what warmth could feel like. He had just been evicted from the men's hostel for beating one of the younger kids.

Adamson remembered this man; the face hidden between the up-turned collar of the coat and the brim of the hat was him.

The woman took his hand in hers, held it daintily. "Barry, I love you very much. You know that, don't you?"

He said nothing. He was cold to her.

"Barry, I want you to come back home."

"We don't have a home. We got evicted."

"But we can make a new home together, here." She held his hand to her heart.

"No we can't. It's over, kid."

For a long moment she stared into his eyes, looking for something, anything that he might be holding back, a laugh perhaps, even a crooked smile, but he gave her nothing.

She cried then. Tears streaming down her face froze before they could run off her jaw. "Barry, I'm pregnant."

He said nothing. He went rigid.

Adamson remembered then that he had decided to never say another word to her.

He punched her hard in the gut. The wind was knocked out of her, she couldn't even scream, and something inside her died. She crumbled into the snow, curled into a ball and lay still, whimpering.

The man just walked away.

Adamson remembered how this story ended. She died.

They didn't find her body until the spring thaw. When the police came to arrest him, they arrived in just enough time to watch him blow his brains out with a pistol.

X

He remembered now why he was in Hell, and with the memory came the pain of the associated emotions, worse than any horror Hell's Overlord had subjected him to, or even the pain of Molly's demon bullet that was ice inside his very veins. Forgetting the kind of monster he had been when he was a man had been his only salvation, his only means of survival, and that had taken decades to accomplish. His mind was the one place Hell's tormentors could not touch, or so he had once believed. Only when he forgot what he had done to the girl he had lied to and cheated on could he be strong again, and rise.

But it was not all lost for Adamson. He was free in a twisted sense of the idea — since he was no longer dissected and tortured in minute portions — he could roam of his own accord in this maze. And there was always the hierarchy in Hell to give him hope. He'd been promoted once, he could be promoted again. He had tens of thousands of paintings or more to explore, gateways leading to many more people who the Overlord wanted dead. As Hell's Assassin, he had purpose again.

All he had to do now was forget, hide himself from the love he had once expressed, the love inside him that made him weak and that he had loathed, but he could only do so by focusing on something other than himself.

In the coming days, he found his next painting; saw his shadow defined for a moment over its subject matter. He stared into the scene from the second storey and at the next victim he was commissioned to murder.

AFTERWORD

My contribution to *Scenes from the Second Storey* came about several years ago when I submitted a short story to an anthology Mark Deniz was editing called *In Bad Dreams II*. Mark liked my submission but felt it didn't fit thematically. However, he liked it enough to ask me to write the opening tale to the Australian collection of *Scenes from the Second Storey*. What else could I say but yes?

I knew nothing about The God Machine or the album at the time, but was intrigued and agreed to tackle the story. When I first heard the opening track, 'Dream Machine', I was impressed with its imagery and realised I already had a story plotted that would be ideal. Trouble was, I'd been listening to another album by another artist, Barry Adamson's *As Above, So Below* (Mute Records, 1998), particularly the track 'Jazz Devil'. I had been hoping to write a story inspired by that song, only I couldn't work out how to bring it together. After listening to 'Dream Machine', suddenly the same idea was speaking to me from two tracks, and so I had only one choice; to combine the two influences into the one tale.

'Jazz Devil' gave me the narrative framework. The main character's name is a nod to Barry Adamson's fine work, although the character is nothing like him. Mr. Adamson in real life is a very fine musician who I admire and respect.

The God Machine's 'Dream Machine' gave me the imagery for the story, such as the Sunday velvet dress, the protagonist talking to himself yet no one listening, the shining star and so forth. The track opens with a sample from the movie adaptation of *The Sheltering Sky*, a film and novel I'd enjoyed long ago that then gave me the idea for the failed relationship between Hell's Assassin and his girlfriend.

I also decided to include reference to the album name, hence all the paintings viewed as if seen from up high, from "the second storey". I suggested to the editors, Pete and Amanda, that perhaps I could include paintings that looked in at "scenes" from other stories in this book. They both liked the idea, and so I included three. I leave it to the reader to work out which story is related to what painting.

Lastly, 'Dream Machine' is part of a series of interconnected horror short stories I have been writing for a few years which include 'Cactus' (*Midnight Echo* #1, 2008), 'The Lord of the Law' (*The Fourth Black Book of Horror*, Mortbury Press, 2009) and 'Hell's Ambassador' (*Black Box*, Brimstone Press, 2008), so naturally they inspired some of the back story in 'Dream Machine'.

BIOGRAPHY

David Conyers is an Australian science fiction author residing in Sydney. His fiction has appeared in *Jupiter, Book of Dark Wisdom, Midnight Echo, Antipodean SF*, and *Andromeda Spaceways* as well as a dozen anthologies published worldwide. He is the co-author of the novel *The Spiraling Worm* and editor of the horror anthology *Cthulhu's Dark Cults*, both published in the United States. David has been a multiple nominee for the Aurealis, Australian Shadows and Ditmar Awards, won the Australian Horror Writers Association's Flash Fiction Award in 2007 and was shortlisted for the Aeon Award in the same year. He is also a reviewer for *Albedo One*, Ireland's magazine of speculative fiction.

www.davidconyers.com

SHE SAID

KIRSTYN MCDERMOTT

Finally, the sound of weeping stopped and Mallory hobbled out of the bedroom on legs that seemed to grow both thinner and whiter with each new day. She clutched an empty baby food jar in one hand and stared at me through the shards of her uneven, grease-black fringe.

"You'll need this," she said. "For the clouds." And she coughed, harsh and hacking, skinny ribs hitching high with each hard-drawn breath, and spat something dark and clotted into the jar. She held it out to me with trembling, blood-scabbed fingers and I took it, trying not to look too closely at the contents.

"Mix it with indigo," she said, as she wiped a smear from her chin.

"Mal?"

"For the clouds."

"Mal, come sit with me a bit." My invitation was less than half-hearted and I hoped the relief didn't show on my face when she shook her head.

"I'm going back to bed, Josh. I'm tired." She paused at the bedroom door, scratched her thigh through the ratty black slip she'd been wearing for longer than I cared to think about. "Do some fucking good with that, yeah?"

The bedroom door closed almost soundlessly behind her. I retrieved a tube of Indigo Blue from the mess scattered over the floor, squeezed about half of it into the jar Mallory had given me. I started to stir, slowly, carefully, blending colour and consistency to something new, something no one had ever quite seen before and as I did, the skin on the nape of my neck crawled. I could already see the paint moving over the canvas, wet and violent and alive, could feel it sliding beneath my brush with a purpose all its own.

I turned to the half-finished cityscape that loomed from the easel by the window: my abandoned, nameless city with its buildings left to rust and rot and ruin, left to cower and hope beneath the threat of an oncoming storm which must surely mean its end. Massive thunderheads little more than charcoal sketches because I'd been uncertain how to render them.

Until now.

As I lifted my brush to the canvas, as I felt the paint flow thick and eager from the bristles, I could see the end, how it needed to be finished. I could see the promise that glimmered beneath the threat, the mercy inherent in destruction. My hand steadied, and worked.

Hours later, I pushed my face into Mallory's neck while we fucked. Her sickly, sweat-stale smell filled my nostrils, seeped down the back of my throat; even then it was better than looking at her. Better than having to meet that weepy, red-rimmed gaze and pretend. But she knew. Turned away as soon as we were done, her fragile foetal curl on the edge of the mattress familiar as breathing now, and I knew better than to try and touch her again. Even if I'd wanted to.

Instead: "I think the painting's done, Mal. I think you'll like it."

She whispered something into her pillow.

I swallowed. "You'll see it in the morning, anyway."

Minutes dragged by unanswered, the dry scrape of sandpaper on skin, and just as I was beginning to hope she'd drifted off to sleep, Mallory sighed and rolled back over to face me.

"I know about her, Josh," she said.

X

Fiona. Fee. My dirty little secret, not so much it seemed.

I'd bumped into her on the street, literally, *crashed* into her as I'd come out of the art supplies place on Greville, head down, suspiciously counting the change the emo kid behind the counter had dumped into my hand. I didn't see the girl 'til I'd almost knocked her over, knocked the breath from her lungs with a small, startled *oh!*, knocked the cardboard carton she'd been carrying from her hands.

Then suddenly, magically, the air was full of feathers.

Thick and white and swirling all around us as though someone had exploded an angel, or a pillow factory, and *oh!* the girl said again, softer this time, and grinned. I was grinning too, trying to apologise as I brushed the feathers from my shirt. A handful had come to rest in her hair and, without thinking, I reached out to pluck them from her ash-blonde curls.

"Sorry," I said again. "I didn't see you."

"Don't worry about it," she told me. "This was so much better than whatever he had planned for them."

She'd been dropping off the box for an artist friend who was working on some kind of an installation to do with animal liberation, or sleep deprivation, she couldn't remember which. Shrugging, the girl shook a few more feathers from the hem of her brightly coloured skirt. I was fixated on her arms, so smooth and tanned, jangling with a dozen or more gaudy plastic bracelets.

"Are you an artist too?" I asked.

"Me?" A coy, sideways tilt of her head. "More an artist's assistant. Admiration and inspiration, that sort of thing."

"And plumage procurement."

"Yes, sometimes that as well." She held out a hand.

"Fiona."

"Josh." Her skin was warm, her grip purposeful. She looked about ten years younger than me, maybe in her early twenties, twenty-five tops.

"Well, Josh, my fine new friend, I think you owe me a coffee." She slipped around to my side, hooked her arm through mine and flashed me another brilliant, straight-toothed smile. "At the very *least*."

I could have said no. I *should* have said no, should have gone straight back home with my tubes of paint and the new Size 4 sable brush I couldn't really afford. Back home where Mallory would have been waiting with her nails gnawed down to the bloody quick and her eyes full of thunder and hurt.

Instead, I followed Fiona to her favourite café and then, later, back to her flat in St Kilda. We sat on her sixth-floor balcony with a bottle of wine, looking out over the bay and arguing, good-naturedly, about whether or not we could discern a curve in the horizon from that height.

"So, you're a painter," she said at some stage. "Any good?"

"Sometimes yes, sometimes definitely not."

"We might have to see about that."

Evening had crept up on us; I could barely make out her features in the growing darkness. But I leaned forward anyway, and kissed her. Slowly at first and then, with her lips moving against mine, more urgently. I caught her hair in my fists, tangled those soft, pale curls around my fingers.

Finally, she pulled away. "It's not going to happen tonight, Josh."

But her smile was wolfish, and more than a little regretful, as she pulled me to my feet and sent me off, alone, into the dusk.

X

Sunk deep into the sagging centre cushion of our couch, Mallory pulled the blanket tighter around her shoulders. A scab on her left knee was flaking and she scratched at it, absently.

"I don't know, Josh. There's something...missing?"

She was right, she was always right. The painting was done, done as I felt I could make it, but it wasn't finished. The abandoned city, the brooding storm-laden sky; it wasn't enough, it didn't sing, or even mutter. More and more, I felt trapped by the canvas, caught within the very oppression I had been attempting to create.

And I couldn't help but think of the other canvas I'd been working on over the past few weeks, the one Mallory didn't know about, could never know about. The painting that currently resided high up in a certain sixth-floor St Kilda flat. My huge, half-finished portrait of a girl with ash gold curls and a grin coaxed straight from a fairy tale.

"I'm done, Mal." I rubbed at my forehead. "It's done."

"No, you're not, and no, it's not either."

I shook my head, refused to meet her eye. The buildings I'd painted reminded me of her somehow. Those empty, abandoned facades agape with broken windows like the teeth she'd lost just the other day. A sharp-pointed incisor and its less interesting neighbour, offered on a shaky, flattened palm for my inspection. *They just fell out, Josh. They fell right out of my mouth.* A childish wonderment in her voice, but also, unmistakably, fear.

"You'll find it," Mallory said from the couch, and sniffed.

"Find what?"

"The way through. You always do, in the end."

"Mal—" I turned, and whatever I was about to tell her slid away as I saw the runnel of blood edging sluggishly from her left nostril. Revulsion kicked at my guts. Revulsion, and something else besides. "Mal, your nose."

She frowned and sniffed again, extended the tip of her tongue above her lip to catch a smear of scarlet. "Oh." Her hands disappeared beneath the blanket for a few seconds before resurfacing with one of her empty little jars, and she leaned forward, one hand pushing her hair out of her face, the other holding the jar carefully beneath her nose. Blood seeped down the clear glass sides as I watched, pooling toxic-thick at the bottom.

And I could see the buildings in my painting bleeding like that. Just like that. Weeping bitter streams of rust and corrosion from every crack and windowless crevice. Not simply waiting for the storm, but falling before it, flowing apart at the edges. Forsaken, even by each other. *Forsaken.* The word tasted swollen and hollow and cold as I whispered it beneath my breath.

It tasted of surrender. It tasted *right.*

"Josh?" Mallory was sitting up again, the jar resting on her thigh. It held an alarming amount of blood. "Yes?" she whispered.

"I think so," I replied. "Yes."

Her lips parted in a faltering, gap-toothed smile and as she lifted the jar up to me, its contents glinting dark and crimson in the failing afternoon light, I leaned over and kissed her, my fingers closing over hers and over the jar, and I tasted the blood still smeared beneath her nose.

And just for now, that tasted right as well.

X

"Let me see." Fiona rose from the wicker chair and retrieved her robe from the floor. It was bright blue and patterned with huge orange flowers, one of which sat over her left breast like a mutant, six-fingered hand as she tied the belt loosely around her waist. I could make out the dark circle of her nipple through the flimsy, semi-sheer fabric.

"Who said the man couldn't paint?" Fiona nudged me with her elbow. "It's beautiful, Josh. Seriously, it's amazing, and I'm not just saying that 'cause it's me. The way you've made it so it almost *glows*, that's...wow."

"It's not quite finished yet, I don't think."

"Really? It looks finished."

The truth was, I didn't *want* it to be finished. I didn't want to give up these mornings in Fiona's lounge room, watching the sun as it spilled through window glass and over her naked curves, watching the rise and fall of her chest deepen whenever she slipped lightly into a doze. But the portrait was too finely balanced now, and I knew if I added so much as a single brushstroke, it could fail.

Fiona was right, it was finished.

"Hey, Josh?" She looked at me sideways, and smiled. "You didn't actually need me to sit for you today, did you?"

I reached out and squeezed the back of her neck. "Not technically, no." My hand moved around to her throat; her pulse beat hard beneath my fingers. "But a little extra inspiration never hurts."

She returned my kisses at first, her tongue giving playful chase to mine. Only when my hands moved down to her hips, sliding through the folds of her robe to grasp at her soft, sunwarm flesh, did she push me away. "It's not that I don't want to," she whispered, her hand trembling on my chest. "But you know if anything were to happen, it would just get too messy. And I try to avoid mess."

"You don't think something has already happened?"

"Josh, you have...complications."

"Let me guess," I snapped. "You try to avoid those as well."

Her eyes widened. Her hand fell to her side.

"Ah, Fee." I looked at her portrait again, so full of light and grace and joy I could barely believe it had been born from my brush. And I thought of the dark, decaying cityscape I'd been working on back home, and the cycle of taut, claustrophobic abstracts before it, and before *those* the grisly series of canvases I'd started within days of meeting Mallory. The ones she'd dubbed *abattoir nouveau* without even the slightest trace of irony.

"I don't love her." I was half-surprised to have spoken the words aloud. "I did once, I think. But not now, not for a long time."

"But you need her," Fiona said. "Or you want her. Same difference."

I shook my head. "I want you."

Fiona sighed. "It's a beautiful painting, Josh. But what if that's all there is?"

"I don't believe that." My hand found hers and squeezed, gently. "There's something here, right? It's not just in my mind?"

She moved closer, rested her head on my shoulder.

"Yes," she said. "There is something."

X

Mallory made a face and dumped the half-eaten jar of baby food onto the kitchen table, pushed it towards the centre. *Apple and Banana Custard*, the label read, though it all looked like the same puréed muck to me.

"I thought that was your favourite," I mumbled around a mouthful of peanut butter sandwich.

"It tastes off," she said. "I'm not hungry, anyway." She sat back and crossed her arms over her chest. The veins on her hands bulged blue against her chalk-dry skin as she clenched and unclenched her fists. Her flesh so wasted away now, I half-expected to hear the grate of bone against bone.

"You should eat," I told her.

She glared at me. "It would be easier if I just left, wouldn't it?"

"Mal—"

"It's not me you want here anymore." Her bottom lip was chapped and tattered and as she spoke the skin split a little and beaded red. "It's her."

"This is your home, too, Mal. I'm not just going to throw you out."

"You can stop being so fucking noble, it doesn't suit you."

Her voice broke on the last words and I couldn't look at her. Instead I stared at the table top, tracing a fingernail over the motley collection of scratches and cuts that crosshatched its surface, some made by me, others by who knows how many previous owners in kitchens past. In the corner was a little heart pierced by two arrows, complete with fletching and tiny droplets of blood suspended from the tips. Mallory had etched that with a compass point one pissed-up night, back when we still got drunk together.

"Mal, this isn't working. We can't keep pretending that it is."

A scrape of chair against lino and then she was sitting at my feet, her fingers picking along the seam of my jeans. "This is what you wanted, Josh."

"No." I swallowed, rested my hand on her head. "Not like this."

"Then it's up to you to change it," she said. "Because I can't do it for you, it's not my choice to make. It's never been my choice."

"I'm so sorry, Mal. I never meant...any of this."

Fingers digging into my thigh, she pulled herself shakily to her feet. "Stupid boy," she whispered, moving around behind me. Her arms draped over my shoulders and she pressed her lips against my neck. "You think she's gonna give you what you need? You think she's all fire and light and fucking glory be?" Her breath smelled of copper and of sour, discarded things. "You need to take into account the common fucking denominator here, my love."

I turned my head away. "Mal, don't. Please."

Mallory straightened, dragging her hands up over my cheeks and across my scalp. She was breathing heavily through her nose, like she always did when trying not to cry. "Go to her then, Josh," she said. "Just fucking go."

X

Fiona answered the door in her robe and for a single, green-tinged moment I wondered if there was someone else in the flat with her. Another painter she was sitting for, or just some guy waiting impatiently in her bed with his dick in his hands, and I couldn't for the life of me have said which possibility cut the deepest.

"What happened to you?" she asked. "There's blood on your neck."

"It's nothing." I rubbed at the place where Mallory's mouth had been less than an hour before. "It's not mine."

"Come inside." She took my hand and I followed her into the lounge room where my painting — *our* painting — still leaned upon its easel, bold and golden and luminous. And I knew I'd made the right decision.

"It's over," I said. "She hasn't left yet, but she will. It's over, Fee, it really is."

My vision blurred and something I hadn't even realised was there uncoiled itself from around my chest and slunk away, defeated. And then Fiona was kissing me, her robe falling to the floor and us falling close behind it, and for a while there was nothing in my head but light.

X

The sun was well into its daily arc by the time I got back home the next morning, but the flat was dim, all the blinds still drawn, and silent.

"Mal?" I called. "Mal, it's me."

The bedroom door was shut. I eased it open a crack and peered through to find her curled up beneath the blankets, tight little Mallory-ball so small it almost hurt to see. Almost. Still no response when I called her name again, little more than a whisper this time, so I closed the door quietly behind me.

I lifted my dead city painting from the easel and leaned it against the wall, face down. Driving home, I'd pictured myself taking to it with a Stanley knife, shredding the paint-stiff canvas to harmless strips, but now something stayed my hand. There was a certain fatalistic grandeur to its darkness that demanded further consideration. So I left it to itself for now and cleaned up all the half-curled tubes of paint and near-empty jars from the floor. I scrubbed my hands with turpentine, digging out the last stubborn dregs of black and indigo and cobalt blue which had taken up near permanent residence beneath my nails.

Then I made toast and ate it thickly buttered over the sink and thought about the look that loosened Fiona's face when she came.

Afterwards, I went to the bedroom again and knocked on the door. "Mal, you awake yet?" No answer, not even the slightest sound of movement in the room beyond, and suddenly everything felt wrong. *Leave, just leave now and don't ever come back.* But instead, I turned the handle and pushed open the door.

Mallory was still in bed, still tightly cocooned in the blankets, and I placed a hand on the bump I guessed to be her shoulder. "Mal, baby, you okay?" She felt odd, sort of *spongy*, and then, as I shook her, she just...wasn't there.

"Fuck!" I stumbled backwards, tripping on some stray bit of crap on the floor, and coming down hard on one knee.

Bolts of pain shot up my leg, and I swore again through gritted teeth, but never once took my eyes from the bed, from the newly flat and barren place where Mallory had been. Ignoring the persistent voice in my head that was telling me again to leave, *leave now, and whatever you do, don't look don't look don't look,* I reached out and grasped a corner of the blanket. Lifted, then swallowed hard, and pulled it all the way back.

Thick and viscous, like treacle or honey left too long in the fridge, the sludge that quivered and spread across the bottom sheet in a shape that too painfully resembled the form of a girl lying on her side. Mallory, the way I'd seen her all too often: curled with knees pressed against her chest, skinny arms hugging her shoulders and her head tucked chin to breastbone like a Bronze Age sacrifice awaiting the slow mummification of peat. I didn't even realise I'd touched the stuff until my fingers were at my mouth, glistening dark and smelling of salt and iron and loss.

She tasted like nothing I could begin to describe.

I crawled to the toilet and vomited until my guts were sore and only hot strings of bile were coming up.

Back in the bedroom, I spotted the little jar I'd stumbled over before and bent to pick it up. And saw under the bed, a battalion of them, tiny glass soldiers guarding a tomb. My breath caught in my throat. Mallory had been eating nothing but that shit for weeks, maybe for months, but still I couldn't believe the sheer number of empties she'd managed to accumulate. I stared at the mess on the bed, then at the jar in my hand, and slowly unscrewed the lid.

It look less than half of them to contain her.

The rest of the jars I collected into two plastic shopping bags and took straight down to the bins on the street. I stripped the bed and threw the sheets away as well. Contemplated burning them, consigning the last of the stains they harboured to fire and ash, but it was hardly a practical solution and I didn't want them in the flat a second longer.

I didn't know what to do with the jars I'd filled.

Briefly, I considered taking them out to the bay and throwing them into the water, or burying them somewhere up in the Dandenong Ranges, deep in the earth where they'd never be found. But something inside me balked at the idea of taking them anywhere, of taking *her* anywhere, so instead I simply stowed them under the bed again. Lined them up against the wall beneath where my head would lie, making sure all the lids were screwed on tight.

I had no idea whether or not she would spoil.

X

It wasn't the light. My flat was dim, sure, the new compact fluorescents overly harsh, but the painting could have been standing beneath the brightest of summer suns and it wouldn't have made the slightest difference.

It wasn't the light; it was what the light exposed.

I rubbed hard at my forehead, wondering how the fuck I could've ever believed Fiona's portrait to hold any real worth at all. Simplistic and garish, it had nothing to say beyond the most clichéd commentary on beauty and the female form, nothing that hadn't already been said by the likes of Klimt and Modigliani — decades earlier and with infinitely greater eloquence. I could imagine prints being sold by the truckload out of suburban shopping malls, disconnected housewives only too delighted to find something pretty and cheerful and just a little bit risqué. Something that didn't clash with their new designer lounge suite.

At best, the painting was vacuous; at worst, utterly mute.

I felt sick.

"Josh?" Fiona called from the bedroom. "You're sure she doesn't want any of this stuff? She's not coming back for it?"

"Just bag it all," I told her. "She's not coming back."

My ruined city reproached me from its place against the wall, and rightfully so. For all its flaws, it at least possessed a tongue.

"How weird would it be if I hung onto this?" Fiona asked from behind me. "Most of her things are kind of dire, but this suits me, don't you reckon?"

I turned, and my throat tightened. I remembered that dress. The bright red fabric dotted with tiny white flowers, the deeply scooped neckline and that row of buttons which ran all the way up the front and which were damn near impossible to undo in a hurry. How long had it been since I'd seen that dress, seen Mallory in it?

"Where'd you get that?" I asked.

"In the wardrobe, shoved behind everything else." Fiona twirled and the skirt flounced around her bare thighs. It fitted her curves perfectly and I seemed to remember it sitting the exact same way on Mallory once. I tried to picture how she looked when we'd first got together, before she lost all the weight, back when there was something beneath her skin beyond the bitter jut of bone.

I couldn't.

"So, too weird?" Fiona asked.

"It's a bit weird," I told her. "But keep it, if you want."

She crossed the room, put her arms around my waist and pressed her cheek against my shoulder. "I don't have to move right in," she said. "You know, if it's too soon. I can find another place." The lease was up on her apartment and her arsehole landlord had decided to double the rent. It'd been my suggestion that she come live with me; anything else just seemed like delaying the inevitable.

"I want you to be here, Fee." I ruffled her hair. Dark roots were starting to push up through the pale blonde, and I tried to imagine how Fiona would look if she ever quit the peroxide habit.

The skin on the back of my neck prickled. I could see how the painting could be saved; moreover, I could *feel* it deep in my guts, the *rightness* of it. The undercurrent of darkness that needed to sit just beneath the surface, the hint of sordid truth behind the beautiful lie that we all want so desperately to believe. But I had to be subtle with it, sound a barely discernable note of unease, just enough to knock the portrait off kilter. Shadows and hollows and the sly insinuation of decay.

Of defilement.

"Ow, Josh, that hurts!" Fiona was struggling in my hands, my fingers digging deep into the soft flesh of her upper arms. I released my grip, watched its ghosts bloom angry and scarlet on her skin.

"Shit, Fee, I'm sorry. I didn't even realise."

"It's okay." She rubbed at the places I'd been holding her. "Where'd you go just now?"

"Nowhere, just thinking." I kissed the top of her head, still thinking. About how to fix the painting, and about the jars that waited beneath my bed. I could see how that dark opalescence would mix with the airy golden tones of Fiona's portrait, how it would give them texture and weight. How it would make them real.

My fingers flexed, ached for a paintbrush.

"I'm going to make chai," Fiona said. "You want some?"

"Hmm? Yeah, sure." My eyes followed the sway of her hips as she strolled towards the kitchen. Just as she reached the doorway, I called her name and she half-turned, her face bright and open and expectant.

"You look good in that dress," I told her.

Fiona smiled. "Thanks," she said.

I listened to the safe, domestic sounds of tea-making and wondered how long the jars would last, how many more canvases Mallory could permeate before she was, finally, gone. Already, my brain was beginning to clutter and swarm with new visions, new ideas, and I got down on my knees to retrieve my sketchbook from where it had slid beneath the couch, a stub of charcoal marking a new page. But my hand was too cautious, too careful, its first little sketch so timid and needy. Frustrated, I flipped the page.

You'll find it, Josh. You always do, in the end.

I nodded. Closed my eyes and tried to recall the sharp, pinched lines of Mallory's body, the lost and broken expression on her face. I'd never drawn her, not once, which seemed a strange thing. And now she was too scattered, too faded, and I couldn't get the pieces to stay together.

Josh?

"I'm sorry, baby," I whispered.

Josh.

"I'm so sorry."

"Josh!"

My eyes snapped open. "Fee?" I lurched to my feet and half-ran, half-stumbled into the kitchen where Fiona was standing over the sink, both hands pressed to her face. "Fee, what's wrong?"

"My nose." She sniffed, loud and wet and awful, as blood started to seep through her fingers. "I need a tissue."

There was more chance of finding a silk handkerchief in this place, so I snatched up a tea towel instead. She waved it away, protesting about stains, but I shook my head — "It doesn't matter, Fee" — and held it gently to her nose. Blood soaked through the cloth.

"Fuck. Here, sit down." I guided her to a chair. "Keep your head back."

It took almost five minutes for the bleeding to stop completely. Half a roll of toilet paper littered the table and floor, all of it bright with crimson blotches. Kitchen as surgical ward, triage tent, autopsy room, with Fiona hunched pale and shaky in the centre, one hand clutched sweaty in mine.

"It must be the dry weather," she said at last.

I nodded, unable to look away from the patterns made by the blood.

"I think I need to lie down," she said.

"Good idea."

I helped her into bed, and she asked me to sit with her for a while, and so I did. Stroking her hair and contemplating the mess in the kitchen, all that blood-soaked paper, and how wrong it seemed to simply throw it away.

Just when I thought she had fallen asleep, Fiona slid a hand from beneath the sheet and squeezed my thigh. "You still want me here, don't you, Josh?"

"Of course." A dry crust of blood stained her upper lip and I licked my thumb, rubbed most of it away. "I need you, Fee." And she smiled, or nearly did. Weary little shadow of a smile that barely creased the corners of her mouth, and I didn't think I'd ever seen anyone look so fragile. Not even Mallory.

"That's good," she said. "That's perfect."

AFTERWORD

When Mark Deniz asked me to contribute to this anthology, I was intrigued, if slightly apprehensive. I've never written a story with such a specific brief before — what if nothing about the song inspired me? I needn't have worried.

The song was a gift.

I'd been carrying half a story around in my pocket for ages, waiting to find the rest of the pieces I needed to put it together. It was about art and muses — masochistic muses to be precise, muses who literally give their entire selves to those they inspire — and it was very, very dark. Too dark, actually; it was flat and black and textureless. The lyrics to 'She Said' reminded me to let in some light, because you can't see the shadows without it. Those last three lines in particular resonated most strongly. Lightness and darkness; the choice Mallory is powerless to make, the responsibility Josh refuses to accept.

Unexpectedly, 'She Said' also turned out to be the most autobiographical story I've ever written, though not in any of the ways you'd think. For that reason, it's both a favoured child, and a feared one.

BIOGRAPHY

Kirstyn McDermott was born on Halloween, an auspicious date which perhaps accounts for her lifelong attraction to all things dark, mysterious and bumpy-in-the-night. She has been published in various magazines and anthologies, including *Shadowed Realms, Southerly, GUD, Redsine, Southern Blood* and *Island*. Kirstyn lives in Melbourne and is a member of the SuperNOVA writers group. Her short fiction has won Aurealis, Ditmar and Chronos Awards and her debut novel, *Madigan Mine*, was published by Picador in 2010.

THE BLIND MAN

FELICITY DOWKER

I can't tell you where it all started, because it didn't start with me. Rage, hatred, revenge, sorrow...these are great and ancient things, bigger than just one man. I can tell you a little bit, though. That much I can do.

X

I was always in trouble as a kid. Once, when I was fourteen, I went too far. It was nothing out of the ordinary at first, just me and Nathan Geeves pushing and shoving behind the school gym, one on one, with the usual audience. It got out of hand when my mates Luke and James grabbed Nathan, held him so he couldn't fight back, and egged me on. I should have just thrown a cursory punch to appease my buddies and the jeering crowd, and left it at that. But I didn't. Something took hold of me, something cruel and wild that was excited by Nathan's helplessness, by the naked terror in his eyes.

My head throbbed and spun, and I saw my father's face, superimposed over Nathan's.

"Please, Greg," he begged. "Don't. Stop."

"All right, I won't stop," I told him. I got a good laugh for that one.

I beat the hell out of Nathan that day. I can still hear the sound of his skull cracking like an egg under my fists, hear his piercing screams, until that last punch when he went limp and silent and Luke and James let him go, watched him slither to the ground and lie there. I broke a couple of my knuckles. That hurt. Nathan wound up in hospital, hooked up to beeping machines and metal pulleys. His face was livid and swollen into a jellied lump. He didn't look a thing like my father any more. His parents thought I was the Antichrist. Maybe they were right.

Broken jaw and nose, the doctors said. Broken ribs. Punctured lung. Fractured cheek bone and skull. Detached retina. Fragments of orbital bone floating behind Nathan's right eye. Cerebrospinal fluid leaking from his ears. Severe brain bleeds with the possibility of irreversible damage. The list went on, and on, and on.

The police came and dragged me from my house, and my mother cried into her tea towel, a low droning *uh uh uh*. I had to go to children's court. My mother didn't come with me. She said she loved me, but she couldn't support me in the terrible thing I'd done. Luke and James ran off to their dads' houses in another state. Suddenly, the crowd that had applauded me working on Nathan was against me, each of them trudging up to the witness stand and regaling the court with their recollections of my savagery. I got one hundred hours community service and a suspended twelve-month juvenile detention term. The local media said it was too lenient by far; a travesty. If this was what I could do at just fourteen, imagine what I'd do in my manhood!

My mother made me lasagne after my sentencing, with extra béchamel. She was still crying into her tea towel, but her *uh uh uh* was happier now. She'd thought she was going to lose me forever, like she lost my dad. He was in jail serving two consecutive life sentences for killing my little brother and sister. They had been two years old. Twins. He strangled them. He loved his crystal meth, did my dad, but it didn't love him much — or my kid brother and sister.

Don't look at me like that. I don't want your pity. Don't assume it's why I am the way I am. It's no excuse. There *is* no excuse.

I knocked on Nathan's door to apologise, a few days after my sentencing. His mother opened the door, boggled at me, slapped me on both cheeks, spat in my face, and slammed the door shut. I could hear her crying from the other side of the thick mahogany. She didn't *uh uh uh* like my mother. She wailed. Her cries sounded like they really hurt, like ropes of barbed wire were being pulled through her tear ducts.

I *was* sorry. I couldn't tell Nathan, or his mother, so I'm telling you. I was very, very sorry.

X

I had to do a minimum of ten of my community service hours every week. I did two hours, Monday to Friday, at The Willows aged care facility. That's where I met Mr. Salioso.

He was a withered old thing, bent into his wheelchair like a weed yanked from its soil and forced into a too-small bucket. He always wore the same tattered brown dressing gown, with little bits of mashed pumpkin on it. No matter what they served for meals at The Willows, Mr. Salioso always had pumpkin on his dressing gown. That was weird, but as I found out, it was one of the *least* weird things about him.

"Hello, Greg," he croaked. He sounded like Clive Barker, post throat polyps. He was wearing hokey sunglasses, despite sitting in the darkest corner of the old folks' lounge. "Thank you for coming to talk to me."

"I don't have a choice," I told him, slouching into the seat next to him. He didn't smell funny, like the rest of the patients here. He smelt...sharp, like a mint candy cane that had been sucked until it formed a lethal point. "I'm doing community service hours."

"Yes, I know," he replied, and we sat in silence for a while. He was smiling, a little curl at the corner of his pale lips. I sighed, drummed my fingers on my thigh, watched the old folks staring into space while cranky staff shovelled pureed mush into their mouths. I checked my watch. Only two minutes had passed.

"So," I said, finally unable to bear it any longer, "What're you in for?"

"This isn't a prison, Greg," Salioso said, amused.

"Isn't it?"

That odd, twitchy smile at the corner of his mouth again. "I've been here such a long time; I don't recall how I came to be here. Someone must have put me here, once, someone who perhaps thought it was the best thing for me."

"Or someone who hated your guts and didn't want to look at you anymore," I said.

"Yes. Maybe that was it."

More silence. This guy was good. I shifted in my chair, sighed again.

"What's with the sunnies?" I reached out to tap on Salioso's glasses, but damn if his arm didn't shoot up, quick as a snake, his bony white fingers like fangs, circling my wrist, biting deep. I gasped.

"I'm blind," he said mildly, giving my wrist one last little love squeeze before shoving my hand back towards me, releasing it. "Can't you tell?"

"No." In my mind, he grabbed my arm again. Crazy fast. Faster than anything I'd ever seen before. "Not at all. You don't move like a blind guy."

"How should a blind guy move?"

"Slow. Careful. Doddery. Unseeing."

"I'm only blind, Greg. It doesn't mean I can't see."

Yeah, right, and what the fuck did *that* mean?

I chewed the inside of my cheek and waited for the two

hours to tick by with excruciating slowness. When my watch grudgingly relented and told me it was two o'clock, I stood up and walked away without a word to Mr. Salioso.

At the door, I stopped, turned, looked back at him.

He lifted a hand and waved at me. Smiling, smiling.

"How was it today?" My mother, bustling around the kitchen, was probably telling herself I was at the old folks' home out of the kindness of my heart. She lived on those little delusions.

"It sucked. They assigned me to this creepy old blind dude. He's really pale, like, you can see through his skin, and he smells funny, not bad, but funny, and—"

"He's old, Greg. He can't help it." She wasn't listening, not really. She never did.

"He could see me."

"I thought you said he was blind?" Well, maybe she listened a bit. She just didn't hear.

"That's what he told me, and he wears blind-guy glasses, but he knew where I was, what I was doing. He told me he could see."

"Blind people's other senses are extra sharp, honey. He could probably smell you, or hear you, or something." She handed me a steaming plate, lamb chops with mashed potato and peas and carrots. Smiled. Ruffled my hair.

Yeah, I thought, that had to be it. He used his other senses.

My dinner tasted funny that night. Like pumpkin.

X

It was my fifth day spending time at The Willows. I crunched an apple in between words. "You can smell me, right? That's how you 'see'. You smell, and you listen, too."

Mr. Salioso pursed his lips, nodded.

"Yes, I can smell you, and hear you. Better than anyone, better, even, than other blind people. I can track your blood, you see. It speaks to me. It paints pictures behind my eyes. In that way, I see you perfectly." I noticed that the orange smears on his dressing gown were so smooth, so clean. Like they'd been put there with deliberate care, fresh that morning, as part of his toilette.

"Track my blood, right. They didn't tell me you'd gone soft in the head, but I guess that's the norm in here." I dipped my head to take another loud bite of my apple. Salioso moved in my peripheral vision, a white-brown-orange blur, and my apple fell into my lap, seeded entrails ripped out, flesh quartered in coarse chunks. Sweet juice dripped from the old man's long fingers. Reaching slowly this time, he leaned into my lap, wiped his hand on my jeans. His smile was close to my face, and I could see the shiny points of his canines.

"Oh," I breathed.

"Yes," he said, drawing back into his wheelchair once more. He was slow now, the movements as careful as the neat smears of pumpkin on his clothes.

Those hours flew, my brain racing with fear, with questions, with excitement. I didn't speak, though. I wanted to say the right things or nothing at all. Suddenly, I cared very much what Mr. Salioso thought of me.

X

"Why do you sit in a wheelchair?" I was proud of that question. I'd worked it out in my head just right as I lay in bed the night before. Not, *why are you in a wheelchair*, because he wasn't *in* a wheelchair. He could get out of it if he wanted to, walk, dance, leap tall buildings in a single bound. I knew it the same way I knew he wasn't human — because it was true. Because all the signs pointed to the truth.

"For the same reason that I wear this disgusting old rag, and for the same reason I smear muck on myself," Mr.

Salioso said. He was minty-fresh as ever, like he'd squeezed a whole tube of toothpaste onto his gleaming fangs.

"It's all part of your disguise."

"Yes, Greg. Very good." He sounded bored, but I knew he wasn't. He'd led me to this point. We were where he wanted us to be, he and I.

"And the glasses?"

"I'm blind. I really am, you know. That happened...before."

"Yes, but they're not essential, are they? And they don't seem very 'you'." I was afraid, of course; always afraid by then. Mr. Salioso wanted something from me in exchange for the glimpse he was permitting me into his truth. That was the way of the world. I knew that at fourteen as I know it now.

Salioso laughed, a little chuff of hoarse breath. "You really are a rather smart boy, aren't you? Not your garden variety thug at all. Why do you conceal your intellect, Greg? Do you *want* everyone to think you're like your father? Is that it? Do you fear their expectations if they look beyond that?"

A sharp chill shot through me. My blood seemed to congeal in my veins, and everything slowed and quietened until all I could hear was the harsh *whumph whumph whumph* of my heart, thudding in my ears. How had he known about my father?

After a long, tense moment, I sucked in a breath and blew it back out, my lips vibrating. Salioso knew because...well, because he was Salioso. He knew because he knew, and I decided that he had mentioned it to rattle me. "The glasses," I insisted.

A pause, and Salioso curled his flaccid lips at me. Approving. "All right. Come closer."

I wanted to run. Instead, I leant into his minty personal space until my nose almost touched his. His teeth were white blurs in my straining peripheral vision. His tongue darted around behind them, pink and moist, tasting my breath.

Salioso lifted a hand and, with one finger, pushed his glasses up onto his forehead.

His eyes were totally black. They bulged, wet and fishy, glistening in his lashless sockets. Cataracts hugged the gangrenous orbs, thick with canker. I swallowed the cry that tried to bubble free from my throat. It slid back down my gullet, heavy and painful.

"The staff think it's an eye disease, contracted in my childhood. That's the story I've fed them, and they've gobbled it up because, like you, they fear fully using the knowledge they already possess." He let his dark glasses fall once more onto his bony nose, and I flopped back into my seat, aware of my rapid heartbeat and the rancid sweat coating my body like frosting. I could taste metal in my mouth. I wondered fleetingly if this panic, this primal horror, was something like what Nathan had felt when he knew I was going to hurt him very badly. And what my little brother and sister...

"I wear the glasses for them, and for the other patients," Salioso continued. "It's a courtesy, you see."

"What—" I found I couldn't speak, and I swallowed several times, rapid fire, *gulp gulp gulp*. "What do you want from me?"

"You came to me, Greg. What do *you* want?"

"I had to come here, and I had to talk to you. They assigned me."

"You didn't have to talk to me like this, though, did you? We could have chatted about the weather, your schoolwork, my festering childhood. We could have discussed nothing at all, if you'd chosen to simply serve your sentence in sullen silence. But you wanted to talk, really talk, and at some point you've got to ask yourself...why?"

Two hours, up. We were over halfway there. I had forty more hours to serve at The Willows, sitting rigid in the seat next to Mr. Salioso's wheelchair. Forty hours to voice the words that had been forming in the swampiest part of my animal brain. I knew Salioso already heard those words and knew what I wanted. He would wait for me to speak the request, though.

It was a courtesy, you see.

X

I dreamed that night.

My mother lay down on the floor and wrapped herself up in the rug like a big ol' sausage roll, and I saw that it wasn't really a rug, but an enormous tea towel. *Uh uh uh.* She wriggled her arms free from the not-rug and waved them around, conducting her own honking sobs. *Uh uh uh.*

"Gweg?"

Oh, no. It hurt, it hurt bad. I didn't want to see them, didn't want to miss them, didn't want to know their pain. But I turned around anyway, couldn't not, and there were my little siblings, Amy and Todd, their hair matching spirals of sunshine, their cheeks pink and round, and I felt my own silent tears start to drip, drip, drip.

Uh uh uh. My mother receded and disappeared, as she always had when we needed her.

"Gweg? Wowee Daddy?" They wanted to know where our father was, and I suddenly thought maybe this wasn't a dream, maybe this was a chance to save them. I lunged for them, gathering them into my arms like the dolls they would forever be. They clung to me with wet kisses and high-pitched giggles, and I ran to hide them in my bedroom, except the floor beneath me turned into hungry sludge, and I sank down, down, down.

"Give them to me, boy." The big bad wolf had arrived and

oh, what big teeth you have, Mr. Salioso. Except it wasn't him, not him, but Daddy, and Daddy had gone mad.

The sludge sucked me into it, devouring me to the neck, and I couldn't turn my face away, couldn't close my eyes, couldn't scream because the sludge filled my mouth with cold malice when I tried. Amy and Todd ran to Daddy, all open adoring arms and puckered-up kissy lips, *luboo Daddy, wowee, Daddy!*

Daddy was a drugged-out demon with popping tendons and bright eyes, and he took off his belt and wrapped it around Amy's slender neck. Then, when she was a broken doll all shattered on the floor, Todd's neck received Daddy's fatal love.

"They're not really kids," he told me as he squeeeeeeezed death into my beautiful brother and sister, who had loved *Play School* and cuddles and chocolate crackles. "They're aliens. You can't see, but I see, I know, and I'll save us."

I let the sludge pull me right under then, and it was orange. Pumpkin. It tasted like mint.

X

I had twenty hours left. Time to get down to business. "Can you bring back dead people?"

"No. Not the dead." Salioso laid a hand on my arm. It felt like frozen clay. "I'm sorry. I can't help them."

I choked back a hard ball of grief. I'd known he'd say that, but I wouldn't have been able to live with myself if I hadn't made absolutely sure.

Tick, tick, tick. The clock on the wall was so loud. How loud must it have seemed to him, day in, day out? Who had put him in this place? Had it been before or after he'd become what he now was? How did it feel to be given eternal life, but be old and blind when it came? Why did he stay at The Willows?

"My father..." That ball again, jagged and hot, surged up my throat. My hands fluttered to my neck, grabbed it, tried to massage the pain away.

"Mmmn."

"He..."

"I know. You don't have to discuss that. I won't put you through it." How kind he could seem. How hungry he was. It rolled off him in silver-bright waves. His fingers were hooked into claws, trembling, eager. "I can see it in your blood."

"I want you to kill him. I want him to be terrified and miserable when he dies. I don't want it to be quick."

"Of course." *Tick tick tick.* "Tell me where he's incarcerated."

"Okay." I told him, and it was done.

X

"Greg." My mother shook me out of my slumber, her voice strange. "Wake up."

"Mmmnh?" She had turned my bedside light on, and as my eyes adjusted, I saw her face. Her cheeks were wet with tears, but she looked...radiant.

"Your father—"

"Is he dead?"

She recoiled a little at that, but only for a moment. "Yes, honey. They found him in his cell an hour ago. They think one of the other prisoners got to him, with a...a knife, or some such. His blood..."

I smiled at her. After a long, long moment, she smiled back.

I guess I'd never really understood how much she'd suffered, too.

X

After they planted my dad in the ground, I was woken in the middle of the night again, this time by Mr. Salioso sitting on my bed. He'd turned my bedside light on, too. He didn't need it to see in the darkness, but he knew I did. A courtesy, you see.

"You're not in your wheelchair." It was a stupid thing to say, but I needed to break the silence. I sat up, clutching my blankets to my chest. The air seemed cold and sharp in my room. Minty.

Salioso gripped my shoulder. I think he was trying to comfort me. He failed.

"Hatred makes us blind, Greg," he rasped. He wasn't wearing his glasses. His black eyes were obsidian mirrors, reflecting my pale, terrified face. "It starts with pain. Our pain, the pain of others, world-hurt, whatever. That's when it begins to grow. The hate, the rage."

"He was a monster," I whispered. Hot tears scalded my cheeks. "He made our lives hell, and then he murdered the two innocent little creatures that loved him the most."

"Yes, he deserved his death, and I was happy to deliver it. But what got him to that point? What pain did *he* suffer, to shape him? He wasn't born a drug-addicted child killer. Maybe he saw something that set his rage to burn...do you see?" He squeezed my shoulder. My bones ground together audibly. I gasped, nodded.

"Like you," Salioso said, and my nod turned into vehement side-to-side shaking. *No!*

"I'm nothing like him," I hissed. I tried to move away, but the blind man held me fast.

"Ah, Mrs. Geeves would beg to differ," he said. For a second, I wanted to ask *who?*, but it came to me. Nathan — who had looked a little like my father. Nathan's mother — her spittle on my face, her loud cries of agony.

"I didn't mean to hurt Nathan. I'm sorry." I was sobbing

aloud by now. *Uh uh uh.*

"Oh, you did mean to hurt him, but you're certainly sorry. Neither fact matters much to Mrs. Geeves. Nathan didn't recover in every way that matters, you see. His body healed. His soul didn't. He killed himself this morning." The words fell from Salioso's lips like thunder, cracking and booming about my head.

I understood, then. Understood everything. I opened my mouth to scream, to bring my mother running, but Salioso's hands were there, sealing my lips. Then his hands were everywhere, impossibly fast, irresistibly strong. He pushed me back down onto my mattress, and his fingers traced loving circles around my bulging eyes. His fangs were bared, his mouth gaping open, too wide, too deep.

"She wants you to live," he said. "She thinks death is too easy for you. She wants you to live, and to suffer."

Salioso's fingers moved like white lightning, and he plucked my eyes out, one after the other in quick succession. I felt the harsh suction and the terrible give as each one went, but the pain took a while to filter through. Shock and the sheer speed of Salioso's movements kept me in blissful ignorance for a short while. Then my body realised that, yes, those long sharp fingers had slid in between my eyeballs and their snug sockets; and no, it hadn't been nice when my reluctant orbs were yanked until their nervy tethers gave way. And, emphatically, the juicy hollows where my eyes had been protested their discomfort as they wept bloody tears and pulsed and swelled with their loss.

The sudden and terrifying blackness of eternity was in me, around me, consuming and surrounding me. Excruciating agony crashed over me in a hard, red wave. I was drowning, my cries for help emerging only as short, wheezy exhalations.

"You saw nothing while you had these." Salioso's voice

came to me as if from a great distance, whooshing through a wind tunnel. There was a mushy popping sound, and I knew Salioso had crushed my eyeballs in his fist. Somehow, that was the worst of it. "It is fitting that, now you have had them taken from you, you shall see all. Blindness is a disease, and it cannot be contained now, but it can also be its own cure, as you will learn."

My mattress creaked as Salioso bent over me. Something firm and wet probed the pulpy beds where my eyes had been. He was licking my wounds. He pressed his lips to my eye sockets then, and sucked hard. The pain was cosmic. I shot into oblivion gratefully.

X

So there you have it. Nothing more than an old blind man's fractured memories, the broken shards scattered before you in hopes that you may make of them a worthwhile picture. There is no moral to my story, I suppose, except that darkness leads to more darkness, pain to more pain. There must be other paths, but not having walked them myself, I'm afraid I can't show you the way.

Salioso did not make of me what he himself was, except for the blindness. And so I will die, perhaps soon, since seventy-four years have passed since I lost my sight and saw everything in the same moment. My mother died decades ago. There is no one else. So I sit and rot here, in The Willows, my days a blur of pureed vegetables, desperate sounds and hospital odours.

Today, however, someone came to visit me. He sat beside me and held my hand. His skin was cold. He smelt of mint.

"You've got pumpkin on your clothes, old friend," he croaked.

"Yes," I said.

We sat in silence, my visitor and I, as the slow minutes

ticked by. His hand in mine was an invitation etched in cold blood. I didn't accept. I wish I had. I hope he visits me again tomorrow.

Perhaps the only way to truly get anywhere in this ruined world is for the blind to lead the blind.

AFTERWORD

The lyrics to The God Machine's 'The Blind Man' immediately affected me, much more so than the music, although I think perhaps the relentlessness of the melody did imprint on my story. The song is a direct piece of prose, weighty despite its succinctness; full of pain, yearning, and a dreadful sort of inevitability. I sucked up that dark emotion and sat with it for a while, and it led me somewhere fantastic and bleak — and unexpected. I had hoped that I would write something beautiful, poignant and complex — perhaps, dare I say, something bordering on lit-ra-cha — and instead I found myself writing something quite different. But that was all right, because what did come forward was blunt and dark, like the song. My human protagonist came to me first, his unenviable — and, worse, somehow unavoidable — life fully formed alongside him. Then came the unblind, undead man who would become a dubious sort of companion, and the tale flowed from there, like a river of...pumpkin.

BIOGRAPHY

Felicity Dowker is a Ditmar and Chronos Award-winner and Aurealis and Australian Shadows Award finalist. Her short stories have appeared in *Aurealis*, *Andromeda Spaceways Inflight Magazine*, *Midnight Echo* and other Australian and international magazines and anthologies. Her limited-edition chapbook *Phantasy Moste Grotesk* was released in April 2009. Felicity is a committee member of the Australian Horror Writers Association and a regularly published reviewer at the Specusphere. She's also a coffee addict, an incurable neurotic and sporadically maintains a blog at:

http://felicitydowker.livejournal.com

I'VE SEEN THE MAN

PAUL HAINES

The man giving the sales pitch is a liar. I can see it in the way the skin sits comfortably over the flesh on his bones, in the slight jowl under his chin, the bulge of the belly beneath his shirt and jacket.

"Yeah, man," he croons. "This is the jizz, the shit, the buzz. This is the *poison* you be looking for."

The whites of his eyes are still white, his hair thick and luxurious. To him, this is simply a job, some cash coming to pay his bills, get his cock sucked, oil his scalp, preen his clothes. He's a liar, every fucking word oozing from his full lips and pink tongue is just more noise getting in the way of what I want and where I need to go.

He nods towards the door, grinning slyly. "This way, man, you'll love it. See the world with new eyes. It's like you're reborn."

He holds his hand out, rubbing forefinger and thumb.

I press the Benefits Card into his palm and he swipes it through the reader, taps something onto the screen, grins a mouth of pearly whites and clean saliva, and hands me back the card.

"Come on in, man. We can give you everything."

Above us the sky looms heavy and dark, like a disease sweeping in under the skin of the sun. I push past him, eager yet hesitant to get back into the Shrine. I hate him. I love him. He is an innocent, a naïve newborn; bless him and his life.

Fuck him.

What does he know about life? What does he know about anything?

X

The first time I went to a Shrine — the original, the one in the abandoned warehouses down near the old docks that started all this — I was terrified.

Back then it wasn't cool and underground, it was just underground, hard to find, harder to get into, and very expensive.

I'd been ushered in, my heart beating and fluttering in my chest, my chakras awash and whirling. The sweat on my palms hot and insistent. Pressure on my bladder. Internal fingers prodding my belly, urging me to throw up the nerves. I expected semi-naked Asiatic women clad in silken veils offering me needles and pipes, a room swirling with the dragon, chased with psychedelic whispers, of me reclining, a sheen of sweat coating the body, head tilted back, face raised in transcendence.

It wasn't like that at all.

It was like this:

The room was sterile. Posters covered the wall. It was footy season and enemy teams were featured. A talking point, just in case we needed one. A dozen fat, comfortable leather recliners lined three of the walls, each with an IV drip and machine. A flat-screen TV was mounted on the opposite wall, so all the chairs and their occupants, the clientele, could see what was on it, although the volume was turned down so low it was only a muted garble. Several nurses, men or women, moved amongst the chairs, adjusting IVs, providing small talk, occasionally stroking a brow, wiping away an escaped tear.

The occupants of the chairs, they're you and me. Normal. Mundane. Everyday. Their faces were creased with wrinkles, smoothed with youth, jaundiced, sallow, sunken, puffed, pristine, flawless, exposed and raw. Hair hung lank, scalps were shaved, stubbled, grey, bleached and *au naturel*. Clothes were creased and clean, labelled and branded, patched, denimed, cotton and silk, baggy, tight, ragged and styled with grime; everything and nothing.

Normal. Mundane. Joe Public. Jane Private. Jesus and Mohammed adrift in a boat crafted from Vishnu's suffering with Thor's hammer, blessed with Buddha's semen and then leased from Lucifer at a cutthroat price.

The occupants of the chairs, reclining, breathing, dying a million deaths with every inspiration, a million more on expiry.

Their souls burned brightly in their eyes.

X

There's only three of us here today, not counting the two nurses controlling the Shrine. A woman in her fifties, me, and Tiki.

I take a seat next to Tiki, and roll up my left sleeve. "How you going, man?"

"Hey, bro!" Tiki's eyes are yellowed, and jaundice shines through the once-tanned pallor of his skin. The Polynesian in the man is slowly leeching out. He's shaved his skull. An IV line snakes from beneath his shirt up to the drip on the stand next to his chair. "Going good, eh? Closer to God, bro, closer to God. Every day. How about you? Haven't seen you around for a couple of months."

"Finances. Hey, thanks for fixing me up with that new card."

"No probs. Should tide you over for about a year before they figure it out. Let me know with plenty of time when you need a new one. Getting harder to get hold of my man in the trade, eh? Business is booming he reckons."

"It's the way of the world, Tiki."

"Yeah, don't I know it. Sorry, bro, I gotta...I gotta...go..." He leans back into the chair, eyes closed, riding the waves. His fists are white knuckles clenching the arms of the chair.

Tiki has been playing this game longer than anyone I know.

X

Why do people take drugs? There are more reasons than there are pharmaceuticals, but I took them primarily for pleasure. Sure, curiosity was a factor, but I was only curious about how it would make me feel. I was never a rebel; I wasn't doing it as a means of defiance, nor enacting a defence mechanism. I had no problems to escape from.

I liked to get fucked up, plain and simple.

Tiki? Well, he was another story. We used to play rugby together at school. He was big, as a lot of Polynesian kids were, and fast too. The by-product of sexual genetic engineering, slung from the vagina of a Samoan/Maori half-breed inseminated by Dutch ancestry that traced itself back to pirates roaming the Indonesian spice trade routes.

He was anything but plain and simple. He'd watched his old man get beaten to death with crowbars outside their garage one wintry weekend. Apparently Tiki's father had overstepped his mark on the local patch, and after ignoring the first warning, had his body bludgeoned as a statement to the rest of the neighbourhood. His mum lost most of her teeth that day, and spent the next few years whoring to make ends meet. Tiki didn't mind the fact that his old lady fucked for a living, but he resented her for bringing business back home. By then, home was pretty much broken, and though Tiki didn't tell me any of this until years later, I knew he was broken too.

But if there was anything you wanted — pot, E, speed, P, heroin, ice — then Tiki was your man. And it was always Good. A-Grade Good.

I'd always figured that Tiki needed saving and I sure as hell wasn't going to do it. Then one day I realised I'd put so much money into Tiki's pockets over the years that I'd lost my house and my wife to go with it. Tiki needed saving, but the bastard turned it all around and tried to save me.

X

"Nice to see you again. It's been a while." Tony is looking clean, his beard trimmed close to his chin. He pulls on gloves, takes a swab, doses it in alcohol then wipes the vein in the crook of my elbow. "What'll it be today?"

"What's on the menu?"

Tony smiles mercurially, raises an eyebrow. "What's not on the menu?"

I suspect Tony gets a kickback from the fake Benefit Cards that are used, and I know he takes a lot of electronic cash payments up front. He's not the dealer, he's the dispenser. A qualified oncological nurse and an auric reader. Quite the package.

"A little sting," he says, as the needle slides into my vein, then he's taping it tight, putting in a block and screwing it off, while attaching another line to the IV pole. "You have a blood sheet?"

"Sorry, Tony, I haven't had one done for a while."

"How come? Dr. Zing not filling them out for you?"

"Finances, you know. Haven't been able to afford to see Dr. Zing lately."

"Well, your blood results will really help me tailor the effect..."

"I know, I'm sorry. What about my chakras? Can you use

them? See what I need most?"

Tony grins. His teeth are white and pristine. "Your Manipura is off, but you knew that." His gloves are off and his hands hover around my body. "And we definitely need to do something about the Vishuddha; the energy is so confused. Have you been having any side-effects with your thyroid?"

"Like what?"

Tiki begins to convulse in the chair next to us. His legs jerk, kicking off the blanket, as his arms shake. His body is heaving, slapping the chair with sudden rapid thuds.

"Shit," hisses Tony between his teeth. "Kara! Get 25 mils of Phenergan into him quick." He turns to me again, a smile curling his lips, his eyes kind. "You should see his Sahasrara. He's almost there. Please, excuse me for a minute."

Kara injects the sedative into one of the taps on the IV. "I'll get some morphine, just in case."

Tony's hands massage the energy surrounding Tiki's head. "Get some warm blankets too. He's going deep."

X

"People hate junkies," Tiki said to me one night while speed was racing through our veins. His dark-brown eyes were both glazed and manic, as he threw back another shot of sambuca. He grimaced. "You know why?"

We were standing at the bar of a seedy joint in Port Melbourne, one where the walls used TAB screens to scare off patrons. Hardcore only. Down and derelict. Make mine a double.

"Because they're junkies," I replied. The sambuca didn't even touch the sides. Lately, nothing seemed to.

Tiki laughed. "Everyone hates them. Selfish motherfuckers. They're not part of society. They do what they want. They waste their life. They flaunt that waste. The junkie is a portal into a world of anarchy. Society can't have that. Society shuns the junkie."

"Sally's kicked me out," I said.

"And why are we doing this, bro?" Tiki hadn't heard a word I'd said. "Because we're looking for something. Something inside. Something to ease the pain."

"She's changed the locks, man. I got nowhere to stay."

"We take all this shit, we do all this shit to ourselves, because we want to belong, bro." Two more shots had appeared before us. Tiki necked his. "Belong."

"She's taken out a fucking restraining order, Tiki! The bitch. Can you believe it? My own fucking wife!"

"Deep down, bro, we all just want to belong. And the more shit we take, the further away from society we fall."

I stared at Tiki. He was lost.

He turned to face me, a thin line of black liqueur leaking from the corner of his mouth, those brown eyes shining and earnest.

"There's a new world revolution coming, bro. If you want in, I can get you in. After this, you'll never want for narcotics again. Guaranteed. And society? They're going to bend over backwards to eat their own shit to help you. This stuff will take you closer to God than you've ever been before. Guaranteed."

I wasn't looking for God. "Can I crash at your place for a while?"

X

Tiki's lying still, the Phenergan kicking in. A thick hospital-issue blanket smothers his body. His skin is so pale now he could be mistaken for an Anglo. Except for the jaundice. The Polynesian has fled in his waka back out to sea, leaving the Dutch pirate behind to pillage the scant remains.

Tony's back, pulling on his latex gloves, dragging the

drug tray towards my chair, its wheels spinning quickly over the carpet.

"If you'd had your bloods, it would make this a much better experience. Tailored to a T. We need to get the clouds out of your Vishuddha, get that sky blue again."

He checks the needle in my vein, then the IV attachments and plugs.

"You thought of getting a portacath put in?" He attaches a saline bag to the hooks on the IV stand. "Makes it a lot easier. We don't have to worry about your veins drying up. Saves us a lot of time pricking holes in you." He grins, all those white pearls.

"Tiki's got infected," I say.

"One in twenty chance. You keep it clean, no problems."

"Finances, Tony, you know. Sally's taking me to the cleaners."

"Tiki sorted you out with a new Benefits Card, didn't he?" Tony injects premeds into one of the plugs on the tap into my arm. "We can use that."

My anus burns and itches for a few seconds as the antibiotics enter my bloodstream.

"A licensed doctor at the public hospital. Even better, it will show up on your medical history, making everything we do look that little bit more authentic."

"Really?"

"Sure. Operation takes about forty minutes. We'll stick a plastic tube into one of those big veins in your chest and bury a plastic nozzle just beneath the skin." He nods at the contraption feeding into the crook of my elbow. "Holes. Punctures. People shake their heads and think 'junkie'. We don't want that, do we?"

X

Doctor Zing was a pharmaceutical paradox of Western

medical science married to Eastern esoteric philosophy. Her office, her official one anyway, seemed crammed with oncology medical journals, Chinese herb manuals, Buddhist meditation guides and biographies about Tom Holt, Ken Kesey, Howard Marks, Timothy Leary and William S. Burroughs.

"Hey, sunshine! Good see you." She leant back in her recliner, a yellowing smile stretching her acne-scarred cheeks. Her hair was tied back in a short, black, greasy ponytail, and she wore dark Gucci sunglasses (with magnified lenses). A faint scent of tobacco lingered in the air around us. "Been long time. You looking good. Your hair grown back already."

"I never lost it." I sat in the chair next to her and nodded. "I've signed them." I handed her the papers. "You'll get twenty percent of my profits from selling the house or on any rents earned. All legit and drawn up like you wanted."

She snatched up the papers, her finger racing down through the text, quickly flipping the sheets until she reached the last page. "Good good. I read over tonight, you come back in morning. I sign them."

"So, when can I restart?"

Doctor Zing laughed, a short, high-pitched series of wheezes. "The ox is slow, but the earth is patient."

She slipped me a business card. The address placed it in the abandoned warehouse complex in Spotswood, down near the river. "For your rituals," she said. She wrote a phone number on a piece of loose-leaf paper, tore it off and handed it to me. "Call this number. They set you up with new Health Benefits Card. Guaranteed for one financial year."

"And then?"

"You still here and you still keen? We get another."

I nodded again, then made to rise from the chair. Her leg shot out, dropping onto my lap. The shoe on her foot was scuffed leather, the heel worn and flat.

"Not so fast."

I tried to put a smile on my face, but inside I grimaced. She wiggled the shoe off in my lap, using my groin as leverage. A warm damp smell rose from her toes.

"You looking good. And you got twenty minutes left before next appointment."

I hated her. But Doctor Zing was the lynchpin and I needed her. I'd done worse in my previous life, before I'd taken my first steps down this path. She could connect us all, me, Tiki, every last one of us sad lost souls looking for a communion we could never get on our own.

How many whores had had to fuck Jesus? How many?

X

Tony hooks up a bag of poison onto the IV stand. He pulls a lime green plastic cover over the bag. On the cover is a smiley face, violet instead of yellow. The pupils of the eyes are no longer black, but each is instead a bright red ladybird. Violet. The infinite. At one with God. Peace. Wisdom. The last colour of the fucking rainbow.

"So what will this do for me?" I ask.

"Mainly bleeding. Mostly nosebleeds, but if you can take the dose long enough we can possibly get you up to a touch of proteinuria. Nothing like a bit of blood in the piss in a public urinal to get the alarm bells fluttering."

"I don't know. Nosebleeds. Public perception of that? Still junkie."

Tony adjusts the taps and the liquid drips steadily into my veins. "We're looking at a combined effect. With the FOLFOX the pigmentation in your skin will go haywire. Depending on the day you'll look day-glo tanned or as pale as priest's cock just before it hits your mouth." He laughs as he looks at me, his eyes twinkling. "We'll up the mixture of the Irinotecan and hope that that finally burns your hair follicles off. You're looking too healthy."

"I know." In the chair nearby, Tiki's face is drawn and pale. Part of his upper arm is exposed, revealing a thick murderous tattoo, a mesh of Samoan and Maori designs fighting for dominance of his flesh. Breath rattles in his chest.

"There's more," Tony continues. "Anaemia is higher with this combination, and the diarrhoea will be constant so you're going to have to take something to counter that. But the anaemia will pay dividends quickly. Increased sweating and production of saliva, hypertension, and neutropenia are almost all guaranteed."

"What's that last one?"

"Neutropenia? A reduction of white blood cells. Usual stuff, but this concentration will really open you up to a lot of other goodies floating out there."

I nod and lean back into the recliner.

"Oh," says Tony. "If you're lucky you'll experience mouth sores and a rash on your hands and feet. The public love the visible signs, remember."

I nod again, then close my eyes. "I'm going to meditate into this, Tony. Can you give us a shot of morphine to help the fall?"

"Consider it done, good buddy."

I breathe in slowly, trying to feel what is happening to my body, the entire cell-death that is occurring right now, in this moment. Thoughts race through my mind; Sally and the house, Doctor Zing forcing my head between her thighs, Tiki closer to God faster than we had imagined, why not me, why not me, why me and the morphine tugs at my blood and drops me an inch, submerging me into the leather of the chair and I inspire all the colours of the rainbow as millions of cells burn in a breath and I expire a vapour of decay and the lights behind my eyes cast yellow Manipura, though it splinters in shards of confusion and depression and I'm in, I'm there, and somewhere Tony is chanting our paths to the Gods...

X

"The living love the dying," said Tiki, back before we began the new path. "The living love those who are being denied their life, and they despise those who are wasting it."

"I don't care. Tiki, you got me all wrong. I don't want to be loved."

Tiki shook his head, thick dreads beaded and dangling. "But you do, bro. Deep down you do."

"Your head's full of shit, Tiki. You're running from your past, not me. I just need some money."

"Do it this way, bro, and you're not going to worry about money anymore."

On the coffee table in front of us, he spread out an insurance form, an application for a Health Benefits card and photocopies of x-rays.

His deep brown eyes were clear and straight. "This'll see us through, bro. Pay for everything."

"You got any money?"

"You listening to me, bro?" The air between us suddenly felt cold and brutal. In the set of Tiki's jaw lay a thousand demons ready to pounce. His fists clenched, then slowly unclenched. He grasped my chin in one of his large hands. The fingers squeezed hard, and I tried to jerk back, but he held me firm. His other hand caught my wrist as I tried to free myself. "I don't think you're listening to me at all. Do you want Sally to take you back?"

"I hear you, Tiki. Jesus, man, that hurts."

He pushed the insurance and application forms towards

me, holding back the x-rays. "There's this doctor I know. She'll set you up with your own x-rays from some dude who's really dying and sort you out for blood tests. Crazy Asian lady. Goes by the name of Zing."

I took the forms, shuffled from his flat out into the streets, and spent the fifty dollars he'd also slipped me just as quick as it took the Vietnamese dealer to spit the plastic-wrapped bag of powder he'd been storing in his cheeks into my willing and waiting and wanting hands.

X

I watched Tiki slowly killing himself over the next six months. I couldn't start yet, as I needed to wait a perquisite number of months before my insurance would cover me for serious illness.

He lost weight, his hair thinned, the melanin in his skin leached away, leaving him pale and smudged. I'd go around to his flat and the toilet would be stale with vomit, the fridge empty, the cupboards bare. Often he'd sit in a threadbare chair in front of the only window that let sun into his room.

"You look like shit, Tiki."

He smiled beatifically. "You look wonderful, bro."

"You any closer to what you're looking for?"

"Every day I'm getting closer."

I flicked through a pile of recent CDs. He had a new widescreen TV, too. "How much did this all cost?"

Tiki laughed. "Nothing. People are giving me all sorts of shit now they think I'm dying."

"How do you turn this thing on?"

"Dunno. I'm not too bothered about it, eh? You want to go for a walk down near the river? The sun looks warm out there, and on a day like today there'll be so much life coming off the water you could eat it."

I had to support him as we took the path through the

park. He managed a slow shuffle, as if his feet were no longer his own to control. Tiki squinted at the sun hovering above, emanating a thin winter heat.

"You can see it in the air, bro. It's everywhere. That sparkle, like a dying bursting born-again synapse. It's *qi*. Everywhere."

He stumbled and sank to his knees. I held his weight and lowered him to the grass. Even though he had shed kilos, Tiki was still a big man. You could shrink the muscle but the bones were still as bruising as they always had been.

"I don't know about this, Tiki. If you're trying to kill yourself, there are better ways."

He folded into himself, his palms pressed to the earth. "Suicide?"

"Yeah, man. Take some pills. Go to sleep. Fuck it, why not just a big dose of heroin?"

"Suicide?" Tiki unfolded like a flower, splaying his arms and legs like petals, opening up unto the sun. "You're missing the point. I want to be a part of life. And it's here, all around us." His fingers curled around the blades of grass, tugging them, caressing them. "God is everywhere, bro, and it wants us to be part of it. Suicide is cheating. The world hates a cheat."

Bags of flesh puffed beneath his bloodshot eyes. Patches of scalp shone where dreads had fallen out. He smiled, and ulcers lined his gums.

I shook my head. "You're dying, Tiki."

His smile widened, then he hacked up a thick wad of bloody phlegm. "Right now I'm dying. Right now. But in three months' time I'll be fine, and I won't forget this feeling. My eyes are open and shall never be closed." He fumbled in his jacket pocket and threw a plastic health card onto the grass in front of me. "Doctor Zing says hello."

I put the card in my pocket and we watched the sun slide

over the water moving slowly downstream and out into the bay.

X

Somewhere in the back of my mind I hear Tony chanting. Somewhere else, the rasp of Tiki's respiration.

The needle in my arm.

The poison in my veins.

No matter how hard I try, the only colours I see are the swirls of blood in my eyelids. Red. Muladhara. The chakra furthest from the divine. I'm kidding myself that I can even see it. It's just blood.

Somewhere in the back of my mind Tony is saying that a significant lack of energy in the Muladhara can make people weak and self-destructive.

Somewhere in the back of my mind I know this is true of every junkie, of every addict. There is no God here. There is no salvation.

Already I feel nausea permeating my every fibre. I don't want to throw up, it's just a low-level sagging of unwell, the very core of my being unravelling on a molecular level. Sally, free and easy, just for fun, just for sex. Give it up come and go and now I'm gone...

But I couldn't.

And here I am, strapped into a leather recliner, pumped full of cytotoxic drugs following in the stumbling footsteps of Tiki's mad dream.

What am I doing?

He's named after a tribal good luck charm. The tattoos on his arms are meant to ward off ghosts. Instead, they fight each other with their greenstone meres. I hear them tearing through the bush, the dull crack of stone on skull as they club each other to death.

I've got nothing but a head full of shit.

I breathe deeper and the red behind the swirls, darker and deeper, phasing into blackest indigo and I'm hot so hot...and there's...I can...hardly...see...

...there's something inside my head, filling me and every breath takes me closer...

purple claws rake my skull

sparkling synapses burst

sharp tiny teeth peel back the layers of my brain like an onion I can smell it sharp and tangy my eyes are watering and thousands upon thousands of them crawl down into the cerebral core oh i can hardly breathe i can hardly bear to be a part of it all

i can hardly

i can

see

Tiki is screaming.

I open my eyes and the harsh brunt of fluorescents overhead flood and overload.

Tiki thrashes in his chair. Tony sprawls over Tiki's chest, trying to restrain him. Froth bubbles from the corners of Tiki's cracked lips.

"Kara! Morphine! Get the fucking morphine!"

I've never heard Tony shout before. Kara rushes from the medical cabinet, squirting syringe in hand. She plunges it into one of the plugs attached to the drip-feeding Tiki.

"Too slow!" Tony yells. Sweat shines on his forehead. I can see it staining under his arms. "Stick it into his thigh. Now!"

Tiki throws Tony across the room, a clatter of surgical instruments shrieking over the floor as the cart overturns. The whoosh from Tony's lungs is a clear and beautiful climax to the cacophony. Tiki swats Kara aside as she attempts to stab him with the needle. She collides with the IV stand, and the drip rips from Tiki's chest. A bubble of dark red blood bursts forth from the hole in his skin above the portacath buried beneath. Tiki stands upright on the chair and throws his arms wide, staring up at the ceiling. He warbles a stream of harsh vowels and guttural consonants that dissolves into a bray of frayed laughter.

He turns to face me and I'm calm, so sweetly safely calm as his rotting mouth parts in a cracked smile. He holds a hand out, as he steps from the chair and towards the door, beckoning me to follow.

Tiki's eyes are a deep violet.

I tear the drip from my vein.

We stagger out into the twilight, the sky streaked with sacral and solar plexus. The man who gives the sales pitch is still here, his hair still luxuriously thick, though his eyes are wide to see us.

He looks back through the open doors, sees Tony scrambling to his feet. "Stop them!"

The man reaches out to grab us but stops short, his eyes caught in a violet shine. Tiki touches him and the man falls to his knees, drops back onto his haunches.

"Get out of here," he whispers.

I'm struggling now. My head pounds with a hundred years of dehydration and the skin encasing my body is too tight, slowly squeezing out my energy. I can feel it pour from my mouth, a steady stream of dancing motes. Tiki drags me with him, effortlessly, a cascade of sound woven with qi. My ears ring, I cannot understand him as he speaks to me in a golden voice of syrup. I'm vaguely aware of the rush hour crowds on the streets parting as we move like water carving sand.

I fall to my knees, riding a wave of nausea too strong to keep my head aloft. I'm going to be sick. Feet move around me, a widening glade of gum-stained concrete in a meadow of tar and asphalt.

"Can you see it, bro?" Tiki's voice is so loud and clear.

The ground rumbles and overhead the tramlines spark. Tiki steps out onto the street his arms held wide, drawing the energy towards him. The ground rumbles, a thundering herd of elephants stampeding through this jungle and the tram hits Tiki in the chest and people are screaming and I can't lift my head, I'm so sick, so sick and I hear his body hit the road, I feel the impact of his flesh shudder through my bones.

I throw up onto the pavement, over my hands, soaking my knees. People are still screaming. The rumbling has stopped. I collapse onto my stomach, then try to roll onto my back, slipping into the gutter. A tram is stopped here, its alarm bells ring. In the gutter, between the cracks of marbled cement, a blade of green grass protrudes, waxily beautiful. A red and black carapaced beetle scuttles from beneath the blade and pauses to greet me. A ladybird. It has tiny sharp teeth. The carapace opens and filigree wings shake themselves free and away it soars into a sky soaked violet.

Nearby lies a pile of ragged clothes, empty save for a crumbling pile of brittle bones and a smear of tattoo ink.

AFTERWORD

I'd heard of The God Machine but not heard The God Machine. The lyrics to 'I've Seen The Man' resonated instantly, a sense of despair and disbelief, a terrible emptiness while others around rallied in their faith. My initial reaction was of someone in a hospital while The Man lingers and haunts them, unseen by others, as that someone slowly dies. I let this seed lie fallow for the next few months.

When the deadline loomed and nothing had germinated, I sat down in front of the keyboard and played 'I've Seen The Man' continuously while I let myself flow. The story unfolded in front me, a tale of despair and disbelief while others around rallied in their faith. I wrote the final two-thirds of the story in silence, the seed returning its promised fruit.

In the last two years of my life, which has been touched with both the fingers of hell and heaven, I have seen the man. I have been the man, I am now not yet the man, I am searching for the man and at times I despair that there is nothing to find — that I shall leave this earth and my loved ones behind prematurely and with nothing.

Can I take comfort in the fact that we are all born with nothing and leave with as much?

No, I cannot, for I love life too dearly for that to happen to me just yet.

BIOGRAPHY

Paul Haines was raised in the '70s, in the wrong part of Auckland, New Zealand. After completing a degree in the frozen, drunken depths of Otago he wound up working in computers and was eventually lured by sex and money to Australia in the '90s. Vowing to never call it home, he now lives in Melbourne with his wife and daughter.

He has won several awards for his writing and is the author of the short story collections *Doorways For The Dispossessed* (2006), *Slice of Life* (2009) and *The Last Days Of Kali Yuga* (2009).

Lately, Paul has been fighting cancer.

www.paulhaines.com

THE DESERT SONG

ANDREW J. MCKIERNAN

Jacob left town at sunrise and walked west, stopping only at noon to rest in the shade beneath an outcrop of blood-red sandstone. As he walked, he fixed his eyes firmly on the dark shapes shimmering deep within the horizon's mirage. By late afternoon, the shapes had become more distinct, but it wasn't until sunset that he finally reached the stand of coffinwood trees and made his camp.

That night, he lay on his pallet, bullets stuffed in his ears to protect against the song, and watched the stars wheel overhead. He plotted lines between points until the ancient symbols he had been taught as a child stood out against the darkness: the Seven Sisters; Old Man Emu; Dingo forever chasing Rabbit, the Stockman with his shotgun never far behind. But the Stockman's eye, which had once glittered brighter than any other star, now grew fainter with each passing night.

There had been other signs, too. The Bedouin's mob down thirteen roos in a week. Young Billy Hollins going walkabout without notice. And only that morning on Main Street, he'd barely avoided stepping on the ruffled corpse of a willy wagtail. Yes, there had been signs, and Jacob was old enough to remember them even if the rest of the town was too young and ignorant to notice.

In the morning, Jacob took a hammer, a length of rope, and a handful of wooden pegs from his swag. Twelve coffinwood trees grew in the stand. Most were old and thick-limbed, roots drinking deep from some artesian reservoir. Jacob circled them, singing softly as he pounded pegs into the hard, dry earth, and looped rope around their tops until he had staked out his claim. When he was done, he sat in the dust and looked back the way he had come. The morning air was crisp and cool, but the town was only just visible on the horizon. Soon, the sun would warm the air, and the town would vanish completely behind a curtain of haze.

Jacob pulled the bullets from his ears and listened to the wind sigh across the desert. Even in the harsh light of day — even safe under the stand of coffinwood trees — he could still hear a faint whisper of the song. He wondered who would be the first to come. Would it be today or tomorrow, when they realised they were in need of his services?

He reached into his swag, took out his tools and lay them on the dirt: an axe, a saw, hammer and nails, and an old wood-plane. And then, he waited.

X

The Reverend Garland Wallace had always thought of himself as a simple man with simple needs, yet his path in life had been a complex one. Complex enough to land him in this dying town, half a century after Judgment Day, still preaching to the damned.

The Reverend took up the pages of his sermon from the breakfast table. Grunting with the discomfort of age, he stood and tucked the pages into his jacket pocket. He grabbed his hat from the rack by the door and stepped out onto the street. He adjusted his collar and set the hat atop his head, all the while watching the far side of the road.

The Bedouin's van was parked outside the General Store. It had once been some kind of mini-van, now converted almost beyond recognition. Brightly woven rugs festooned its sides, covering doors and windows to keep out the heat.

Dipole aerials and single-wire antennas sprouted like an echidna's spines from a rack on the back. Four children scrambled across the roof, securing supplies and equipment with old and over-stretched octopus straps. Their laughter filled the early morning quiet, work looking more like play as they clambered over and around each other. Four camels stood at the front of the van, tethered to its steering column by a complicated series of harnesses and custom bridles.

That was the Bedouin's entire camp, packed and stacked and ready to roll. Very unusual, unless he was planning to move his family on; and that possibility brought a smile to the Reverend's lips.

The Reverend strode across to the General Store's verandah. He could hear the voice of the Bedouin inside, talking to Mrs. Sheffield about flour and salt. The Bedouin's wife sat in the front passenger seat of the van, black *asaba* wrapped around her head, a swaddled baby at her breast. The side door of the van was open, rugs rolled up to reveal the Bedouin's two eldest sons seated in front of a bank of small monitors. They chattered incessantly into the headsets they wore, joysticks held tight in their hands. On the monitors, seen from a dozen different overhead viewpoints, a large group of roos bounded across a plain.

"Where're ya movin' the mob?" he asked, but neither of the boys turned and the Bedouin's wife ignored him.

Kangaroos were the Bedouin's livestock and the only pastoral animal still surviving in abundance in the country. His family herded the animals using a fleet of semi-autonomous rotorcraft drones emblazoned with the distinctive markings of the Israeli military. The Reverend had no idea where the Bedouin had obtained them, but they were effective. He had seen them buzzing around the roos like over-sized wasps, driving them from one watering hole to the next.

The Reverend watched the tiny monitors, looking for familiar landmarks, listening hard for the sound of rotors in the distance. He could hear something. Not the drones. Their sound was obviously mechanical; a soft electric hum and the flit-flit-flit of blades through dry air. No, this was a sweeter, earthier sound. The wind, skipping across dunes or whistling around an outcrop? That had to be it. But, somehow, it didn't sound like a natural phenomenon. More like a song, with rising and falling notes and a constant rhythm. A flute maybe? Or flutes? Because the more he listened, the more he heard. Layer upon layer of harmonising notes; a cascade leading deeper and deeper until the song became a low rumble in his ears. The Reverend tilted his head and closed his eyes, listened close to find its source, felt himself falling into the song...

"Reverend, do you mind?"

He snapped his eyes open. The Bedouin's wife was staring at him, the baby asleep in her arms. The sons were still fixated on herding their charges and had not moved.

"Reverend Wallace?" The voice came from behind. "I hate to rush the day, but you're standing in a doorway through which I'd dearly like to pass."

The Reverend turned. The Bedouin stood just inside the store, arms full with sacks of flour and salt. He was smiling, though the Reverend had always thought it a wily smile. Grey-white whiskers, as wiry as horsehair, grew in a well-manicured moustache and beard, framing the Bedouin's brown face and peeking out from beneath the white *kufiyyah*-cloth covering his head.

"My apologies for disturbing your daydreams, Reverend. If I had known this thoroughfare was your place of internal reflection I would not have intruded, but," he looked down at the sacks he was carrying, "these goods are beginning to weigh heavy in my old arms."

The Reverend rolled his eyes. He'd seen the old Arab lugging twice that weight and for twice the distance.

"You're no older than me, Azim, and a good deal less infirm, so stop the poor-old-foreigner act."

"Older by a day, and wiser by a year," Azim smiled and shrugged, "but then, arrogance diminishes wisdom so they say; which would make us about even."

The Reverend stood aside and Azim straightened his back, stepped lightly to the van, and hefted the sacks onto the roof with ease. Reverend Wallace envied the man his health, but the envy churned through his mind as contempt. Contempt for the man. For his way of life. His religion. Contempt, most of all, for his very presence in this town and for its acceptance of him. Couldn't the townsfolk see that this was exactly the sort of heathen that had damned them all?

"I notice you've packed up your tents, Azim. Not enough *djinn* around to keep folk frightened? Off to peddle your superstitions elsewhere?"

"I don't peddle 'superstition', Reverend Wallace. I've never met a *djinn*, or an *afrit*, or a *ghul*. Never met anyone who did. By 'superstition', do you mean such things as Judgment Day, whores of Babylon, and great dragons rising from the earth?"

"That day has come and gone, Azim. Just look around you. The End Times are no longer prophecy, they're history. Why do you find that so hard to accept?"

"Because I don't know a single person who was lifted up to Paradise. Because I stand before a holy man of God and I see that he is still here with us. Surely you *are* a holy man? You wear the cloth. My God, my God, oh why hast thou forsaken him?"

The Reverend bristled. He always did when caught for any length of time with Azim. He couldn't help it. The man's sheer disrespect for the Almighty caught in his craw like a fish-hook.

"Not all of God's men have lived perfect lives." The Reverend tried to keep his voice calm. "And some have been left behind for a purpose."

"Which one are you, Reverend Wallace?"

"Both," he answered quickly, proud that he understood his place in the scheme of things. "I wouldn't be fit for God's purpose if I had not first endured the pain of sin."

Azim laughed.

"Oh, and sinning is so much the better part of repentance, isn't it, Reverend?" He turned back to his van, reaching up to tighten the final straps. "To answer your questions: yes, we are moving on. This town is not the place for us at the moment. It isn't the right place for *anyone* at the moment, but I doubt you'd listen to my 'superstitions' about such matters. Maybe you'll listen to Jacob instead?"

"What's the undertaker got to do with anything? He's just an old drunk."

Azim laughed again and turned back to the Reverend.

"Allah willing, my *bayt* will pass through here again. I hope you're still here when we do, Reverend. It would be a shame to return and find nothing but another ghost town."

"What's that supposed to mean?" the Reverend asked, but before he could receive an answer, someone called to him from back down the street.

Aida Hollins was running through the dust, skirts in disarray. By the time she reached him her steps were shuffling, her breathing heavy. Sweat slicked her hair and ran down her red face and neck, moistening her dress until the top was almost transparent.

"Reverend Wallace," she gasped, breasts heaving beneath thin fabric. "You have to come...please, you have to come."

"Now, now, Mrs. Hollins, you haven't run all the way from the homestead, have you? Come, I'll fetch you some water."

He reached out for her arm, catching just the barest touch of sweat-slicked flesh before she pulled away.

"No, you have to come now. It's Billy. He came back this morning. But I don't think he's okay, Reverend."

"Then fetch the doctor, madam. That old quack's more qualified to cure illness than I am."

"It's Doctor Marshall who told me to fetch you. Says you should come right away."

The Reverend watched her for a moment — the fit of her dress across her hips, the gentle curve of her neck — then looked away. Azim was still standing close beside his van watching and, most probably, listening. For the first time since the Reverend had known him, the Bedouin was not smiling.

"Ahh, well then, Mrs. Hollins, we'd best be on our way immediately. It's a rare thing for Doc Marshall to be wanting my advice."

He stepped off the verandah and strode back down the street, hoping Aida Hollins would follow.

"Reverend Wallace," Azim called.

The Reverend stopped, but he didn't turn. He didn't want to look at the Bedouin again. Didn't want to see his mocking smile, or worse, the other face that had slipped into its place — a face of concern, and worry, and fear.

"What is it, Azim?"

"Just a piece of advice...if you'll take it?"

The Reverend nodded for Azim to go on and stared down at his dust-covered boots. A dead bird, black and white, feathers ruffled and crawling with lice, rested between his feet.

"My advice is merely this, Reverend: believe what you see and lay aside what you hear. Keep that in mind for the sake of the town. Lay aside what you hear. Today just might be the day they finally turn to you for help. And if they do, may Allah help them all."

Damn him! The Reverend kicked at the bird's corpse, imagining it was the Bedouin.

X

By noon, Jacob had felled the first of the old coffinwood trees and had begun to strip away its bark, enjoying the sweet, almost cinnamon scent of the wood.

Earlier, he'd seen the Bedouin's mob of roos heading north-west, escorted by their fleet of buzzing drones. Now, the caravan was materialising out of the haze, drawn slowly by its team of mangy camels. If Azim was leaving, then things had already begun, and it wouldn't be long before someone from town showed up at the stand. Jacob would have to work faster, stripping and cutting the wood, planing it flat into planks ready for sizing.

Jacob watched as a small, dark shape separated from the caravan and flew towards him. It landed only a few metres from his camp, rotors throwing up a willy-willy of dust. Jacob went to it, crouching to remove the small bundle strapped to its undercarriage. He smiled into the camera mounted on the drone's front and waved. He stood and looked back to the caravan, kilometres away across the flats, and waved at it too. And then the drone took off, buzzing away into the distance.

Jacob unwrapped the package. The pouch of tobacco and rolling papers made him smile. The small flask of rotgut made him laugh. Azim had never encouraged his drinking before, but he guessed these were exceptional circumstances. The flask was tarnished and dented with age. His fingers ran across the small badge soldered to its side: a dagger thrust downwards through an upturned boomerang, the words *'Strike Swiftly'* engraved across its arms. It was a gift Jacob had given the Bedouin many years ago in a land that no longer existed.

The paper the package had been wrapped in was covered with handwriting, large and chunky like it had been written with a stick of charcoal.

Moving NW, 170km.
19°39'0"S, 134°12'0"E.
See you there if you can make it.
Better to leave sooner rather than later.
Remember Tel Aviv. Remember Sydney.
Believe what you see, lay aside what you hear.
Your friend,
Azim.

X

The Reverend crouched down beside the Hollins' homestead, Doctor Marshall at his side. Aida and George Hollins were behind them, unable to stay still for a second, and their constant movement was annoying.

"For the Lord's sake, will you two just stop? How can we do anything with you both pacing around? George, do you have a torch? It's blacker than Hades under there."

"Yeah, I think there's an old wind-up one in the shed."

"Well, go get it will you? And Aida, fix us some tea."

Billy Hollins was under the house somewhere. They could hear him humming. It was a tune the Reverend found familiar but couldn't quite place. There was another sound too; a wet, tearing sound that set the Reverend's nerves on edge.

"How long's he been under there, Doc?"

"Aida heard the hummin' this mornin', when she first got up. Billy went out to check the dam levels four days ago and didn't come back. Should'a been just a day trip. George said he's done it on his own a hundred times before."

"Then why call me? The boy's probably dehydrated. Delirious, by the sounds of it. And here I thought *you* were the doctor. Let's just get him out of there and get him some water."

"Listen to what he's humming, Reverend. Recognise it?"

He stooped lower, stuck his head into the darkness and listened.

"It's an old hymn!"

"Yeah, thought it was. Haven't heard it since I was a tyke. They used to sing it on ANZAC Day. Any idea where Billy mighta heard it?"

"Umm, no...I...not from me, no."

"Might've noticed people 'round here don't have much patience for your preachin', Reverend. While they're looking for some sort of hope, all you do is tell 'em they're already damned. If you've been poisoning that boy with your crap, it isn't just George Hollins you'll have to deal with."

George came up behind them, cranking the torch.

"What'll I have to deal with?"

"Nothin' George. Just hand us that torch."

Aida had come back from inside the homestead and crouched down beside the men. There were tears in her eyes and a hitch in her voice when she called out.

"Billy? Come on out, honey. I've made lemonade...Why won't he come out?"

The Reverend took the torch and flicked the switch. He pointed it into the darkness. The bright light threw shadows from the brick pilings. Dust and cobwebs filled the spaces between them like veils.

"Over there," Doctor Marshall pointed, and the Reverend moved the beam.

Light fell across Billy huddled in one corner and Aida screamed.

The boy's face was that of an old man; skin dry and

brown, tight as leather against his skull. His clothes hung from his thin frame in tatters. Smears of something dark were spread around his lips and the remains of a small kangaroo sat in his lap. The roo's body was torn open, scraps of bloody fur scattered in the dirt. Billy hissed as the light hit him, screwed up his eyes and held the roo tight to his chest.

The Reverend screamed too, his voice adding a deeper harmony to Aida Hollins' high-pitched squeal.

"We gotta get him out," the Doctor said. "George, you're gonna have to give me a hand here."

George wiped his palm across his face, held it to his mouth and nodded. He was holding his breath, eyes wide as saucers. Aida was weeping — a pitiful sound, the Reverend thought — and she'd moved back beneath the shade of an old ghost gum.

The Reverend held the torch tight with both hands, though it did little to stop the shaking, and George and the Doc got down and crawled under the house. Billy didn't move as they approached but he seemed tense, muscles like cords of rope against his thin frame. His humming became an increasingly guttural growl and the two men hesitated. They whispered to each other, planning how they would approach things, but the Reverend saw Billy tilt his head and was sure the boy could hear every word.

George began speaking softly to his son, as gently and fatherly as he could manage. He moved one way, and Doc Marshall moved the other. But the boy wasn't fooled for a second.

Billy twisted sideways, threw the kangaroo carcass at his father, and scuttled for a darker recess. George scrambled forward and grabbed one bare ankle. Doc Marshall grabbed the other and they dragged Billy backwards through the dirt and dust and blood-stained fur. The boy screamed; a dry screech that reminded the Reverend of trains braking suddenly and unexpectedly.

The two men emerged backwards from the crawlspace, hauling on the shrieking boy's legs. Billy dug his fingers into the dirt, nails ploughing furrows as his legs emerged into the sunlight.

And then his screaming stopped. His movement stopped. Even George and Doc Marshall stopped. They looked at the Reverend who nodded them on.

"Come on, he's given up. Let's get him out of there."

They pulled Billy out and turned his body over. His flesh was as tough and hard as well-cured papier-mâché. His lips were pale and cracked, like stitches drawn tight across his teeth. His eyes were closed, wrinkled lids covering sunken sockets.

Doc Marshall felt at the boy's wrist and neck. He pried for a moment at the lips, then looked up and shook his head.

"I think he's dead, George. Looks like he's been dead for years."

George Hollins stared at his son's corpse and his bottom lip trembled. The Reverend went to place a hand on the stricken man's shoulder but stopped himself, not knowing how it would be received. George had never been one for religion, but hard times might change a man's perspective. Then again, such an obvious sign of God's wrath...well, George just might turn on him.

Aida Hollins collapsed against the trunk of the ghost gum. The Reverend could hear her humming softly to herself.

"We'll have to get him back into town," Doc Marshall was saying. The Reverend barely noticed. He was too busy listening to Aida's gentle melody, and to the sound of the desert that whispered beneath it like a song.

X

The sun was setting when Doc Marshall and Reverend

Wallace rolled back into town, the Doc's dung-powered ute juddering on ancient suspension. Billy Hollins' body lay in the back, shrouded in an old sheet. It shifted with each new jolt from the road, sliding from one side of the tray to the other.

The townspeople had gathered in the street and they crowded in on the ute as it slowed. They all wore looks of concern and some called desperately for the Doctor's attention. The Reverend sat quietly in the passenger seat, ignored and glad of it for once.

"Step back, step back," the Doctor growled, trying to push his door open. The crowd moved back a step but their talk didn't falter. Patrick Anderson and Jenny Buckland had both disappeared during the night. Something had killed three of Andy Paulsen's dogs, and the other two refused to come out of their kennels. Tony Camilleri had gone out to the Olsen farm this morning to fix their generator and no one had answered, not even old Maggie Olsen, who never left the house.

The Reverend stepped from the ute and went around back to check on the body. Nobody wanted to confess their calamities to him. They didn't yet see that his faith might be their only salvation. But he would begin by doing the right thing by Billy Hollins and his family. The boy would need a proper funeral. He'd need a beautiful eulogy and a new sermon. And he'd need a coffin.

He left the body and moved onto the porch of the undertaker's store. There was a 'Closed' sign on the door and a note tacked beneath it:

```
Gone west, 20km
Old coffinwood stand.
Bring any bodies to me immediately.
Don't forget to bring a spade or two!
              - Jacob
```

Damned drunk, the Reverend thought. They'd never make it 20km and back before sunset, not if there was a body to bury in hard, rocky soil. They'd have to leave it until morning.

Damned ignorant, useless, drunken abbo, the Reverend fumed. *What a day to go on a bush bender.*

X

Most of the time, Jacob heard the song as *Cockleshell Heroes*, the adopted march of his old regiment. If he listened too long, it was like they were somewhere just on the far side of an outcrop, calling for him to join them on the parade ground. He wondered what that said about his psychology; that such a song would have so strong an influence. A song, that at any other time, he could only match with thoughts of desert raids and bio-bombs, bleeding children and crumbling walls.

Faint lights were beginning to appear in the distance as the town prepared for night. The song would be louder there, Jacob knew. It would find the cracks in their walls and in their minds, and what everyone heard would be different — a lullaby, a hymn, an old television theme or a forgotten Top 40 hit. But to all of them, it would sound like the call of everything they thought they had lost. To them, it would sound like heaven.

X

All afternoon and into the evening, Reverend Wallace stood over the body of Billy Hollins and preached the Word of his Lord. He spoke piously and fervently, referring less and less to the old, leather-bound Bible clasped loosely in his hands. The words had been sunk deep inside him many years ago: now, a well-spring had been tapped and verses sprang forth, fizzing with life after fermenting for so long in the bile of his own guilt and shame.

He supposed it had something to do with having a congregation again.

The townsfolk had followed the body into the old church; a procession of the curious and confused. They'd left the carrying to the Reverend and Doc Marshall, preferring instead to continue their gossip while Billy was laid out on an old trestle table in front of the pulpit. They stayed to ask questions of the Doc — questions for which he had little or no answer — and most left when they were sure he knew no more than they did. Many, including Doc Marshall, left when the Reverend stood to say a prayer for Billy Hollins. But enough of them had stayed, and the Reverend was heartened to see Aida and George still sitting amongst them.

"We are like the harlot-wife of Hosea," he told them, perspiration dripping from his brow. "We have violated the obligations of our divine marriage to God. And like any dutiful husband, God has turned his back on us."

Candles and lamps had been lit throughout the church to hold back the night. Their presence added significantly to the room's already stifling heat but threw barely any light. The Reverend could only count eight people sitting in the gloom, though there might have been more in the shadows. He wiped sweat from his eyes, placed the Bible on the chest of Billy Hollins' shrouded corpse, and leant forward as if addressing each and every one of them personally.

"We've always known those rules and obligations, but it is a knowledge that we have chosen to ignore. The Lord God said: *My people are destroyed for lack of knowledge; because thou hast rejected knowledge.*"

A couple of the townsfolk were nodding at his words. Aida Hollins swayed to the cadence of his speech; George looked like he was asleep. Warm desert winds blew through the rafters, whipping up a sound that reminded the

Reverend of organ music.

"But, my people..." And here he paused to look around, catching as many eyes as he was able, palms resting across the shrouded body as if in benediction, "...there is still hope! For God has also said: *I will have mercy upon them that have not obtained mercy, and I will say to them that were not my people, Thou art my people; and they shall say, Thou art my God!*"

The Reverend closed his eyes, enjoying the soft scattering of applause and whispered amens. Someone was weeping; it sounded like George Hollins, and the thought that it might have been him affected the Reverend most of all. He breathed hard and tried to regain his composure. He could feel his own tears starting to flow, mixing with the hard-earned sweat of his fervour.

Beneath his fingers, the bed-sheet twitched.

It might have been just a fold of fabric shifting in a draught, or movement caused by the weight of the Reverend's own hands. He might even have been able to ignore it altogether, had the sheet not moved a second time.

The Reverend jerked his hands from the shroud and opened his eyes. The Bible on the boy's chest was moving, slowly and subtly, rising and falling like a boat on a gentle tide. He watched, unable to move, as the book shifted and fell to the floor with a thud.

The congregation started; chairs scraped against the floorboards, necks craned forward. The body twitched again and a corner of the shroud fell away, exposing dry and flaking skin drawn tight across a bony hand. The fingers curled and uncurled with a sound like scrunching paper. The body shuddered — once, twice, three times — and someone screamed.

Reverend Wallace was frozen in place, arms half raised towards his congregation. Some of them scattered, tripping over chairs in a race for the exit. A few stood still and open-mouthed, as transfixed by this miracle of resurrection as he was.

The figure sat up on the trestle table, and the shroud fell away. The Reverend took a step back. To see that face and think the boy might actually be alive? It just wasn't possible. There was nothing of God's mercy written on that withered flesh or in the sunken, staring eyes.

Aida and George Hollins were both weeping. They called to their son between sobs, advancing uncertainly towards the trestle table. Billy turned to watch them, cracked and bloodied lips parting in what might have been a smile. Aida tried to smile too, but the Reverend could that see her belief was fading.

"That's not our son..." she mumbled, "That's not our boy..."

The thing on the table looked her in the eye, held out its arms, and began to sing.

The voice was harsh and gravelly at first, but it smoothed out with each new note until it was as fine as the desert sand. Aida heard a lullaby; George, an old Elvis track to which he'd once courted his wife. Everyone in the room heard a different song — tunes that comforted and soothed them, sounds from their past and their dreams. The Reverend heard it as the hymn Billy had hummed from beneath the floorboards; as the soft drone of organ music and the buzz of rock and roll; as marching tunes and jazz. He heard it all and knew this demon's trick for what it was. *Believe what you see, and lay aside what you hear.* That was what the Bedouin had told him, and he stumbled away even as the others were stepping closer.

It went for Aida Hollins first. The creature tensed its ropey muscles and sprang from the table. Desiccated arms wrapped around Aida's neck and she stumbled backwards. Sharp teeth gnashed at her throat. The Reverend tried to get around the trestle table, but George was in the way. The man was humming, hips gyrating in time to a song only he could hear. Aida screamed, her shrill voice mixing with the wind as it rushed through eaves and half-open doors. Candles spluttered to sparks and the desert song echoed louder through the near-empty church. It was calypso and reggae. It was Wagner and Bach. It was the sound of heaven, and the Reverend fought hard to ignore it.

He pushed George away and the man staggered, feet tangling in the sheet that had once been his son's shroud. Aida thrashed and screamed at the creature crouched on her chest. It pinioned her arms above her head, face nuzzled deep into the crook of her neck.

The Reverend started forward. His foot came down on the tail end of the shroud and the linen wrapped tight around George's ankles. The farmer's arms flung out, groping as he fell, and he came down hard against the wall. A lamp dropped from its hook and shattered. Oil and flames spread quickly across the old hardwood floor. George tried to stand and run, but the shroud was already alight. He screamed and stumbled, arms pin-wheeling as he fell back into the spreading puddle of fire.

The demon looked up from Aida's throat. Its face and claws were slick with blood, lips drawn back in a snarl. Aida's screams had become gurgles.

The Reverend grabbed the Bible from the floor and hurled it at the thing that had once been Billy Hollins. The book flew true, opening at the last moment like a dove spreading its wings, and slammed into the thing's face. The creature tumbled from Aida's chest and scurried for the shadows. The Reverend tried to follow but the heat had become too intense. George had stopped screaming and thrashing, his body a beacon of fire that lit the room.

The Reverend went back for Aida, but she was already

dead. He took her by the legs and dragged her from the church. Her skirts rode up over her head, but he averted his eyes. He stayed low, crouching beneath the churning smoke and flame, until he fell, coughing and spluttering, onto the street.

X

Jacob threw a handful of leaves into the boiling billycan and waited. He'd seen the smoke rising from the town first thing. That visitors would follow seemed almost certain, and his mum had always taught him to make sure the kettle was on when guests were due. By the time Doc Marshall's sputtering ute arrived, Jacob was onto his second cup.

Sunlight glared across the ute's windscreen. Jacob couldn't see the Doc in the driver's seat, but he waved anyway. Two people sat in the back, slouched against the tailgate: Tony Camilleri and Andy Paulsen. Both held long-handled spades. A sheet-wrapped bundle was in the back too, about the size and shape of a body.

"So, you found Billy Hollins, Doc?"

The driver's side door opened. The man who got out wasn't Doc Marshall. It was that smug bastard who called himself a Reverend.

Tony and Andy were already out of the ute and lowering the tailgate. They handed Jacob their spades and hefted the body from the tray.

"Where do you want us to put her?" Tony asked.

"Umm, over there, beneath the big tree on the left."

The two men set their backs and carried the body away. Jacob turned to the Reverend.

"What does he mean, *her*? What about Billy Hollins?"

"It's *Aida* Hollins, Jacob. Aida is the one who died. Oh, we found Billy Hollins all right. He was the one who ripped out her throat."

Jacob turned and followed the body to the old coffinwood tree. "I need to take measurements," he said. "For the coffin." And he unwrapped the shroud from the body.

Nobody had thought to close her eyes and they stared up at him like dull, upturned saucers. Her face was pale, lips blue, but neither were dry or cracked. There were no signs of dehydration or rapid cellular desiccation. A number of ragged tears at her throat indicated the obvious cause of death.

He reached out and gently closed her eyes.

"She's okay," he said, realising immediately how that would sound to the others. "I mean...she's not going to become one of them. But we'll bury her here anyway."

The Reverend stood behind him as he ran a tape measure down the length of Aida Hollins' body.

"You seem to know something about this, Jacob. That filthy Bedouin told me as much. What sin have you committed to bring this evil down upon us?"

"It's not *my* sin, Reverend. A sin of men, for sure, but nothing of my doing."

He stood and went back to the newly planed planks he'd stacked beside his camp. He chose a few lengths and sat to mark them up for cutting. The Reverend followed, stomping furiously through the dust.

"This town might be the last refuge of God's people on earth! The dead are rising! And you? You choose to be cryptic?"

"What happened to Billy Hollins, Reverend? Where is he?"

"I...I don't know. We took his body to the church. It was too late to bring him all the way out here. He was dead, Jacob. But he got up and tore out Aida's throat. He started singing, like the sound that's been coming off the desert. What in God's name is all this?"

"Billy? What happened to him?"

"There was a fire. He ran off."

"And George?"

The Reverend shuddered. "The fire. There's no way he could have got out."

"This might sound callous, Reverend, but it's the truth: if even an ounce of your Faith is true, then George and Aida are the lucky ones. They're not infected and they're not going to come back. The rest of us are stuck here for now, and things are only going to get worse unless you do as I say. How many more people are missing?"

"Ummm...Patrick Anderson and Jenny Buckland went missing yesterday. Tony couldn't find anyone at the Olsen property, either. This morning, there were six more unaccounted for. But some of them...they might have died in the fire, too."

"What about Doctor Marshall?"

"Couldn't find him. Had to get Tony to hot-wire the ute."

"That means about twelve, at least, including Billy Hollins. We can still save them though, Reverend, if you trust me."

The Reverend nodded, though Jacob didn't see much trust in his eyes.

"You need to go back to town with Tony and Andy. Get as many people together as you can and search all the houses. Search the cupboards and pantries. Under the floorboards. Cellars too, if they've got them, and sheds. Anywhere it's dark and cool, that's where you'll find them."

"And then what?"

"Drag 'em out into the sunlight. That'll immobilise them. Their metabolism is too fast, and they dehydrate quickly, so they go into a sort of torpor to conserve energy. Get them into the sunlight and you'll have enough time to get them all back here."

"And what are you going to do to them here?"

"Bury them...that they shall rise again on the third day."

The Reverend bristled at the misquote. That this man, who made his living from death, should try and throw the Bible back at him!

"Steady on, Reverend. I'm not exactly making fun. They're afflicted with a bacterial infection that's trying to over-write their DNA. If I bury them here, in coffinwood for three days, they *will* rise again. The trees contain *eugenol*, a strong anti-microbial that will kill the bacteria. The water the trees drag up from down deep will soak through the wood and rehydrate the bodies. They'll wake up! They'll be fine!"

The Reverend shook his head. This was all too much. It was exactly the sort of scientific mumbo jumbo that had damned the world in the first place.

"This is a joke, isn't it? Satan is breathing down our necks and you're ready to deny his hand in this? We are stuck here in this Hell, and *you* want to resurrect the dead? Death is the only door the Lord has left open to us. Why would you want to deny people the chance of entering His Kingdom after all this suffering? Why does that amuse you so much?"

"You think those people are dead, Reverend? You think that their suffering has ended? You saw Billy Hollins! He looked dead, but did he act like he was? Is that the way you measure your God's mercy? By what Billy has become? By what he did to Aida?"

The Reverend spat at the ground and turned on his heels. "I'll not listen to this! You know nothing of God's mercy!"

"They're not vampires or zombies, Reverend. They're not minions of Satan. They're people who need our help. Take Andy and Tony back to town with you and do what I said. Find them, bring them here. And do it before nightfall. Do it before the desert starts to sing, Reverend, because I'm thinking that you're the sort of man who'd be quite susceptible."

The Reverend stood with his back to the undertaker.

"What *is* that sound? It sounds like...like, everything that ever sounded good."

"It doesn't sound like that to everyone. It isn't always heavenly choirs. But it *is* their best weapon. Applied Neurotheology: sound waves modulated to increase the flow of *Dimethyltryptamine* in the pineal gland. In some people it induces a religious experience, makes them compliant. Easier for an invading force to subdue a target community."

"What? You're saying this is some sort of military weapon they are using?"

"They *are* the military weapon, Reverend. An experiment in mapping extremophile DNA onto the human genome. It was supposed to make better soldiers and if you don't get back into town soon, your position is going to be overrun. And then whose souls are you going to save?"

X

On the way back to town, the Reverend thought a lot about what Jacob had said. He didn't believe all of it, but a lot of it could have been true. That mankind had been used as a tool to engineer his own destruction was no surprise at all. None of it changed the fact that the Lord's wrath was upon the world when what they really needed was His mercy.

I will have mercy upon them that have not obtained mercy...

He let the quote roll around in his mind until it picked up the rhythm of the tyres against the desert's gentle corrugations. It took on the melody of the wind whistling through the windscreen, and soon he was whistling, too.

About a kilometre from town, he stopped the ute.

He stepped out, looking across the red sands, and called to Tony and Andy.

"Listen," he said when they reached his side. "Just listen for a moment. Can you hear that? That's the sound of God's mercy."

X

Jacob had barely been working an hour when he heard the ute returning. Tony and Andy hopped from the back and walked over to where Aida Hollins still lay beneath the shade of a coffinwood tree.

"What's going on? Back a little early aren't you?"

The two men ignored him and picked up their spades. Jacob turned back to the Reverend, who stood beside the ute, head tilted to one side.

"We need your wood, Jacob. We've come back so that we may have mercy upon those who have not obtained mercy. Your hard work — carpentry no less! — will allow me to save them from this eternal Hell."

"What are you going to do, you sick bastard?"

"Jesus said: *And he that taketh not his cross, and followeth after me, is not worthy of me.*"

It was all the explanation Jacob received before a spade smacked into his head from behind.

He floated through dreams of waking up inside his own coffin buried deep beneath the earth. He dreamed of his fingers scrambling at newly hewn wood, splinters breaking off beneath his nails. Of the air growing stale and his chest getting tighter, tighter, tighter with every breath.

When Jacob finally did wake the dark confused him for a moment, and he thought he really had been buried alive...again, for the dream images were largely memory and not fantasy. But it was only the darkness of night, and his fire had gone out. He felt the egg of pain on the back of his head and checked his hand for blood. The lump was large and tender, the hair around it crusty, but his fingers came away dry.

The moon hadn't risen yet, but the stars were bright enough for him to see that his camp was in disarray: tools stolen, the hewn planks gone and at least four other coffinwood trees cut down and taken away.

The wind was blowing strong from the east, warm and full of grit. So loud and clear was the desert song that Jacob spent a frantic moment searching the dirt for his bullets before he realised they were already in his ears. He groped around in the dark for his swag and felt inside for the handgun that went with the bullets. Its clip was already full, apart from the two in his ears, but he checked it anyway before sliding it into the waistband of his jeans.

The town was a beacon of shifting orange light on the horizon. Jacob began to walk towards it. He sang tunes Azim had taught him — tunes especially written to counterpoint the whisper of the desert. If he walked hard, he'd reach town by morning. Maybe then he'd be able to save some of the people the Reverend seemed so intent on murdering.

As the eastern sky grew lighter and Jacob drew closer, the morning winds brought with them the sound of gunfire and the smell of burning coffinwood. By the time Jacob reached the first building on the outskirts, he could hear shouting and screaming, and the singing of hymns.

He'd removed the bullets from his ears at the first sign of light on the horizon and inserted them back into the clip of his sidearm. The desert song was still strong, though it would fade with the coming of the sun, and he preferred the comfort of a full weapon.

He slipped silently between shadows — the old stealth training rushing back — until he reached the corner of the town's wide main street. Doc Marshall's ute sputtered past and he crouched low and hard against the wall of the old fish-and-chip shop. Tony Camilleri was driving and Andy Paulsen sat beside him. Four or five bodies had been stacked in the tray.

The ute pulled up at the far end of the street. The Reverend was waiting there, standing beside piles of smouldering ash and wood. Three or four other fires still burned; heavy wooden crosses planted in the hard-packed dirt, flames eating and blackening their crossbeams and the remains of the figures nailed to them. Another cross had already been constructed from the planks of Jacob's coffinwood, lying in the dust beside where the ute was parked.

Tony and Andy dragged a withered body from the tray — *Doc Marshall*, Jacob thought, *they got Doc Marshall* — and laid it along the length of the fresh cross. They took its arms and straightened them out along the crossbeam. The Reverend took up a hammer and a handful of nails. He knelt down and hammered the Doc's desiccated right hand to the coffinwood. The Doc's eyes widened and his cracked lips opened with an unearthly scream. Tony and Andy sang as they held the thrashing body down, and the Reverend secured the other hand to the cross with a single stroke of his hammer.

Jacob stole a little closer, ducking behind the cover of the church's charred remains. The Reverend hammered the final nail into the Doc's thin ankles, and the three men lifted the cross until its base dropped into a hole they'd dug in the street. The Doc, hung by his arms, finally fell still, the rays of the morning sun forcing his transformed body into torpidity.

The Reverend held his Bible tight to his chest and took a

battered jerrycan from the back of the ute. He shook it and clear liquid sprayed onto the dried skeletal husk hanging on the cross. The thirsty flesh drank it up, grew momentarily supple and new, and then the body began to convulse. Arms and legs jerked; tugging, pulling, tearing on the nails that held them in place. The grainy smell of home-made ethanol drifted through the air past Jacob's hiding place.

Andy Paulsen took a lighter from his pocket and lit a taper of newspaper. In the moment it took for it to catch, Jacob was on his feet. He fired off a quick shot that went wide, but it was close enough for him to adjust on the run. He sprang from behind a charcoal-covered wall and ran for the ute. His second shot caught Andy in the chest.

Andy looked down in surprise at the large hole that had opened in the front of his T-shirt. Jacob had just enough time to see the taper fall from Andy's hand and go out before he was sliding in against the ute's grille.

He stayed low, listening to Tony and the Reverend's confusion and panic, then popped his head up and looked back over the bonnet. The men were both looking off into the buildings that lined the street. Neither of them had seen him come up on the ute.

Tony turned to take something from the ute's tray and Jacob ducked. He heard the clack of a shotgun opening, shells being fitted, snapped shut again. He could hear the body of Doc Marshall struggling on the cross; a sound like crumpled wrapping paper settling in a garbage bin.

"It's that Satan-born-black-atheist-motherfucker of an undertaker!"

Jacob bent lower and crawled away from the voices. He kept the body of the ute between himself and where he estimated they were standing. He looked back to see Tony's boots and the cuffs of his jeans heading off towards the ruins of the town hall. The Reverend shuffled around somewhere at the back of the ute. Jacob couldn't see him and hoped he was looking the other way. He counted three, waited for Tony Camilleri take two more steps, tensed his muscles to stand and—

"Hey! Tony! He's on the other side of the truck!"

The Reverend was crouched at the back of the ute. He'd bent to pick up Andy's lighter and was relighting the taper. For an instant, he and Jacob locked eyes through the shadowy space between the tyres. The end of the taper caught the lighter's flame and Jacob stood without thinking. He turned to where Tony had been and fired. The man was considerably closer than before, his shotgun raised to shoot from the hip, but Jacob's line was still good. Tony took the bullet in the throat and the shotgun fell from his hands, discharged into the air, buckshot tearing shreds from his face.

Jacob swivelled his aim to the rear of the ute. The Reverend was backing towards the coffinwood cross. The taper still burned in his hands.

"The wind hath bound you up in her wings, Reverend," Jacob called and lowered his weapon. "Wasn't it your God who said: *For I desire mercy, and not sacrifice; and the knowledge of God more than burnt offerings*?"

The Reverend laughed.

"Don't quote scripture to me, heathen! I *am* offering these souls mercy. I am giving them the mercy of a true death, so that they might rejoin the Kingdom of God and be forgiven their sins."

"But who will forgive *your* sins, Reverend? Who are you really trying to save? Not these people — we could have done that, I told you how. You're certainly not trying to save yourself! All you're trying to save is your own twisted idea of God."

Jacob edged along the side of the ute. He kept his

handgun down and his eyes on the burning taper.

"These people are not evil. They are not damned. They're just infected! A bacterial infection; I know how to cure it! Please, just stop listening to the song. If you really want to save God, or yourself...if you want to save anyone, just lay aside what you hear, Reverend."

"Ahh! You and that filthy Bedouin! It's your lack of faith that damned us all here in the first place!"

The Reverend spun on his heels and stepped towards the cross. The taper spluttered and flared with his sudden movement. Flames had already consumed most of the rolled newspaper and spread down his hand to the cuff of his suit. Jacob dropped his weapon in the dust and dived at the Reverend's back.

The two bodies met with a slap and a grunt. The air rushed from Jacob's lungs as they hit the ground, his arms still wrapped around the Reverend's waist. He gasped for air and grabbed for the Reverend's still flaming hand. The Reverend twisted, taking Jacob with him, and their bodies rolled through the fuel-soaked dust. Legs kicked out and connected with the jerrycan, sending it toppling. More ethanol poured out, soaking the ground.

Jacob saw the sudden bright flash of ignition an instant before the heat washed over them. He let go of the Reverend and rolled away. His trousers and shirt were already on fire, and he could smell hair burning. He rolled until the flames were out and patted a shower of sparks from his head. The cross was in full flame now, Doc Marshall's body little more than a blackened husk nailed to the flaming crossbeam. The Reverend lay at the foot of the cross, arms outstretched as if in prayer. His cleric's suit blazed and the body did not move while flames consumed it.

Jacob sat in the gutter and looked up at the flaming crucifix. Like the Reverend, he hadn't saved anyone in the end. He pondered this and watched the fire burn. It didn't quite have the power of the desert song, but it was captivating nonetheless. So captivating that he didn't notice when the flames caught at the ute, licking their way across the tray to the vehicle's methane fuel tank. In fact, when the tank exploded, the concussion was so swift and violent that he barely noticed anything at all.

X

Eight days and nights, moving across the desert sands. North west, 170km, that's what the Bedouin had told him and he knew he must be close...or he'd already passed the spot.

His water had run out three days ago. But that was okay, he'd gone longer than that without water — in the deserts of China and the Middle East. Occasionally, he thought he could see the dark wasps of the Bedouin's drones floating far off in the mirage. He imagined that they had seen him. That, even now, the caravan was coming back for him. He knew this was only fantasy, though. That the drones were just illusions of the heat. The same heat that drew moisture from his body and left him feeling dry and listless.

When Jacob grew too tired and weak to walk any further, he sat down on the edge of a dune. Soon, the sands would cover him, and he would sleep. If he was lucky, one day, a good rain would come, and he would rise to walk the desert sands again.

AFTERWORD

The God Machine — what an awesome band, and one I came to quite late, long after they'd split. 'The Desert Song' is the one track on the album I come back to time and time again. Despite the simplicity and sparseness of its lyrics, there is an underlying complexity that just sucks me in every time — the middle-eastern intro and biblical quotes, burning crosses, all that shooting and killing, and then there's the driving drum beat that holds it all together so magically.

When I was asked to provide a story inspired by that song for this anthology, it didn't take long for all those musical and lyrical pieces to fall into place. With my love of Spaghetti Westerns and a long-time interest in theology, the main basis for the story came fairly quickly: a battle between two conflicting ideologies that culminates in an old-style shoot-out. The biblical quotes from the book of Hosea — and the verses that surround those quotes — hint at a land and people rejecting, and rejected by, both God and rationality. This led to the characters of Jacob and The Reverend, and to the battle they have over the forces of knowledge and superstition. And the Australian Outback was just too good a setting to pass up for a post-apocalyptic tale.

BIOGRAPHY

Andrew J. McKiernan is an author and illustrator living and working on the New South Wales Central Coast. His work appears here and there, like a slow-growing fungus.

www.andrewmckiernan.com

HOME

MARTIN LIVINGS

Jack sits, dead, in the passenger seat of a white sedan driven by a familiar stranger. It's hot in the car, hot like an open oven, hot like a burning lake of oil; rivulets of sweat trickle down his brow and back, along his arms. His wrist itches and aches where his watch strap digs into it, but he doesn't dare look at it, doesn't want to know the time. Half past death, a quarter to hell.

"How are you holding up, soldier?" the man asks him, without taking his eyes from the road ahead, straight and featureless as the barrel of a rifle. On either side of the road, misty buildings stream past them, their walls transparent. Nebulous tree spirits line the street, barely there at all. And, beyond and beneath and behind them all, the desert, always the desert, dry, flat, dead. Dead like Jack.

Jack looks down from the road ahead, at his once-pristine army dress uniform, rumpled by heat and sweat. There, in the middle of his chest, the shirt is torn and burnt, hanging away in ragged flaps. Beneath that, the gaping hole in his chest. His fingers flutter unconsciously to the wound, feeling the jagged edges of his shattered ribs.

"Jack?"

Jack looks up at the driver, a well-dressed man in his middle years with dark, thin hair greying and flat against his scalp. Small, delicate glasses sit on the bridge of his thin nose. He wears a stylish dark blue suit and seems blissfully untouched by the heat that torments Jack, who feels like he should know him. The man keeps watching the road.

"Jack, I asked you how you were holding up." There is a searching quality in the man's voice, a piercing lighthouse beam of concern that makes Jack shrivel in his seat.

Jack doesn't say anything, can't find the air in his ruined chest. He wants to ask where he is, who the driver is, where they're going, but there's dust in his throat, sand in his lungs. He shrugs instead.

"Not too far to go now," the man says. "Nearly there." He glances across at Jack.

Jack flinches away from the driver. The man's eyes are carnival mirrors, each one holding a twisted, misshapen reflection of Jack, throwing it back at him like a foul curse. He turns, looks out his window instead, anything to escape those mirrored eyes. Outside, the ghost houses pass them by, their fences swirling with pale luminescent smoke. They stand above the arid sands on foundations long dead, faded memories of brick and wood and concrete. Only the desert is real now. The desert, and the road, and the heat.

The car slows, pulls over. Jack feels the bump as it stops, and the buildings around them emerge from the smoke, become more real, more solid. It looks like a service station, a low-slung building with huge glass windows and doors plastered with garish advertisements for a thousand things a dead man no longer needs. The driver turns to Jack, he sees it in his peripheral vision, but he doesn't return the look, doesn't dare meet those eyes again. "I'm sorry," the man says, "but we need to get some petrol. Can I get you anything? Some water?"

Water. Jack's dry mouth and throat cry out for it, but he controls them. He can't trust anything, not from this man, this *thing* that looks like a man. He shakes his head.

"Suit yourself," says the man, and climbs out of the car.

He walks around and pumps some petrol into the tank, stands casually in the mist, the buildings languidly fading in and out of existence around them. The harsh clunk-clunk-clunk of the bowser makes his head hurt. Then it stops, and the driver puts the nozzle back and walks into the smoke, towards the hazy shop. In a second or two, he's gone. Jack holds his breath, waits for the man to reappear, but he doesn't. Then Jack reaches for the door handle, expecting it to be locked, but it clicks and opens beneath his hand.

Outside, the air is even hotter than within, drier, dustier. He coughs as he steps out of the car, wobbles on his feet as if he's never walked a step in his life. He leans against the vehicle for a moment, then pushes himself off. He walks away, away from the car, away from the phantom petrol station. Away from it and towards the only thing that's real. The road and the desert beyond.

He stands at the edge of the road, swaying a little. His head spins. The sweat is under his watch band again, making his wrist hurt. Even outside the car, he can smell the stink of his corpse, the flesh rotten, blood congealed and tacky. He looks down at his chest, sees flies buzzing around the open wound. He feels sick at the sight of them.

He looks up, up at the road, and glances to his left. There's a car approaching, a dirty black car, dented and rusted, travelling fast down the straight, barren highway. Then a noise to his right distracts him, a sharp rhythmic drum roll. He recognises the sound immediately, looks in its direction. There is a jeep approaching, an army jeep painted pale yellow and brown, desert camouflage colours. The muzzle-flash of its rear-mounted heavy machine gun flickers like a faulty light bulb. He hears the triple-bangs of the bullets, the gunfire, the sonic booms, the impact explosions. He looks down and sees the road at his feet splinter, shattered pieces of rough bitumen dancing like startled crickets. He turns back to his left as the bullets finally find their target. The dark car shudders and shivers beneath the assault, metal torn, glass shattered. It veers off to the side of the road.

His side of the road.

It's coming right at him, collision course, but he feels no fear, just a curious detachment. It slides sideways in the soft sand at the road's shoulder, engulfed in a plume of dust. The cloud reaches Jack, slaps him in the face, and he closes his eyes, flinches away from the stinging sands. When he opens his eyes again, the car has come to a halt.

Jack hears footsteps to his right. He turns and sees that the jeep has stopped, maybe ten metres away, and a man in army fatigues is jogging towards him, sidearm drawn and at the ready. His pale helmet is low on his face, shading his eyes. The soldier runs straight past Jack, close enough to reach out and touch if he wanted, and approaches the ruined black car. He looks through the shattered windscreen, at the dead man slumped behind the wheel. The driver doesn't look much older than Jack, maybe in his thirties, with olive skin and dark hair. He's dressed in civilian clothes, his white button-down shirt soaked with blood. Sunglasses cover his eyes, a small mercy. The soldier carefully walks around to the side of the car, to the rear door. He reaches out and opens it.

No...

There's a man with a shotgun crouched in the back seat, swathed in black robes. Only his eyes are visible, dark eyes, almost feminine. Jack hears the man's battle cry, high-pitched and filled with terrible rage. Then the shotgun goes off with a muffled bang and the soldier stumbles backwards, away from the car. He lands hard on his back in the dirt, his ruined chest already soaked with blood. The chinstrap of the soldier's helmet snaps, and it comes loose and rolls aside.

Jack sees the man's face, lying there in the reddening sand, the horrified expression, the pain. The moment of death.

It's Jack's face. As he knew it would be.

He watches himself die in the blood-stained dirt, transfixed, but at the far edges of his awareness something else is bothering him. A deep drone, barely audible at first, but getting louder. It fills his head, makes his vision blur. He closes his eyes and covers his ears with his hands, hunched over on the side of the road. It gets louder, more insistent.

Strong hands grasp his shoulders and yank him over backwards. He yelps and tumbles, flails blind and useless at his assailant. A hot gust of air rushes over him, dragon's breath, filled with the stink of smoke and oil. Then the deep drone becomes deeper still, and slowly fades to nothing. Jack is on his back, and that man, that familiar stranger is standing over him, looking down at him with those damned mirror eyes. In them, Jack looks tiny, pathetic, like a frightened child.

"Jesus, Jack," the man gasps, "that was bloody close! Are you okay?"

Jack doesn't respond, just climbs to his feet. His legs are shaky. He turns away from the man, back to the road. The black car and jeep are gone. *He* is gone. His body, dead in the sand.

"Come on," the driver says, "let's go." He puts his hand on Jack's shoulder. The man's touch scorches like a hot iron, straight through Jack's uniform to the tender flesh beneath, and he twists away. He looks once more to the road, to the desert, but he knows now that there's no escape there, no escape anywhere.

Defeated, he returns to the car.

They pull out of the station and continue to drive in silence. Jack doesn't know how long they've been driving now. It feels like days, weeks maybe, though the sun's never gone down, the temperature's never dropped. It's always been hot and bright. Jack would give anything to see the sunset, to be wrapped in the cool night air. Instead he's here, in this car, with this man-shaped thing behind the wheel. It's his fate, like that story of the man who spends eternity pushing the rock up a hill. No, more than his fate. His *punishment*.

He sees something on the road in front of them. There, in the distance, almost lost in the ripples of heat haze, is another car. It shimmers and becomes the army jeep, on the same side of the road as them, coming fast.

He looks over at the driver to see if he's noticed the oncoming jeep, but the man has changed. He's now the dark complexioned younger man, the driver of the black car, his large sunglasses covering his eyes. Sweat trickles down his face. He looks frightened. The car has changed as well, become older, the seats upholstered in cracked brown leather, a musty, *used* smell filling the air. The heat, though, the heat is the same. The heat is always the same.

Jack looks back to the road ahead, across a bonnet now black and dirty and dented, and sees the flashes from the back of the approaching jeep. Chunks of the road ahead leap into the air. Then bullets pierce the bonnet of the car, holes appear like magic tricks, pop pop pop. The windscreen explodes inwards, shatters into a million geometric pieces. The driver jerks back and forth in his chair, and splashes of blood burst from his white shirt, shockingly red. He doesn't make a sound, not so much as a grunt. The car swerves, a little at first, then more, as the man's dead hands pull it this way and that. Jack knows it's going to crash.

No...

Then another bullet, far behind all the others, finally finds him. It enters him, pierces him. Violates him. It doesn't even touch the edges of the hole in his chest, but he still feels his heart explode, his dead ghost of a heart, like the houses on the street outside, gone yet still there. The seat against his back rips open, and a sound he can't quite identify comes from behind him, a horrible animal-like shriek that makes his guts twist inside him. He gasps.

"Jack?" a voice asks him, a familiar voice, still filled with that quiet concern.

Jack looks over at the driver, the dead man with the bloodied white shirt, and he's gone, replaced again by the man in the dark suit with mirrors for eyes. He's not sure which is worse. The windscreen is whole once more, the bonnet intact. But the sounds still ring in his ears, echo and hum. He shakes his head, looks away from the eyes, those looking-glass eyes.

"It's all right, soldier," the man says, his attention mercifully back on the road again. "We're almost there. Almost home."

Jack's chest hurts. If he had a heart, it would be breaking. This was too cruel. All he'd ever wanted was to go home, all through his time overseas. And now he's dead, and home is nothing but a distant memory, a heat mirage on a long desert highway. A brutal illusion.

The car slows again, pulls into a driveway. A house appears out of the mists, red-bricked and tin-roofed. Three windows and a door, painted in nostalgic watercolours in Jack's eyes. He watches as they pull up in front of it, mesmerised and appalled.

It's his house. He's home.

The lie is almost perfect. The gardens aren't as lush as he remembers them, the roses wilted and faded by the ceaseless sun above. The windows are dirty, the path dotted with scattered brown leaves. But it's so close, so damn close, that it makes him feel dizzy. He wants to cry, but there are no tears in him, he's as dry as the desert, dry as old bones, dry as dust.

The driver gets out of the car, then walks around and opens Jack's door. Jack steps out, gravel crunching beneath his booted feet. He looks around, at this house surrounded by thick blue vapours, the house he grew up in. No, *not* the house he grew up in, just a good likeness, it has to be. The man leads him away from the car, towards the front door.

He's only taken a few steps when the door opens, and he sees his parents.

For a moment, one wondrous moment, he *believes* it, believes it all. The mists disappear and he's in the front yard of his childhood home, surrounded by the streets and houses of familiar memories. There are the musical sounds of birds coming from the many native trees and bushes planted all around. Cars drive past at a sensible speed on the road behind him, making soft comforting roars. He can smell the lemon tree in the front garden, the sharp citrus tang in the cool autumn air. And there, on the front door step, are his mum and dad; older, yes, but still his mum and dad, still real. They look at him and...

The make-believe world fractures and fades when he sees his parents' eyes. They're the same as the driver's, terrible silver-plated mirrors embedded deep in their sockets. He is trapped in them, once, twice, three times, four. Each reflection smaller and more misbegotten than the one before. Most of all, he sees the hole in his chest, dark and deep and decayed. These...these *things* masquerading as his parents, these monsters in human costumes, walk towards him, their arms open, ready to gather him up like a helpless baby, carry him away into his own private hell. The mists roll in again, the suburban paradise engulfed once more by the desert and the heat and the smell of old blood and rotting meat.

Jack turns away from them, from the house and the people and the lies, turns back to the car. All he wants now is to be driven away from here, anywhere, anywhere but here. But the car is wrecked, peppered with bullet holes, tyres half-buried in the sands. The windscreen is a ruined glass jigsaw puzzle, jagged pieces scattered across the front seats, across the bloodied corpse of the olive-skinned man behind the wheel. Jack's hands are hot and sore from firing the heavy machine gun in the nearby jeep, battered by the recoil. He holds his pistol out in front of him with both hands, arms straight like he was trained. He approaches the back door, releases his gun with one hand to open it up. Pulls on the handle, and inside...

No...

The dead woman looks like she's in her twenties. She's dressed in a traditional Islamic hijab, all black, but the veil has fallen away from her face, revealing high cheekbones, those beautiful dark eyes. Her mouth is slightly open. A bullet has struck her in the temple, torn away the flesh and bone there, leaving a ruined jagged crater the size of a man's fist. Jack can see fragments of her skull, and beneath them, the sponge-like pink tissues of her brain. The side of her face is painted bright red. One arm is flung back on the seat, a blood-splattered finger raised to the sky.

The other cradles her baby.

The child is wrapped in a blanket, once white, but now stained with blood, its mother's and its own. Its head lolls to one side, small chubby hands held out, palms up, imploring, begging, pleading. It's been struck in its tiny chest, the impact of the bullet all but quartering the baby. A jumbled bloody mess lies in its lap, and it takes Jack an awful moment to realise that it's the baby's internal organs, guts and lungs and heart, all shredded up and spat out by the force of the gunshot.

Jack hears a noise, a sickening high keening like an animal caught in a trap, and for a second or two he thinks that the child is somehow still alive, wailing for its dead mother. But the sound isn't coming from the baby. It's coming from Jack. He feels something crumble and fall deep inside himself, in his chest, like he's collapsing into himself.

"Doctor?" a voice so much like his mother's says softly from somewhere behind him, thousands of miles away. "What's wrong with him?"

His wrist still itches and hurts, where his watch strap digs into it. He scratches at it, but there's no watch there. His fingernails dig at the bandages, and blood blooms beneath them again. From far away, he can hear their voices, the creatures with his parents' faces and mirrorballs for eyes, concerned, worried. Gentle hands on his shoulders, on his back, soothing. He doesn't feel them, can't feel them. Can't face them, can't see himself reflected in them. Can't.

His heart is gone. His heart is gone, and he can never go home.

AFTERWORD

It began later than most.

Picture it now — a dark and stormy night, a mad writer hunched over his parchment, quill freshly torn from the scaly flesh of a wild roc clutched in his gnarled fingers. A single drop of red ink falls from its tip, splashes on the papyrus beneath.

All clichéd up, and nothing to write.

What's that? A whisper on the wind? A desperate plea for help? Shane's fallen down a well and can't get out? But how can I, a mere scribbler, a purveyor of filthy lies, help?

I listen, and the wind tells me. Finish what he started, it breathes into the writer's ear. Complete the circle.

And then it sings him a song.

The writer's first cynical thought is that Visual Audio Sensory Theatre ripped off the opening of 'Home' for its much more widely played song, 'Touched'. His second is that it cries out of dust, and heat, and desert sands. A picture forms in his head, vivid, stark. Black car, wrong side of the road. And a wayward soldier, on his way to his promised land.

Home is where the heart is. But where is home when your heart is gone?

BIOGRAPHY

Perth-based writer Martin Livings has had more than sixty short stories published in a variety of magazines and anthologies. His short works have been listed in the Recommended Reading list in *Year's Best Fantasy and Horror*, and he's had stories in *The Year's Best Australian SF & Fantasy, Volume Two* and the 2006 and 2008 editions of *Australian Dark Fantasy & Horror*.

His first novel, *Carnies*, was published by Lothian Books in June, 2006, and was nominated for both the Aurealis and Ditmar awards.

www.martinlivings.com

IT'S ALL OVER

L.J. HAYWARD

"That's it?" James asked.

Ron — of Ron's Bait and Tackle — smiled proudly, floppy hat perched precariously on the very back of his head. "That's it." He slapped the side of the rust-speckled Land Rover, the sound distressingly hollow. "It's a beast. Absolute bastard to handle, but it'll get ya where ya goin'. Look at that tread on those tyres. Deep enough to bury a cat in. Never had no complaints."

Not yet, James thought, eyeing the old 4WD with growing trepidation. When he'd called ahead and enquired about hiring a vehicle, Ron had assured him the Rover was the perfect way of getting into the more remote parts of the coast. But this corroded antique wasn't anything like the new, polished 4WD with leather upholstery, air-conditioning and iPod dock James had imagined.

"You had off-road experience?" Ron asked, blind to James' worry.

"I was in Kakadu last year."

Ron's eyes lit up. "Fishing? Hear the barra up there are monsters."

"I went to see an Aboriginal elder."

"Still," Ron said with a dismissive wave of the hand, "Kakadu's nothing like the headland. Not a lot of room for mistakes out here."

"Not a lot of room for mistakes in the Top End, either."

Ron conceded the point with the barest tilt of his head. "But, not a lot of room out here, period. Tight as a duck's arsehole. Guarantee, you'll get one end or the other stuck in the bush."

"How bad can it be? The last technician got out there."

"And he came back by helicopter," Ron said patiently. "You heading out alone, or is someone else going, too? A girlfriend, maybe? To keep you warm at night." He winked outrageously.

James ignored the spike of old pain unblunted by time. "Just me."

Ron eyed him for a moment, then nodded sagely. "Come on, we'll get you loaded up." He opened the back of the Rover with a loud screech of old hinges. Compared to the exterior, the inside was immaculate.

"What's all this?" Ron asked as they began putting in James' equipment.

"Very expensive." James winced as Ron dumped cases carelessly on top of each other. "Cameras, computer, night-vision lenses. That—" he rescued a small box from Ron and put it in his backpack, "—is vital to my survival on the headland."

"Bit small for a camp oven."

"It's a satellite phone."

"Swanky. So, what do you need all this stuff for?"

"Research."

"You some sort of scientist? Thought you said on the phone you was a student."

"PhD student. I'm working on my psychology thesis; *The Development and Perpetuation of Ghost Stories Within the Socio-Psychological Structure.*"

Ron grunted. "In English?"

Putting his pack on the front passenger seat, James said, "I'm studying why people insist on believing in ghosts."

"And you have to go out to the old lighthouse to do that? Nobody out there to study."

"No, but there are, reportedly, ghosts." James examined the map Ron had given him, checking to make sure he knew where he was going.

"That techie that went out there the other month, he said something 'bout a ghost. Made him jump off the lighthouse. Can you believe that?"

Folding up the map, James said, "That's what I'm going out there to discover."

X

The engine in the old Land Rover growled as its tyres clawed at the washed-out, near vertical dirt road. Saltbush crowded in on either side, dense in the middle and frayed by harsh ocean winds on the borders. Heavy grey clouds hung low over the headland, lit from behind by the setting sun, hints of orange and pink sneaking in around the edges.

Dust and smashed insects on the windscreen reduced visibility. Not that there was a lot to look at. Even if there had been something to break the monotony, James couldn't take his eyes off the road. It was a narrow, brutal track — two wheel ruts so deep the chassis scraped the ground in places. The Rover had to plough down a forest of grass and germinating scrub, and a good portion of the uphill leg had vanished in the recent wet season.

Exhausted by the lack of power-steering and the treacherous road, James took a moment to admit a newer vehicle would have been trashed by the hostility of this place.

It really was the arse-end of the world out here. And only an hour's drive from the tiny cluster of houses the locals called a town, where Ron's Bait and Tackle's only competition was the no-name service station that proudly displayed two vending machines and a single freezer of ice-creams in faded wrappers. There had been no one else on the road, just the occasional letterbox declaring the bush-crowded tracks leading back into the trees actually went somewhere.

The sat-phone rang.

Startled, James let the steering-wheel slide through his hands. The tyres lost traction, squealing on the soft dirt. The Rover slid back a metre or so before James could push the brake in far enough to have an effect. Heart beating thunderously, sweat soaking his hair, he craned a look over his shoulder. Through the dirt-encrusted back window, all he could see was a short length of track, then only scrub where the road turned. If the car had rolled that far back, the saltbush would have caught him — for maybe half a minute. Enough time for him to get out, but not enough to save the equipment.

Beyond the pitifully thin screen of scrub was a vertical rock face he'd passed earlier.

Turning the steering wheel, James angled the tyres and gently accelerated. They skidded and then, just when he thought it wasn't going to happen, they caught and the Rover lurched forward. The bonnet crashed into the saltbush, sharp-tipped twigs scratching against the metal.

Left leg stretched painfully far to keep the brake depressed, James swore. Damn Ron and damn his know-it-all attitude.

Struggling with weariness, James carefully extracted the nose of the Rover out of the scrub and got it pointed back in the right direction. Inch by tortuous inch, the beast scrambled up the steep track. Toward the peak, the engine coughed and spluttered. Terrified it would stall and he'd roll all the way back to the cliff, James pumped the accelerator.

Stones flying up, the Rover jumped forward. Before James

could ease back, the world vanished from sight. Nothing but sky filled the windscreen and the front of the Rover fell forward.

With a panicked scream, James jammed both feet on the brake and the Rover juddered to a stop. The engine rattled and died.

In the abrupt silence, only James' hard breathing let him know he was still alive. He might not have fallen off the edge of the world, but it was pretty damn close to it.

Past the bonnet, and very far below it, was the headland. A narrow spit of land jutting out into the South Pacific, like Australia was giving the world the finger. Or maybe it was just fate giving *him* the finger.

The saltbush thinned out and was replaced by a single, annoyed-looking tree. Coastal weather had blasted away some of the grass, leaving the rock bare in places, glistening red and gold under the pearlescent sky.

This was about as far from civilisation as you could get and still be on the continent. There were no beaches to bring in campers, no easily accessible areas for fishing, no picturesque islands to frolic on. Nothing but cold, grey ocean, inhospitable cliffs and the lighthouse. A few mental 4WD enthusiasts might find the drive enjoyable, but James suspected the locals didn't let many folks know about the track.

No. It was just idiots like him who cajoled maps out of old suckers like Ron. And lighthouse technicians who broke their legs trying to escape ghosts. At least the sparse plant life would have made it easier getting the chopper in and out.

James made the painfully slow descent. Controlling the downward-tilted 4WD was easier: the uphill climb had let him get to know the vehicle, and now he could see what he might run into if he lost control. All the same, his legs were sore and his arms aching by the time he reached the bottom.

At the base of the hill, the track disappeared, leaving an expanse of wind-flattened grass. Out of the protection of the saltbush, the wind pushed at the car, trying to force it off the headland and into the water.

In this wind, a chopper rescue wouldn't be so easy after all.

X

The caretaker's cottage was habitable, if barely. The roof in the bedroom had caved in, but it was solid everywhere else. Wind howled through the breach, bringing stinging salt and grit with it. James dropped his backpack and sleeping bag and hauled the bedroom door closed. The fine particles settled to the stone floor, laid well over a century ago when the lighthouse and its squat companion were built. The furniture was of solid, polished pine; heavy table with thick legs, carved doors on the cupboards, brass-handled tallboys and a writing desk.

He headed out into the harsh weather again and backed the Rover up to the entrance of the lighthouse. The door was unlocked and stale air rolled out when he opened it. Coughing, he switched on his torch and shone it around the ground floor. Cobwebs were strung like Christmas decorations from wall to wall, from ceiling to floor. The lighthouse had been automated in the eighties, but still required regular maintenance. Since the last caretaker had left, no one had been out here bar the occasional technician, and even then they'd only stayed for the minimum amount of time.

James checked the room and found nothing unusual. Dust, spider husks, dried remains of mice. There were faint footprints in the dirt, leading directly to the stairs going up to the lamp room. There were no tracks leading out again.

Following the footprints, James went up. The lamp was

off, its reflective cup an empty, staring eye looking out over the wind-tossed, barren ocean. There was nothing out there. No fishing boats, no freighters, definitely no pleasure cruises; just a wide openness, a vacuum waiting to be filled.

Shivering, James turned from the lamp and looked around. This room, with its big glass walls and modern fittings, was clean except for a scattering of dried leaves just inside the door to the balcony. The door was open, swinging back and forth, clacking against the frame. James stood there for a long time, wondering what had been going through the techie's mind when he rushed through this door and jumped from the balcony.

According to the papers, the man, delirious from exposure and pain, had claimed a ghost had chased him from the lamp room. His doctors had confidently assured the media he was just suffering from shock.

James didn't believe in ghosts, but he *did* believe in a certain social mindset that created a support frame and allowance for the propagation of the ghost-myth. One person claimed they felt a shiver walking past a room where someone may have died, giving the next person the suggestion that they too might feel something, allowing their subconscious to expound any slight disturbance into a haunting based on a wealth of preconceived notions. He also believed in the gut-deep reactions fear could induce. He wondered if that's all ghosts were — a psychosomatic response fleshed out by stories people had read or heard.

Closing the door, he returned to the ground floor and brought his gear in from the car. His watch said it was close to six p.m. but the light outside was indeterminable; a perpetual dusk created by the clouds that seemed permanently attached to the sky — or perhaps tethered to the lighthouse.

He set up cameras with night-vision lenses, a laser

detection grid, digital thermometers and pressure pads at the bottom of the stairs, under each narrow, frosty-glassed window and just inside the door. All the while, the wind billowed around the lighthouse and rushed over the aging body of the 4WD. It was almost musical; a slow thrum of bass and distant, shimmering cymbals. James kept waiting for it to build into something more, a realisation of the rhythmic potential, but it didn't. It remained constant, settling into a buzz in the back of his head, an annoying, nagging sensation of whispers barely heard.

When everything was set up and switched on, James was grateful to leave the lighthouse and make his way back to the cottage. It was close enough that he could remotely pick up the equipment readings on his laptop. He did his best to distract himself from the background drone by testing each instrument read-out and adjusting the volume on the alarms. But soon there was nothing left to do but wait.

Dinner was a sandwich and a bottle of water, pulled from the esky Kristen had given him when he'd first talked about an overnight stay at the lighthouse. That had been six months ago, not long after the techie's talk of ghosts had made it into the media. Six months since Kristen had suggested he go check it out as part of his thesis. Six months since the accident.

Abruptly not hungry, he put the food away and checked the laptop. Everything was normal, no disturbances in the lighthouse, earthly or otherwise.

Settling down to read, he realised the book he pulled from his pack wasn't the text book he'd thought he'd brought. It was a worn copy of Edgar Allan Poe short stories.

A flutter of uneasiness disturbed the small portion of food in his stomach. Opening the ratty front cover, he saw the neat handwriting he knew so well.

This book belongs to Kristen Mathers. Hands off!

He hadn't seen the book in such a long time. How had it shown up here, now; while he was lost in some remote, unpopulated part of the world trying to scare up a ghost, all because she'd said he should? The first time in six months he'd managed to pull himself together enough to leave the house, and somehow this book had made its way out here with him.

It meant nothing. Perhaps the book had fallen into his pack during the first round of preparations; forgotten in the flurry of bad news and pain that had seen the trip cancelled.

James put aside the book and all of its related baggage, reached for his laptop and called up his file on the lighthouse. He'd collected every story about the haunting of this place, read them so many times he could almost recite them.

Haunted lighthouses weren't exactly rare, though the instances of paranormal events had dramatically dropped since the vast majority became automated. Dropped, but not ceased. Lighthouses were perfect feeding grounds for any number of psychological responses. The majority of stories came from past caretakers, men who spent a lot of time alone, cut off from the rest of the world, exposed to the borderless, vast wasteland of the ocean. It gave them time to think, to inhabit a world entirely created within their own psyche. In such a place, it was easy to see how the smallest thoughts, the most insignificant of fears could be magnified and sharpened into weapons. The wind through the trees might be a voice, the unfamiliar sounds of the cottage cooling in the night could be footsteps on the stones.

So many logical explanations, but those who experienced these things were so adamant the answer was supernatural. It was the solidity of their convictions James wanted to test.

It was still early, but he was tired from the battle to get here and from setting up the monitoring equipment. Hands behind his head, he closed his eyes and waited for sleep.

X

He dreamed. A confusing replay of his journey to the lighthouse, mingled with his conversations with Ron and his thesis supervisor. What road to take off the highway, what equipment to use to record any ghostly activity. Then he was in the Rover, struggling with reluctant gears and washed-out wheel ruts.

"You should go out to that lighthouse." Kristen sat in the passenger seat, reading her book of Poe.

"What lighthouse?" he asked, looking back to the windscreen. It showed an image of the weekly round-up of football scores. He picked up the remote and flicked through the channels.

Kristen stretched, arching her back against the couch. "The one they were talking about on the news. Where that technician jumped and broke his leg. He said a ghost made him do it." She made spooky "woo woo" noises, laughing at his pained expression.

"It wasn't a ghost." James tossed the remote to the coffee table. "It was—"

"His repressed fears of being alone," she cut in, an all-too-familiar teasing in her tone. "I know that's what you think, but how can you be so sure? I mean, what if there really was a ghost?"

"There was no ghost because ghosts are a figment of our imagination. A manifestation of our fears of losing loved ones, of being alone, of dying, of any number of things. People don't want to believe that death is the end of everything, so they invented religion, the afterlife and ghosts."

"Or," she said patiently, "ghosts do exist. This is your thesis, Jimmy. Shouldn't you explore every aspect of your chosen topic?"

"Now you sound like Prof Temperly."

"Only to be expected. We are a pair of very smart people." Kristen smiled sweetly. "Of course, if you're afraid, you shouldn't go."

"Afraid of what? Ghost stories? I don't think so."

"That's right. You're James Franklin, scared of nothing." She waved the book under his nose. "The man who can read Poe before bed and happily turn out the lights."

He swatted the book aside. "They're just stories."

"Then what are you afraid of?"

"Sharks. Global financial downturns. Road rage."

"No," she said, serious. "I mean, what makes you wake up in the middle of the night, sweating, your heart racing a million miles a minute, your blood like ice in your veins? What shape would your ghosts take? What do you truly *fear*?"

His dream sense changed and he fought it, somehow knowing where it would shift to. He was with Kristen again, her twenty-third birthday and the night everything changed.

Dinner in an expensive restaurant, slow dancing, a leisurely walk home via the old covered footbridge in the park where they'd first met. His perfectly planned evening interrupted by a rain shower that caught them out in the open. It was fun at first, to laugh and skip through the growing puddles, but Kristen quickly grew cold, shivering in her silky dress.

"We've been out here long enough," she said as he encouraged her on. "Let's just call a taxi."

"The bridge is right here, we can warm up under the cover," he said, racing up the bridge and stopping at the edge of the arching shelter.

Kristen clattered up in her heels. He playfully blocked her way, keeping her out in the rain.

"Jimmy! Let me in."

He just smiled and didn't fall for her attempt at a fake-out.

"This isn't funny," she said. "I'm cold and wet. Why won't you let me in?"

"You need to answer a question first."

She stood back, arms crossed, her stern expression marred by her chattering teeth. "What are you? The bridge troll?"

James dug in a pocket, pulling out a small satin drawstring bag. "Sort of. Kristen Mathers, to cross this bridge, you have to answer the following question." He opened the bag and upended it over his palm. A ring fitted with a small diamond tumbled out. Kristen's eyes widened in shock. "Will you marry me?"

"Yes!" She squealed and threw herself at him.

A lot of happy laughter and breathless kisses later, he relented and called a taxi.

She went to the taxi and opened the door, but it changed, morphed into a pine door in a stone wall. She stepped through, turned and, mouth extending grossly wide, screamed, slamming the door so hard it rebounded open on an aching, black void.

X

The unfettered howl of the wind woke him. He sat up, dust and grit whipping into his face.

He spluttered and turned his back to the wind. Shivering from the last, horrible image of the dream, James pulled in several deep breaths, trying to calm the racing of his heart. The image of her distorted face, the mindless horror in her eyes, seemed etched into his mind, overlaying the truth. They had piled into the back of the taxi, dripping wet, grinning like fools — but they hadn't made it home that night. James hobbled through the door two weeks later on crutches and without a spleen. Kristen...hadn't.

He scrubbed at his eyelids, clearing away the grit and memories. The dark was relieved only by the ambient glow of his laptop screen displaying a star-field screen saver. It quivered as it was beaten by the wind. His pack was on its side, spilling clean clothes, the edges of the material rippling in preparation for flight.

The roar of the wind was enough to drown out any alarms that might have been sounding. Slapping the laptop, James banished the screen saver and saw that all systems were still running, showing no disturbances. The only activity was in the cottage.

Invisible battering rams trying to force him down, James clambered to his feet and staggered toward the door to the bedroom. It was open, letting the outside world in. His nose was full of grit by the time he reached it. Putting himself between door and wall, he shoved against the might of the wind, slowly forcing the door closed.

The doorknob came free in his hand, the wood of the door, cut through with termite tunnels, had broken around it, leaving him with no way to secure the door. Unless...

Letting the door slam open again, practically swimming through the maelstrom of air, he went to the writing desk. It was solid pine and built to last, so heavy that James nearly threw his back out moving it, and more than sufficient to keep the door closed.

Becalmed, James lay down and tried to sleep.

X

The wind woke him up again.

If anything, it seemed harder and louder. His clothes were fluttering about the floor and the computer had shifted a good foot away, its screen awake and glowing brightly.

James stared at the writing desk in the pale light of the laptop. His heart gave a single, loud thump of shock. The desk was back where he had gotten it from.

He had moved it in front of the now wide open door.

Hadn't he?

Perhaps it had been a dream. It had to have been. The beginnings of his own psychosomatic response to the isolation and the ghost stories?

Head hunched down between his shoulders, James hauled the desk against the door, ignoring the voice in the back of his head swearing black and blue that he'd done this before. He checked the computer to make sure it hadn't been damaged. It was fine and it told him the lighthouse was quiet. The moaning wind outside said it was all natural, just the world behaving as it always had.

He didn't sleep, just dozed, half stimulated, half lulled by the gusting wind, blearily checking the laptop every now and then. He listened for anything unusual but heard nothing coherent in the blustering.

The crash brought him fully aware a moment before the wind came roaring back in.

It wasn't the bedroom door. The desk still sat firmly in place across it. Instead, the front door banged back against the wall. The wind bellowed through the opening like a kid throwing a tantrum. It caught his scattered clothes and tossed them helter skelter. His laptop skidded toward him.

James grabbed the computer, shut it and rolled to his feet. The wind pummelled him, buffeted between walls and ceiling. He headed for the kitchen, but that door slammed open, rebounded and banged shut.

There was another sharp crack. Behind him, the writing desk toppled forward, its legs broken. It hit the hard floor with a shattering crash, the straight lines of its top skewed into conflicting angles. A couple of brutal shoves from the wind pushed it out of the way and the bedroom door flung open once more.

Hammered from all sides, James clutched the computer to his chest, snatched up his mostly empty pack and hauled himself to the front door. The wind tore at him so hard it felt as if it would rip the clothes right off his body, yank his hair out of his head. He had to grab the doorframe to keep from being pushed backwards. Eventually, he managed to clamber outside.

The sweeping beam of the lighthouse cut across his vision, blinding him. He blinked his eyes back into focus and saw the Rover groaning under the assault. The grass of the headland was flattened, given barely a moment's respite to stand up again. The lamp swung around and James closed his eyes before it could cut through his night vision again. When it had passed, he checked on the single tree. It leaned so far over, it was a wonder its roots were still in the ground.

The Rover was not going to provide security, so James headed for the lighthouse.

Alarms screamed the moment he stepped inside. James jumped in surprise, fumbled the computer but caught it before it could fall. Leaning on the door to close it against the wind, he opened the laptop. The pressure sensor by the door was signalling a weight. Him. The laser grid was detecting something in its final crossbeam. Him. The camera facing the door was showing a pallid-green man. Him.

Turning the alarms for those systems off, James let out a long-held breath.

The entire ground floor of the lighthouse was rigged to detect one thing or another. If he was going to stay in here he would have to turn some of the sensors off.

His first night back in the proverbial saddle and it was all going disastrously wrong.

James deactivated the laser detection system but kept the pressure pads and cameras running. He set himself up under the stairs, waving to his image captured by a camera, then settled down on the hard floor to wait out the rest of the night.

It was quieter in the lighthouse. The sound of the wind had been cut dramatically by the thick stone walls. He could just hear the hum of the lamp machinery and that was a pleasant thing. At least the wind wasn't the be all and end all of his world anymore.

Yet, it was almost too quiet now.

He needed something to distract him. The laptop had only his work files on it, no games. But the sat-phone had Sudoku. Scrounging through the pack he found the phone. The message icon flashed at him, reminding him of the call earlier in the day.

He was about to check the message, but paused when the computer beeped.

Nothing on the cameras apart from him. Nothing on the pressure pads. But the digital thermometers had detected a four-degree drop by the door. The camera covering that area showed nothing. The other thermometers recorded a steady twenty-three degrees. Another beep and another drop by three degrees. It was now sixteen.

Perhaps the wind was coming in under the door, chilly enough to cause the drop.

Cold spots supposedly came with ghosts. But a significant drop in temperature could always be explained away. A faulty thermometer, a cool breeze, a leaking cooling unit on a freezer.

The spare thermometers were in the car, so James scavenged one from the far side of the room. As he approached the door, he knew it wasn't an equipment fault. The second gauge rapidly counted down to match the increasing chill creeping across his bare arms. Standing to the side of the pressure pad, he knelt down and felt along the gap under the door. A hint of the wild wind outside, but the air coming in was warmer than sixteen degrees.

"*Jimmy.*"

James jerked back, landed on his arse. The second thermometer hit the floor and broke.

Breath pluming visibly in the cold air, he waited, straining to hear something more. Only the thrum of the wind, the clatter of branches. Then a patter of footsteps.

Before he could think, the patter increased to a run, then to a stampede of dozens of feet. Only when it grew into a thundering horde did he realise it was rain.

A small, weary, relieved laugh escaped him. Just the wind and rain. Nothing else. As he stood up, he realised the cold spot was gone. His breath no longer misted and the thermometer showed the temperature rising back to normal.

James returned to his place under the stairs. The computer showed the new temperature readings and no other activity. After a quick adjustment to exclude his little area, James turned the laser detection back on.

Almost immediately it began to register movement. Flickers here and there in the lasers. James searched the room. Nothing. But something was out there, interrupting the laser grid for microseconds at a time. The wind eddied at the base of the front door, but not enough to affect the lasers. Misted rain forced through tiny cracks by the wind?

He turned the lasers off and walked around the room. No fine spray of water from anywhere. The reflectors had no grit on their surfaces; the power to the laser itself was strong and steady. Retreating, he turned it back on.

It was worse this time. Many more lightning-quick flutters.

"*Why won't you let me in?*"

The thermometer alarms on the laptop sounded all at once, but the temperature was dropping so fast James didn't need to be told by any meter. Goosebumps lifted every hair on his body in a single, unsettling wave.

The computer blared out another alert. Images from the three cameras flashed across the screen in rapid succession. Every new motion in each camera pulled its window to the front, but there was so much flickering movement that each window was instantly replaced by another.

James scanned the room, heart thumping wildly. He couldn't see anything in the dark. He turned back to the computer, clicked on one camera window and stared at it. In the background, the other cameras continued to register movement, but the one he was looking at showed nothing. He clicked on one of the others. Again nothing, but the previous one now alarmed madly.

Letting them cycle naturally, James stared at the screen, trying to catch a glimpse of what was triggering them. They fluttered by too fast.

Forgetting the computer, James grabbed the phone again. He hit a button and the screen lit up. Turning it around, he shone the weak light into the rest of the room. Nothing, nothing, nothing.

There!

The light died. He lit up the screen. Pale light sliced through the dark and showed him...nothing.

To one side, the computer continued panicking, responding to all the activity picked up by the sensors. James wanted to turn off the alarms, but couldn't take his eyes off the room. He kept flashing the phone light around, trying to find something, *anything*, to explain this mess.

A new alarm joined the cacophony. James glanced at the screen. A pressure pad, the one by the door.

He pointed the phone at the door and lit it up.

She stood squarely on the pad, wet, dripping water that vanished before it hit the ground. She wore the same dress she had that night, the one they'd had to cut off her, but it was whole now, plastered to her slender body with rain.

"Kristen."

James' throat tightened. His heart was wild, his muscles both loose and tense.

He remembered the God-awful day he'd woken up after the surgery. Learning about his injuries, then being told about Kristen. Comatose, her prognosis not good. Sitting beside her bed, amidst the machines that breathed for her, that fed her, that said she was alive with their beeping and hissing.

"This," he'd said then, "is what truly scares me. Losing you."

The phone died. Darkness folded in and she vanished. James hit the keypad again. Light blossomed, revealed an empty space. She was gone.

Gone in the blink of an eye, in the last flicker of light from a mobile phone. But she had been there.

No, no, no!

Not Kristen, his beautiful Kristen.

Her doctors had only given her a month or two to live, even sustained by the machines. She'd defied them all, though — living for four months, then five, six.

He couldn't deny it. He had the recordings to prove it. The pressure sensor, the thermometer readings, the camera footage — his own eyes.

Ghosts existed. He'd proved it. Kristen was his proof.

But for that be true, she'd have to be...

Hollow, James sagged against the wall. All of the alarms had gone quiet, the only noise now was the rain and wind.

He stared at the phone in his hand. It had shown her to him, shown him that she was gone.

The message icon flashed.

"Jimmy."

James jumped to his feet, phone up, pressing buttons at

random, lighting up the room. It was empty. The computer was silent, registering nothing.

A soft step on the stairs above him. Another, heading up.

He raced out, swung around and onto the stairs. The alarms jangled but he ignored them. She was upstairs, that was all that mattered. He'd find her again, he'd see her one more time.

At the top, he dodged the beam of rotating light. He circled the glass room, the lamp trailing along behind him, giving him all the light he could ever need. Around he went again but she wasn't there.

On the third circuit, he found the door to the balcony open. He skidded to a stop, breath held in fear.

The light swept over him, flared on the iron railing and there she was, silhouetted against the night.

James stepped through the door, took the two steps to the railing and the light moved on, leaving him alone. She was gone again.

The wind was rising, stealing the breath right out of his body. He turned to look into the lamp room. The light swept by and he flinched back, eyes squeezed shut. His body touched the railing. It creaked and shifted under his weight.

A cold, cold hand touched his chest.

James jerked back. The railing cracked and he fell.

X

The helicopter landed in the bright morning light, artificial wind flattening grass barely relieved from the brutal ocean gale. Two paramedics leaped from the still quivering machine and raced past the overturned 4WD to the body lying at the base of the lighthouse.

"He's alive," one announced, fingers against James' neck.

"Compound fractures to both legs," the other said.

Between the paramedics, James stirred. His eyes opened

briefly and his lips moved, then he lapsed back into unconsciousness.

"What did he say?"

"Sounded like a name. Christine? Crystal? Something like that."

"Here's the phone," the other paramedic said, prying the satellite phone from James' tight hold. The screen showed the last number dialled — Ron's Bait and Tackle.

As the paramedics got the unconscious man ready for transport, the phone rang. With the chopper engines building back up to takeoff, the paramedic scurried away from the noise and answered it.

"James?" a woman asked.

"Who's this?" the paramedic shouted.

"It's Jennifer Mathers. Is James there?"

"He's not available at the moment. Who's calling?"

"I left a message yesterday. Please tell him it's very important. It's about Kristen. She's awake."

AFTERWORD

What was it about 'It's All Over' that inspired my story? A moody atmosphere? A doomed love affair? A hint of ghostly despair?

Truthfully, I have no idea. Perhaps it was because I was reading about haunted lighthouses at the time. Maybe...probably. Still, the subject melded with my sense of the song — isolation, captivity, wide open spaces, dark days, false dawns, an out-of-control tumble down the rabbit hole into a strange new world where up is down, east is west and ghosts are real — or not.

I don't believe in ghosts and I'm not sure I want to. The power of imagination is undeniable, as is how easily it can be manipulated. I worked in a hospital that occasionally closed a wing when there weren't enough patients to warrant the staffing. One night, a colleague came back from walking through the empty ward pale and trembling. She had "felt" the ghost which haunted a room — a cold spot, fingertips down her spine, a sensation of being watched. When it was my turn to walk through the empty ward, I felt a chill at a certain room. My hair prickled and my stomach quivered. I hurried back and told my colleague.

"That's the ghost!" she said.

"It was freaky! I'll never look at room twenty-eight the same way again," I said.

"Twenty-eight? No, it's room thirty-five that's haunted."

So. Not a ghost. Just a dose of the I-want-to-believes and a measure of suggestion. But, what would happen to the power of that suggestion in an isolated place you couldn't leave, where there were no boundaries for your wild

imaginings and where the past lies as close as a lover?
    Your guess is as good as mine.

BIOGRAPHY

L.J. Hayward lives and writes in southeast Queensland. She's had stories published with Eneit Press, Aurealis Magazine and Morrigan Books. Like Robert A. Heinlein, she feels that writing isn't something to be ashamed of, but she does do it in private and washes her hands thoroughly afterward.

TEMPTATION

TRENT JAMIESON

The old steel chimes are ringing like you would not believe. They always do around the bridges: a warning and a promise. The Dark calls. It calls and promises.

Wind's howling and midnight's singing. Bolland and Smirker race and rush and stumble through the dark to the bridge they must cross, like all the bridges before and all the bridges after.

The ruined city stands behind them, the bridge ahead. The pair run shoulder-to-shoulder, breath rough in each other's ears.

Bolland is tall but hunched down low, grey woollen scarf round his neck. But even that and his beard can't hide a face scarred with the boiling fingerprints of a death that didn't get a good enough grip. Smirker is short and dandied-up, wearing gold in places prominent. Not death-marked in any way that you or I could tell.

Onto the bridge, past a sentinel who doesn't give them a second look. There are worse things about on that wind and in that dark than these two bridge-crossers. And that's the impression they like to make. To cross a bridge is to cross it fast and quiet. To not give into temptation, to not give into the Bads.

A person could spend a lifetime crossing Victoria Bridge, or failing to.

Used to be a swift passage, but the stony bridge is cluttered now with narrow, labyrinthine lanes walled with corrugated iron: roofed and dark. Hot as sin in summer, those bleak black laneways. But it's winter, the ice-hearted dead of winter bound in the dead of a clattering night. Wind trying every which way to tear the bridge down and drown it in the slick and shadow-scrawled river beneath. Conspirators in decay, the wind, and the wet, and the dark. And there, on the bridge, Bolland and Smirker's burring breaths are ropy and pale: and everything round them is sharp and cruel and ringing.

The two men make the turnings, eyes casting about for the Dark and its promises; dipping their hats at the ladies they meet, scowling at the gentlemen, who (following propriety) scowl back if they can manage it. No good men are about this night. The bad sticks to everyone, sticks and sinks beneath the skin; and everyone knows it. The bridge is in need of crossing. Desperate need.

They come to an open space, maybe a third of the way in. There's cold clean air, and a rough square of sky. Something passes beneath the stars. Not cloud, but huge and horrible, like living oil. Smirker crosses himself — a less puissant cross than the one they'll soon use. Bolland yanks him under cover. There's a distant howling: thunder pitched too high. The iron rattles, and even the white stone of the bridge buried beneath it all shivers a little.

Still, Smirker ducks his head out again and watches — damn the world and consequences — as the stars come out beneath the viscous Dark and its hurried, hungry flight. These two, below, bridge-crossers professional, are as nothing to it. Scarcely a flea on the mangiest dog. But sometimes fleas are irritant enough or the Dark bored and desirous of easy crushings.

Bolland releases a breath, and pulls his scarf about him, more to warm his hands than his neck. Work to be done. There's a bridge to cross. Not just a bridge, the last one. Six weeks travelling this time, following roads scarcely deserving of the name, coming up south, from the border ranges, and down the murky hinterland. Winding through the iron-cloaked bridges, finding things contrary to all negotiations but the knife.

He rubs at his death-marked face and rolls a cigarette, his fingers stiff and cold. Still, he manages it, and admires the job a moment, before glaring over at Smirker.

Smirker pulls out his shiv, the casting one, with its sharp point and dull edges, and pricks a finger tip, all the while mumbling, mumbling under his breath. The cigarette tip ignites.

Smirker reaches out and snatches it from his mate.

His blood. His right to first smoke.

Smirker breathes deep and quick. The smoke's heat, its breath, crashes against the Bads that have sunk into his flesh. They slide from his pores, swift and shuddering, one slips from his eye (pain, but a good pain) and stumbles, shrieking, tiny feet slapping on the iron, down and away, racing ahead along the bridge. They'll try to get back in. But not for a while.

No amount of vigilance can keep them all out. But, handing the smoke back, he's feeling virtuous, cleansed.

Bolland, hunched even lower now, drags on the cigarette. He coughs as a single, scrawny Bad slides from his lips to his boots. Bolland dips and pinches his fingers closed over its loose-skinned shoulders, then he's nailing it to the floor with a shiv of his own.

The Bad struggles there, little limbs flailing. He twists its neck until it stills.

Bolland puffs up his chest. Always the purest, despite his haggard face, despite his foul tempers.

Jealousy. Jealousy. Smirker loses his smirk for a while. Bolland doesn't make the sort of deals he does. The kind that muddy you, regardless of your intent. Bolland bears the cross he can't.

Another scar in the iron. This time the wall, on the edge, cold winds rattling, lifting from the shining trembling river. The wind blows low or shrill, dependent on the angle of its approach, which is various, though this time of year it always blows hard and cold. Smirker shivers sympathetically, remembering the south and the bridges there round the city of Wish. They'd crossed those, each and every one of them. He had the cuts to prove it: little souvenir cicatrices.

Bolland lifts his head and sniffs. He frowns. All manner of foulness on the wind.

Smirker plays with the gold bangles on his wrists, a counterbalance to the howls of the gale, the banging iron. They reach another turning.

There's a baby crying, then chuckling, in the dark ahead. Both men catch each other's gaze and nod.

Smirker stops jangling his gold.

Bolland checks his weapons. Pulls out a book of poems, whispers his way through a couple of them, voice cracking. The cachinnation stops, a long finger extends towards him from the shadows. Smirker stamps his boot on it, it quivers beneath his heel.

Another finger lashes out of the dark. Smirker stomps down on it, too. Unsteady. He swings his gaze to Bolland, who shrugs. Then Smirker flips, flung onto his back and two fingers shoot towards his eyes, faster than he can raise his hands.

A flash of movement, a brittle crunching. Bolland stomps on the fingers with his greater weight.

Something screams in the night, and Smirker's a long time getting to his feet, for all that he's trying. He's all gasping breath and clumsiness.

Bolland's unsteady upon all that fury. He looks to Smirker, then down to the fingers.

Smirker slides his knife, the long, killing one, through the air. A bleak pain runs up his arms as he swings down.

The silence is swift in coming. No time to hunt it out, though somewhere, some tempted thing weeps. Speed is of the essence.

Bolland nods. Smirker smirks, though his hands shake with a deep-bone shaking.

Another cigarette that judders on the lips for a couple of drawn breaths. Fresh Dark drips from Smirker's skin. They pass the corpse-thing; broken-fingered, huge-eyed and large-mouthed. Another few twists of laneway, cold, though the iron's slick and wet. Then, up creaking, half-rotten stairs. A swift ascent.

There's a small bar at the top, a sign at the entrance offering *Beer and Felicities: Old Time Songs Sung With Fervour*. But there's no one in there, and the only song is the wind, ceaseless in its shrill inquiry of the bridge. Smirker figures that's the oldest song of all. Then even that dies away to nothing.

The silence is so loud it crams their skulls or takes something fundamental from them: an absence of pressure, a dreadful aching subtraction.

Smirker glances sidewise at his mate, but he's running his fingers thoughtfully over the sign. Smirker waits until he can stand it no more and slaps a hand upon his back. Bolland's grin is idiotic. Smirker knows what his mate is seeing, the shadows of happiness, the promise of drink and song. But there are webs inside that bar and shuffling scuttling things and eyes that reflect light.

Bolland takes a step towards the door. Smirker slaps him hard. The eyes narrow, grow familiar. He nods a thank you.

They leave the bar. Take another set of stairs down. The

iron laneways grow twisty again. They know they're close. Both feel it. Which is good. Which is terrifying.

Smirker always forgets how terrifying it is. His guts are loose. His eyes water. He wishes he were anywhere but here.

They reach the middle of Victoria Bridge. Smirker considers all of the bridges they have crossed. The mates they lost along the way to corrupting influences, to death and weariness: the compound weight of crossing bridges. They're different every time. Even the same bridge is different.

Here, in the middle, there is sky again, peeking through a tear in the iron. It looks as though something erupted from this point and launched itself at the heavens. The stars, few as they are, are familiar.

There's no comfort there. These stars have spun their chill light upon the firmament, and watched the dreadful passage of all the dreadful nights of their lives.

Bolland coughs.

Smirker nods his head. He peels his mate's jumper and shirt from him, running his rough hands over the knotted skin of his spine. Smirker traces circles there. The flesh gooses. He pushes down and the skin gives way. He sinks his hands to his wrists in flesh. He can feel his mate's heart pounding, knows his own is racing, too. Blood roars in his ears.

Smirker's seen other men fail, in such horrible ways. He has found their corpses mummified upon the centre of bridges. Men and women, their bodies fused together as his and Bolland's are fused. To die that way, well, the odds are they will, and sometimes the dying would be a relief, from the tedium and the terror of this good work.

The temptation to halt, to rest, to give into the Dark washes over him. He pauses. Feels Bolland beneath him. Just to end it. To stop all this struggle.

Maybe that is what has happened to all those bodies fallen.

The bridge holds its breath, waits.

Smirker breathes deep, maybe he will give in to temptation, but not tonight, with Victoria Bridge creaking around them, the wind cold and strong across the river, and home so close he can smell it, can taste it in the back of his throat.

His fingers close around the bony cross, and his grip is good.

Bolland groans beneath him.

Smirker yanks, feels the sucking pressure of Bolland's flesh. The cross comes free, the last movement is the easiest. He stands with it in his slick hands. The cross is warm, but it's a fast-lapsing heat. It gleams in the moonlight, luminous as snow or the stony heart of the bridge, not a drop of blood upon its surface.

Bolland falls to the ground. The wound already closed. He rolls on his back. Looks at the cross above him. Smirker cannot hold his gaze, not just then. He'd kiss him, hold him, drown in him, but there is no time.

And he has held him, and he has drowned in him, and there will be time for kisses later. Perhaps.

Already the bridge is shuddering, rage building.

Smirker helps Bolland up. The quaking bridge almost knocks him down again, but Smirker doesn't let that happen.

Both pairs of hands close about the bony cross.

They lay it down in the middle of the road. The cold becomes less cold, the wind stills. For a moment. Just a moment.

And then there is clamour: clamour and rage. Death throes for a hundred cruel Bads.

Things tumble from the stone, like the darknesses that had inhabited their flesh, though bigger and clawed. And some of them aren't dark at all, but pale and palpitating: maggot flesh with teeth and vivid eyes.

And how they scream and spit.

All these things witnesses to this betrayal or that, this grim thought or that cruelty. They know of violence, they know of pain. They rush at the pair, desperate and demanding.

Bolland's sword is out, a blade he'd made himself from the folded bonnets of cars.

Smirker remembers that: the weeks in some long-ago dead town, the crease-faced industry. He had already loved him then, but he loved him more after. Bolland straightens, swings the bonnet-sword around his head, slashing out at first this great Bad then that. The movement is hypnotic; he is no longer the bent and hobbling thing, weighed down by the gestation of the cross. He is glorious and swift.

Smirker's breath catches in his throat to see it. His friend, his lover, with his cross released. He is like a bird. He is like one of the poems in the book: all brevity, beauty, and precision.

A poem with a rusty sword.

Smirker draws a hot line across his wrist and lets the blood fall upon the cross. There is a soft sound like a breath, but carried the length of the bridge. Everywhere that regretful softness sings and moans.

Fire rises from the stone. Clear at first, before birthing smoke. Then it erupts from the bridge with a hiss.

The Bads-various fall back.

But not all of them.

Smirker ducks as his mate's sword whistles over his head and strikes a Bad down. Night spills from it like blood, it screams and scuttles to the gap in the iron. And there it hisses and spins, and snatches at Smirker's hair with icy fingers. It yanks. Smirker's neck creaks. He closes his fists about its wrists. His fingers burn. He kicks it in the chest. Handfuls of hair are lost with that booting. His head stings, but the Bad is tumbling over the edge into the water far below

It's time for getting out, and getting off.

So the two men run.

They sprint. They fairly fly. Down and around the last twists and passages of the smoking bridge. And there are other folk, fleeing with the Dark tangled in their hair and clothes. The air stinks of piss and smoke and screams.

When they can, the pair aids those in need. Cut away the Bads with the long knife or the sword, but mostly, it's about the flight. These petty things can be dealt with later.

They reach the other end: shaking and pale.

The bridge is crossed and they have made it from one shore to the next.

They stumble onto a dirt road: dawn hours off. Fires burn, weak and windblown, all the way to the shantytown. People gather staring at the bridge. They nod as the pair pass.

Even now the Bads are building in Smirker's blood, but the sky ahead is clear, and his mate for all his coughing and shaking, remains by his side.

Smirker and Bolland pick up their pace, boots scraping and slipping on mud and gravel, Bolland already hunching down.

Dawn draws near but night is never far behind. The whole world's a temptation.

A month, two months if they're lucky, of break. Cold wind's still blowing, stinking of smoke and Bads, undone and patiently re-knitting, and the chimes are ringing like you would not believe.

AFTERWORD

This was a tough story to write. The song, while it's called 'Temptation', is without lyrics, and has an energy that suggests action rather than temptation to me. So, I decided to try and write something that was essentially a story on the run, and one without dialogue. The story makes a deliberate use of repetition, of words and images occurring over and over again, because...well, I was trying to be clever and reflect the repetitive nature of the instrumental piece.

Does it accurately reflect the nature of the song and the title? I dunno, I guess that's up to you, but I had a hell of a lot of fun writing it.

BIOGRAPHY

Trent Jamieson has had more than sixty short stories published over the last decade, and won two Aurealis Awards. His most recent stories have appeared in *X6*, and Jack Dann's anthology *Dreaming Again*. His collection *Reserved for Travelling Shows* was released in 2006, and book one of the Death Works Trilogy, *Death Most Definite*, will be released by Orbit Books in August 2010. He lives in Brisbane with his wife, Diana. Trent's blog is at trentonomicon.blogspot.com

OUT

STEPHEN DEDMAN

Suri had only just learned to walk when the engines cut out.

We'd been accelerating at .5 g for nearly two years and were cruising along at .9 c, but even with time dilation, we had twelve years of cruising — in free fall — ahead of us. It made no difference to the sleepers, of course, and everyone who'd been accepted as crew had spent enough time in microgravity that they were confident they wouldn't get space-sick. The cryo-chambers were completely computer controlled, so the doc — Suri's mother — only had to check on a couple at random every few days, unless an alarm sounded, and none ever did, so she had plenty of time on her hands. Maybe that was the problem.

Some scientists sneer at medics, say they're really just technicians; they don't use scientific method enough, don't experiment, they just do what their training and experience tell them should work until they notice it doesn't. Maybe that's true. The Roys — Suri's parents — weren't like that, though: they'd never have gotten berths on the *Chandrasekhar* if they were. I don't know for sure that Suri was an experiment, but the pregnancy was so conveniently timed that I'm more than a little suspicious.

(A month or two earlier would have been even better, of course; left them some margin for error. Not that they were the sort who made errors, or admitted to them.)

Suri was carried to term and born in gravity, of course, without her mother needing to spend all that time in the centrifuge. And she was toilet-trained damn quick, too. If you've ever tried to shit or piss in free fall, you'll understand. I'm glad they re-engineered that part of me: an arsehole is a wonderful piece of design, considering the materials you have to work with, but that doesn't mean it can't be improved upon with some variable-friction memory plastics.

Anyway, Suri was a smart kid, and curious, and she was the only kid around, so yeah, maybe we all spoiled her rotten. Particularly after the gravity was switched off.

Free fall's probably the best toy a kid could have — not that gravity can't be fun and doesn't have its uses. But Suri took to free fall like a mermaid to water, thinking and moving in three dimensions like she'd never had to worry about which way was Down. If her parents hadn't insisted on her doing exercises in the centrifuge so she'd be in shape when the engines kicked on again and we decelerated...

Yeah, I know. That was just a, what do they call 'em, a thought-experiment. Like Schrödinger's cat. I'm no physiologist, but I know it's supposed to be a bad idea; I've seen holos of the animals they brought up in free fall from birth. Shit, I used to think *I* was a mess until I saw those. Some of 'em, I couldn't figure out what sort of animal they were meant to be, and I don't know that they knew, either. Of course, it wasn't like they had parents that could teach 'em how they were supposed to cope. Maybe if...

Okay, I know. I'm not a scientist, but you spend long enough with no one but scientists to talk to, some of it rubs off. I guess it rubbed off on Suri, too.

X

Suri's mother didn't much like her spending time with me, though I think that had more to do with my just being a tech, without a doctorate, than with being a hyb or an Outer. But Suri liked me. Maybe it was because I'd had more time in free fall than anyone else, or maybe it was just because I look so different from everyone else, like some toy you can pull apart and put together again. Not a good idea to try that with real people. Yes, I'm joking. Can't you tell?

Anyway, I didn't spend any more time in the centrifuge than I had to, either — which wasn't all that unusual, a lot of the crew thought free fall was more fun than the shitty exercises we had to do — and even when I did, I didn't always bother changing limbs. All of my muscles were augmented enough that I could cope with being in a Down. Maybe Vina Roy thought it was bad manners my having four hands when everyone else had two. Or showing off, or setting a bad example...I don't know. Back when I was a kid on Earth, I know I envied people who had legs, but I didn't think they should stop walking around just because I couldn't. At least, I don't think I did. But no one could make me wear feet when I was in free fall. And since we'd stopped accelerating, I was spending more time Out.

I used to have to go Out — on the surface of the ship — for some jobs even when we were accelerating, but it was a lot safer once we were cruising. Even if something went wrong and my ties broke, the ship was enough of a Down — I mean, it had a little bit of gravity of its own, and we were between stars, so there were no other Downs to worry about — that I didn't have to be so careful. When the engines weren't blasting away, I went Out whenever I could think of an excuse.

For one thing, it's quiet. Even if I turn the gain on my ears down to zero, when I'm inside a ship I can't really get away from the noise completely. Outside, I can. That much silence used to scare me — I used to play music whenever I was Out — but not anymore. Now, I just enjoy it. Sure, I have to stay in radio contact with the ship, but no one bothers me all that often. The quiet is...it just feels right. You know most of the universe is quiet like that. It's like the sky. The sky is *meant* to be black, so you can see the stars — and see them properly, not like on Earth, where there's so much light pollution and air pollution and noise pollution...I mean, people talk about the beautiful blue of the sky on a day on Earth, but that's just blotting out what's really there, trying to forget that most of the universe actually exists. And Mars is worse. It's like we're building walls all around ourselves, up and down and...

Sorry. When you don't have to breathe, sometimes it's hard to remember to stop talking.

Anyway, Suri and I became friends. She used to ask if she could come Out with me, and I had to explain about how she wasn't vacuum-adapted like me and there weren't any suits for anyone as small as her and we couldn't make one — not until she stopped growing, anyway, and she was growing at least as fast as a Martian kid. Her parents didn't even like her going near the windows, because she didn't have a shipsuit...but she loved looking at the Out — at the stars.

Yeah, just as much as I did. Bear with me, okay? I'm getting there, but it's important that you hear my side.

I don't remember how old Suri was when they told her we were going to another Down and weren't going to be on the ship forever; five or six, maybe. She was seven or eight when they told her that the skies there would never be bright blue, like those on Earth — cloud cover will be the only thing that keeps the ultraviolet down to a safe level — and I remember how she cried. For weeks after that, she'd spend as much time in the window rooms as she could, which was whenever there was someone else there to watch over her. A lot of the time, it was me.

And she was ten or eleven when they told her that living on Taranis would mean living in .94 gs, and that after we started decelerating in about two years time she might never get to be in free fall again...

X

Her parents blamed me; said I was a bad influence. Said she picked up spacer terms from me — Down for a planet or any gravity well, Out for free fall — and a lot of other stuff they thought she was too young to know. Maybe she did. Maybe not; she read a lot, and stuff about spacers, or by spacers, probably meant more to her than anything written about living on a Down.

Don't forget, this was a kid who'd never known Earthian gravity. Or even half a g. I know you're a Downer, so maybe you can't understand what this must be like, but I don't blame her for freaking out; I don't blame anyone.

But I never interfered with her lessons or her exercises or anything else she was supposed to be doing. You've seen her education scores; you know how smart she was. Anything that interested her, like computers or astronomy or biotech, and that was part of her world, she just soaked up, 'til she could've done nearly half the crew jobs on the ship. Theory stuff, thought-experiments; not so much. She liked to learn by doing.

Maybe she could've coped with being stuck on a Down, given time, but she was only thirteen when they switched the engines on again, and teenagers don't think like us...

X

Growing up mostly in free fall, even on a shitty shipboard diet, Suri had gotten tall enough to wear a spacesuit by then...and before you ask, no, I didn't teach her to use one. Like I said, she was a reader, and if her parents tried to restrict what she read, she got around them easy enough, like any smart teenager. Or most of the dumb ones I've known, come to think of it. But I digress. Point is, she didn't need any help from me, or anyone else, to get one out of the locker. Or to open the airlock. Shit, I don't think there was a manual control in the ship that she couldn't have figured out, and that was all routine stuff.

Besides, why would *I* need to know how to check out a suit? Air-tanks and a flightpack, yeah, if I was going to be Out for more'n a few hours, but not a suit.

Anyway, by the time anyone noticed she was missing, the ship had been decelerating for hours at a quarter g, and even with the telescopes we could barely see the suit as it headed further and further Out.

Sure, there would've been air left in the tanks, but the flightpack was probably out of fuel and there was no response from the radio.

Her parents would've stopped the ship and turned it around if they could, but they knew it wasn't possible. Even if you could've over-ridden the computer, we would've been left without enough fuel to make it into orbit. You probably heard her mother say I should go Out after her to try to bring her back, but even she must've known that'd be a one-way trip.

Not that I wasn't tempted, mind, especially when the alternative was another six years on board ship, under watch and under suspicion and with Vina Roy's hate poisoning the air...I mean, even *I* have to breathe, occasionally. But everyone knew there was no one else who could do my job. The ones who thought I'd helped Suri get Out probably thought of me as a necessary evil...

Until now, of course. What use is an Outer hyb when everyone's living on a Down?

X

It's not a particularly attractive planet, is it? Even from this height.

I know a lot of people think that leaving me up here on what's left of the ship is too kind, and the only ones who're in favour of it are the astronomers. Even though I'd be fuck-all use on a farm; oh, I could probably do some routine tech stuff, or shovel shit, but nothing I was designed for. I don't know what Vina Roy's been telling them about me, but I can guess. Stuff about the drugs my mother took, and whether they twisted my mind like they did my body. Stuff about surgical addiction, when I got over that years ago. She probably says I'm a sociopath or something just because I don't think of other people as being the same as me. Maybe she hopes that I'll space myself rather than spend the rest of my life on a Down. Come to think of it, given the choice...

But, you see, I know something she doesn't. If she'd ever bothered looking in her own cryo-chamber, she'd have realised it wasn't empty. Suri shut herself in there, a few hours after she sent that empty suit into the Out with the flightpack jammed on. And while she's been asleep all this time, she's now legally nineteen, and she can make up her own mind where she wants to spend the rest of her life.

Maybe she'll decide to go Down to Taranis; there's gravity, sure, but there'll also be people, some of whom aren't really that much older than her. I won't blame her if she does. But maybe she'll stay up here on the ship, where there's just me and the Out. At least for a while. You can ask her yourself when they wake her up.

Until then...it's been good talking to you, Captain. Been a relief to get Suri's secret out of my system at last. And I must admit, I'm looking forward to seeing Vina Roy's face when she hears the truth.

No, don't bother getting up. I know my way out.

AFTERWORD

The lyrics of 'Out' immediately suggested a need to escape, and the idea of someone seeing only walls and being unfamiliar with a blue sky made me think of a spaceship — specifically, someone who'd lived their entire life in metal rooms and corridors with occasional glimpses of a black sky. Born on a generation ship, Suri only knew of Earth through what she'd read and been told. I'd used 'Down' and 'Out' as spacer jargon in 'Spin', many years ago, so I made my narrator a cyborg adapted to the zero-gravity 'Out'.

It seemed inevitable that Suri would choose to escape the ship rather than face a long life being weighed down by gravity, but I wanted to put a twist in the ending that let her survive, and maybe even be happy. Suicide just seemed too easy a way Out.

BIOGRAPHY

Stephen Dedman is the author of the novels *The Art of Arrow Cutting*, *Shadows Bite*, *Foreign Bodies*, and *A Fistful of Data*, as well as more than 100 short stories published in an eclectic range of anthologies and magazines: an up-to-date bibliography and other information can be found at www.stephendedman.com.

Stephen is the proud part-owner of the Fantastic Planet sf bookshop, and teaches creative writing at the University of Western Australia, where he completed his PhD in English (he's still waiting for the paperwork to be completed on his nomination for sainthood). He currently lives sixteen metres above sea level with his partner, Elaine, a few thousand books, and a finite number of cats.

EGO

ROBERT HOOD

"Don't do it, Stefan. Please. Just let me go!"

"Go if you want. It's not up to me."

"Don't do this, you stupid bastard!"

"Go! I won't stop you. But you'll be back eventually. I know you'll be back."

"Fuck you!"

As the door slammed shut, Merrin was still screaming at him.

Her cursing had defined Merrin in the end — and had reconciled Stefan Clemens to her departure. What was the point in agonising about it? If all she could do during his time of need was swear at him, what sort of relationship had they had anyway?

His fingertips dragged through the condensation on the window, leaving a column of parallel lines that sliced through the reflection of a gaunt, desperate-looking man. The man might have been in his late 40s, though in fact he was only 36. Stefan stared past the lines and the man, out into a darkened street where the rear lights of Merrin's car were lost in the gloom, swallowed whole and in an instant.

He wondered if he should worry for her. She'd been so angry. You can't drive attentively in that state, and accidents happen. The road that ran past Stefan's house dipped just beyond the southern border of his property and swept around and up again, performing an elaborate turn before cresting Dolamite Hill and ceasing to be. Beyond the hill, where lay a group of houses known optimistically as "The Village", there was, tonight, simply darkness. Was the power out? Not Stefan's. Nor the single streetlight in front of his house. Its glow radiated outward in a dim circle, casting a cold sheen over the bitumen and the roadside bush. Another stood sentinel a hundred metres on, but it flickered badly. Beyond that, dark poles were silhouetted against occasional snatches of sky or disappeared against the dark bush backdrop.

"You're a heartless bitch, Merrin," he muttered, his lips brushing the chill glass of the window. "Learn compassion."

If there was a reply, he didn't hear it.

Merrin had always been a bitch. Perhaps he'd loved her for it. But she needed to gain perspective. Would she find it, out there in the dark? If she did, she'd be back — he was sure of that. They belonged together. Some sort of change would be necessary if they were to continue, and it would need to be her who changed. He was helpless. He had unavoidable needs.

Cancer was spreading freely through his bowels, despite what the doctors said. Sometimes he could feel the evil growing in his flesh — its tendrils scratching at the walls of his intestines and eating great chunks of healthy tissue from his lymph glands. It was remorseless. Surely Merrin should have felt some kind of pity for him, even if her actual affection had died.

Something moved on the glass. Ill-defined patches of darkness and light shifted and clarified. A car? The puke-yellow glimmer told him whose. But it wasn't Merrin coming back. She was still running from him, running from the inevitable. There was only one place she belonged and that was here, with him. He imagined her Toyota cutting through the night, at the edge of Seadale now, a small town only notable for its beach, everything else — its heritage pub, small supermarket, burger joint and lone Italian café — being boringly standard. Merrin was moving fast and erratically. A wheel scraped the gutter near Tognetti's Roundabout (she always did that), drawing the gaze of late-night diners in the café there. The car swerved on the damp surface and Stefan held his breath.

As Merrin turned out of the skid, Stefan saw her pasty face lose the momentary panic that one moment of dark possibility had injected through her body. She'd pay attention for a while, to the road, to where she was going. A streetlight caught the echo of anxiety in her blue-green eyes.

"What the fuck am I doing?" she'd say to no one.

Stefan smiled to himself. She'd be starting to question her actions. Starting to regret them, perhaps. She must know that leaving him, this act of petty melodrama, wasn't right, but it needn't be terminal. Stefan could be forgiving, if she gave him good reason to be.

Come back!

The images on the window glass became dim and muddled, but there was enough clarity for him to see that though she had a chance to turn, to come back, she didn't. She sped around a corner, wheels screaming on the bitumen. If she didn't return now, he couldn't be held responsible for what might happen. Death could be absolute.

The vision of her disappeared.

He grunted, rubbing his hand over the glass and smearing the scene to oblivion. So be it then. Let her fade! Let the outside world abandon him! Stefan had whispered its eulogy long ago, and the fact that it was as sick as it was had been the main reason he'd bought this place. The house was relatively isolated, dug in against the hills on a narrow strip of land between the escarpment and the ocean — though not so isolated that he had to travel more than ten minutes to find a supermarket. He had no intention of growing his own food or any of that shit. Okay, sure, if the world were doomed, having a supermarket within walking distance wouldn't be much use. But right now, he didn't want to think about self-sufficiency. Fuck it, anyway! He'd be dead soon enough and when he carked it, the world could follow him to oblivion.

In the meantime, no one left him, not until he wanted them to. Not the world. Not Merrin. She'd be back. While the world turned, what she'd lost would torment her. One way or the other, she'd be back.

He'd really had such hopes for her. She's not like the others, he'd thought. Relationships were hard. None of his had worked out. And it wasn't his fault. His mother had been right — women were self-centred, emotionally damaged by a male world that idolised them, incapable of consistency or loyalty, unable to understand where their best interests lay.

"You have to teach them, Stefan," his mother had said as she died of the cancer that ate away her lungs. "You have to be constant, true to yourself."

So far it hadn't helped. Merrin was the fourth. They'd all left him, though he'd done his best to keep them with him. With the others, he'd tired of the effort and let them go. It took more strength than he had to keep them from leaving. Drained him. With the others, he hadn't cared enough in the end. Now only dusty memories remained. He had no intention of doing the same with Merrin. He loved her. He wanted her to stay.

Damn it! Come back!

His mobile rang. He spun around as though it had cursed him and glared at it where it lay, buzzing and warbling against the surface of the table. Who'd be ringing at this hour? It was 10:32 according to the digital display on his clock. He never talked business after nine at night and his few friends knew better than to call this late. "Bugger off!" he growled. But the ringing continued.

Perhaps it was Merrin. He strode over to it, grabbed the phone and looked for the caller's ID. The number was withheld.

Jabbing the connection button, he growled, "Who is this?"

What might have been a voice whispered at the edge of his hearing, dim and distant. It was more like an energy surge somewhere far away, an accident of the system that had for a moment mimicked humanity.

"Who's there?" he asked it.

Silence. Someone was on the line. He could feel them. The feeling confused him somewhat, though, because an intuitive reaction told him that it was Merrin. A vague ambiance suggested her, yet it didn't exude the strong sense of presence that he knew contact with Merrin would have.

"Is that you? Has something happened?"

Suddenly, the line went dead. Whatever, whoever had been there was gone. Stefan snarled at the phone and threw it away, hard. It smashed on the wall and clattered over the polished floorboards.

Then, out of the resonance of its fall, he heard the sound of a car pulling into his driveway. Its tyres ground on the dirt, broken stone and detritus from the surrounding trees snapping under the vehicle's weight.

He didn't move, eager for some indication that this might be Merrin, returning to him. It was a delicate and awkward moment and required all his concentration. The engine died. A car door slammed. Footsteps, tentative, first diminishing, then pausing. Then coming on again, in his direction. Up onto the front porch, provoking a hollow sound in the wood. The footsteps stopped. Someone knocked against the doorframe.

Still Stefan waited silently.

More knocking. If it were Merrin, why would she knock? Yet he could smell Merrin. Not with complete clarity — the impression was similar to her but subtly different. Would a return have changed her that much?

Pounding on the door.

A dark shape appeared against the frosted glass.

"Stefan, I can see you, for God's sake." The voice was female, once again evocative of Merrin, but not her. "Let me in."

Alice, Merrin's younger sister. Genetic factors gave her some of the qualities of Merrin and the confusion that caused in Stefan's interaction with her made him uneasy in her presence. Sexual attraction fought with the annoyance that always remained in her wake. She had an air of disapproval about her even when she wasn't actually criticising him.

"Damn," he muttered. She was exactly what he didn't need right now. What if Merrin came back while she was here?

"Stefan?"

"Okay!" he yelled. "Okay, keep your pants on."

He let her in. As she pushed past, she shot him a glance that was dark with suspicion. It was a look that once again reminded him of Merrin. Despite the chill that had permeated the outside air, she was wearing a low-cut top and Stefan couldn't stop his gaze from exploring the smooth contours of her cleavage. Why did she dress like that? Didn't she know how much it confused him? Why was she always trying to tempt him?

She moved away hurriedly as though catching some hint of his thoughts. Closing her coat around her and turning away, she said, "This place is so friggin' cold. How can you stand it?"

Her hair was dark brown and frizzy, so unlike Merrin's

short black style that with her profile obscured, Stefan was momentarily freed from the uncomfortable illusion of intimacy that she provoked.

"I'm not cold," he said.

She turned and he could almost hear her thinking, *You're the coldest fuckin' person I've ever met.* She didn't say it out loud, though. Merrin would have.

"What do you want at this hour, Alice?" He slammed the door and led the way into the lounge area.

"I want to talk to Merrin."

"Merrin? Now?"

"I want to know what's going on." She faced him, her features determined. "I haven't heard from her for ages, months. She's not answering her phone and doesn't return my calls. I've even written, for God's sake!"

"Maybe she doesn't want to talk to you."

"Don't give me that, Stefan. We've always been close."

He shrugged, but said nothing.

"Just get her for me, will you?"

Tossing a gesture toward the nearest chair, he said, "You want to sit? Can I take your coat?"

"I just want to see her."

"Well, she's not here." He paused. "Book club or something—"

"But the car's in the garage. I looked."

"That's mine."

"When did *you* get a license?"

"Months ago. It was Merrin's idea."

She snorted sceptically. She'd never considered him capable of anything useful. Stefan shot her what was no doubt an overly theatrical frown.

"It's some sort of literary retreat. I wasn't really paying attention. She'll be away for a few days."

His answer seemed to punch the wind from her belly.

Alice gave an exasperated groan and slumped into the chair. After a few moments, her head turned upward slightly and dark eyes studied him. They were no longer aggressive but pleading.

"What's going on with her, Stefan?" She made a helpless gesture. "Please. She's been so distant. I don't want to lose her."

"I'm sure everything's fine," he said. "She's just been distracted."

"Distracted?"

"Work. You know how it is."

"No, I don't know how it is." She stood and came toward him. "We've spent most of our lives together, Stefan. We've always been close. Suddenly, she's not talking. It just doesn't feel right."

"What can I tell you—?"

"You can tell me what the problem is. I know there's a problem. I can feel it."

"People change, Alice. Their priorities shift." He gazed past her, trying to avoid meeting her eyes without being obvious about it. "Merrin's undergone some big changes lately. Personal crises."

Alice was close now. He sensed her like an infusion of pheromones. Her hand slapped against his chest to draw his attention back to her.

"What sort of changes?"

My God, he thought as he looked into her face, her eyes are so like Merrin's. Is that Merrin I'm seeing, hidden behind the differences?

"Come on, Stefan, don't bullshit me! I'm her sister."

Her lips were far more sensual than her sister's. He couldn't stop himself studying them as they formed words, emitting sound like an exotic perfume. The fleshiness, the flash of white teeth, the hint of tongue...

Tears welled into his eyes.

"Stefan? Are you all right?"

He turned away, embarrassed.

"Oh, God," Alice whispered, softening. She grabbed his arm. "Did she leave you?" He didn't reply. "She actually dumped you?"

Stefan imagined that his backward stare was cold and indifferent. "Yes," he said. "I guess she did. She dumped me."

"It's just a break, right? While she sorts herself out?"

"Maybe. Sure." The tears runnelling down his cheeks were genuine, at least. "She'll come back. She has to."

"I'm sorry, Stefan."

He grunted. "Sorry? Don't go all Mother Theresa on me, Alice. I know you've never liked me."

"Stefan—"

"I've got nothing but bad vibes off you since we first met. It felt like hate. So don't try to tell me otherwise, just 'cause your sister has decided she agrees with you."

Her fingers gripped his arm tightly. "That's not true, Stefan. I don't hate you. You just..." She released her grip and stepped back a pace. In its anxious uncertainty, her face reminded him so much of Merrin. "You make me nervous, that's all. I don't know why. When you're around, I feel..."

He waited. His silence refused to let her off the hook.

"...wrong, Stefan. That's all. I feel wrong."

Wrong? Stefan tried to decode what the word meant, but found that his mind wouldn't function properly. It was a confused tangle of passion and despair. Yet this might be a revelation. Alice bit her lip, pushed her hair back with a sweep of her right hand. Clearly misinterpreting what he was feeling, she slipped off her coat. His eyes caressed the soft skin on the exposed top of her breasts. "Look, how about that cup of tea?" She held out her hand. It was trembling slightly. "I think you need to talk this through."

On an impulse, he entwined his fingers in hers. She didn't pull her hand away. Yes, there it was; he could sense the truth in the heat she radiated. She was Merrin, but more than Merrin. Perhaps that had been the problem all along. He'd ended up with Merrin, when it was her sister he should have had in his bed with him. She was warmer, more sensual, more in tune with his needs. Perhaps she was the one who could free him of the cancer that was consuming him.

"Okay," he said. "Let's talk."

When inhibition finally fell away and her pity became desire, the sex that followed was energetic, passionate and only slightly awkward — for Stefan, nostalgically similar to the experience of fucking Merrin, though somehow more satisfying. Afterwards, he drifted into a warm hazy comfort zone, listening to her breathing as she slept beside him. He stared at the ceiling, where darkness waited for a shape to be consigned to it. His despondency had retreated, at least for a time. Merrin was suddenly irrelevant and for all he cared, she could stay away. He didn't need her, anymore than he had needed the others.

But the despair was there still, just out of sight, waiting for its moment to return.

He was nudged back into full wakefulness by the sound of a car. Light streamed in through gaps in the blinds. He glanced toward the bedside clock, but a blade of deep shadow cut across its face. Must be some time well after midnight. Why would anyone come here now?

Could it be Merrin?

With Alice still there beside him in their bed, he was suddenly afraid. What would she think? Fucking Merrin's sister had sated the lust in him but his dismissal of Merrin herself in Alice's favour now seemed like lunacy. Once again, it was Merrin he wanted. Merrin he needed. And now, perhaps, she'd returned to him.

He slid from beneath the tangled bedclothes, not caring if he woke Alice, and stumbled toward the window. As his fingers touched the blinds and began to ease the vertical slits apart, the light suddenly cut off. What he saw beyond the glass was Alice's silver Prius sitting cold on the gravel, the rest of the driveway empty, darkness everywhere, gnarled eucalypts silhouetted against the lighter night sky, the curve of the road and the patches of dim sheen spread by the streetlights. No other cars.

He grabbed his jeans off the floor and awkwardly pulled them on. Barefoot, he shuffled from the room, across the hallway and into the lounge area. The air had grown colder, and the chill increased as he approached the front door. He hesitated, hand halfway to the lock.

Something thudded against the glass, though there was no shadow visible to indicate a solid form on the other side. Stefan listened to the external silence and his own laboured breathing. Then the wind became audible, shrieking across the porch. Hanging pot-plants rattled. He switched on the porch light.

Nothing.

Cautiously he opened the door, bracing himself against the turbulence. But now there was none. The night was still and breathless once more.

"Merrin?" he called.

From somewhere out in the night, where darkness consumed the contours of the road and the silhouettes of the trees, a voice whispered his name.

Stefan felt his stomach spasm and the nerves throughout his body tremble. He stepped back. The distant darkness seemed to expand, consuming the trees and the last of the streetlights. All that remained was the dimming luminescence struggling into the night from his porch.

He could swear someone was standing out there, right at the far edge of visibility. Was it Merrin? He didn't think so. There was an aura, a deep and hateful chill emanating from it, as clear to him as the press of the doorjamb against his back. Suddenly desperate to be out of its sight, he retreated through the portal and slammed the door shut, leaving the porch light on to give him warning should the thing out there come close enough to cast a shadow.

Trying to control the panic building in him and struggling against the tension screaming through his muscles, he backed across the room like a supplicant begging leave of a king. The luminous rectangle of light that was the glass panel on the door revealed nothing. He breathed out. But in that moment the wind rose again and there was shrieking carried on it.

A floorboard creaked far down the hallway. He glared in that direction. Alice was up and headed for the basement.

Forgetting his imaginings and the phantoms lurking in the wind, he ran after her, finding her pulling on the handle of the basement door. Fortunately, he'd locked it before she arrived. He always kept it locked and kept the key hidden. Didn't want unwelcome visitors stumbling down there. Until her last few days with him, not even Merrin had been allowed through that door. It was his place, his sanctuary.

Alice spun around at the sound of his footsteps. She looked cold and vulnerable — a white shape huddled in the gloom.

"What the hell do you think you're doing?" he growled.

"You weren't there — and I heard a voice." She glanced around anxiously.

"It was the wind," he said.

"No. Someone...someone was calling for help. Behind this door."

"You imagined it," he said, moving closer. "The wind was

rattling the hanging plants on the porch. I got up to check the windows were shut."

"What's down there?" Her fingers rapped against the wood.

"Storage. Just rubbish, that's all. The stairs are old and termite-ridden. Not very safe. So I keep it locked."

Alice put her left ear against the wood. "What if someone got trapped?"

Close enough now. He reached out and grasped her arm. "No one goes down there!" he growled. "No one can."

She squealed and pulled from his grip. "What're you doing?"

"I said to forget it! There's nothing—"

A shrill scream cut him off, echoing from beneath the house. Its familiarity choked the words in his throat.

"Let me go!"

Alice slapped her hands against the door. "It's her! It's Merrin."

"It can't be Merrin," Stefan responded distractedly, without much conviction. "You're imagining things. It's just the wind."

"Don't do it, Stefan. Please!"

"Surely you can hear that!" Alice grabbed at the door handle and pulled, trying to wrench it open. "It's her!"

"How can it be her, Alice? Merrin left me. She's gone."

She glared at him, eyes full of shocked comprehension. "You locked her down there, didn't you? You fucking locked her down there!"

"Of course not—"

"Fuck you!"

"Open this door, Stefan. Open it now!"

Coldness filled Stefan then, dampening the heat that had made him want to strike out at her.

"All right," he said, "if that's what you want."

He took a few steps backward until he came to an antique cabinet and extracted a bunch of keys from somewhere in its depths. Shoving Alice aside, he unlocked the door and flung it open, revealing a set of stairs and a pit of darkness. The only sound emanating from that darkness was a low rustle, like rats scurrying for cover.

"Merrin?" Alice called, leaning through the doorway.

Stefan grabbed her and nudged her onto the stairs. "You think I'd lock her down there? Well, go on, take a look!"

She resisted, but he was strong. As she stumbled onto the second step, Stefan reached out and flicked a switch. Dim red light took some of the fear from the place, replacing darkness with the shadowy contours of stacked boxes, broken furniture and a sea of clutter.

"I'm sure I heard something," she said uncertainly.

"Go on!" He pushed her, gently, but she lost her footing on the narrow wooden step. Stefan steadied her, allowing her to get her balance again. Her skin was soft under his fingers.

"Is it safe?" she asked.

"Not very." He shrugged. "That's why I keep it locked."

Alice frowned at him then leaned into the gloom.

"Merrin?" she called out. "Is anyone there?"

Stefan's mind had become a whirlpool of conflicting impressions — images of Merrin, her car driving away, his fist rammed against a cupboard, love-making, blood slipping in runnels along the contours of rough brick walls, laughter both happy and manic, wind shrieking through the tops of trees. As Alice moved downward under her own steam now, confident that he wasn't going to slip away, Stefan turned quickly and locked the door. Alice didn't notice.

"Merrin?" Alice called again.

In the silence Stefan could hear her breathing.

"See?" he said. "Nothing."

She moved down another few steps, her bare feet hesitant on the rough wood. Stefan watched the contours of her back, the tense curve of her buttocks, but he felt no desire for her now. That passion had left him, replaced by an interest that was almost compassion. Perhaps he would give her one last chance.

"Let's go back upstairs," he said. "Aren't you cold?"

She glanced over her shoulder, her face a featureless silhouette. "I want to make sure."

He sighed — then slipped past her and continued down the remaining steps to the bottom. Alice followed him into the basement.

"Do you see Merrin anywhere?" he said with what he imagined was an injured sarcasm.

Alice ignored his tone. "It stinks down here. Smells like a dead animal."

"Probably rats."

"What's over there?" She gestured beyond a pile of boxes that formed a sort of inner wall. Red light emanated above the barrier, indicating a largish space.

"More junk. Why don't you look for yourself?"

She disappeared along the improvised corridor. Stefan listened to the scuffing of her feet on the concrete floor, the shallow nervousness of her breathing, the whispers of something dark and unseen in the shadows...

Then all noises stopped. That moment of silence lingered, exuding an anticipatory tension. Stefan felt the cancer within him beginning to stir.

When the silence broke, mere seconds had passed, yet it seemed to Stefan like minutes. Alice's scream amplified itself in a ragged attempt to find release, echoing from the walls, off the ceiling, out of gaps in the junk. He ran toward her. She turned, face contorted with fear and anger.

"What's up?" Stefan asked.

"Don't come near me!" She backed away, cringing into a corner. She tried to cover her nakedness now, as though they'd never been intimate. Tears streamed down her cheeks, reforming her skin into an unattractive mask he barely recognised. "You killed her!"

He followed Alice's trembling gesture. The flaccid human ruin chained to the wall was wearing Merrin's face and body, but emaciated into a skeletal mannequin by lack of food and water, and now beginning to rot. The sight came as no surprise, of course, though it did, as always, evoke a momentary regret. He ignored the older, barely recognisable corpses chained beside her. Three of them. As Stefan's gaze returned to Alice, it became cold and unforgiving.

"That's not Merrin," he growled. "It's what she left behind."

"You killed her, you bastard! You killed her!"

He stepped closer. This caused the terror in her eyes to overwhelm the rage. She grabbed at something — a broken broom handle leaning against the wall — and swung at him. He batted it aside, so fiercely it spun out of her grip and crashed into a box of discarded crockery. His blows turned on her, keys scoring across her cheek. She shrieked as she crashed to the floor.

"You're so like her." It was disgust he felt now. "Hard. Critical. Colder than I've ever been." He stepped toward her in one fluid movement and kicked her in the gut. The cancer in him screamed along with her. Bending down and ignoring her whimpers of pain, he pounded his fist into her face. Blood from her broken nose sprayed over the floor.

"You think I'm so shallow that I'd value her body over her spirit, her essence? I'm not that kind of man. I love and I love deeply. She should have seen that, understood what it meant, before she turned away from me." He gestured toward Merrin's corpse. "That's nothing. She could've stayed and I might have forgiven her, but no! She chose to leave me." He grunted bitterly. The dim lights flickered, while a voice breathed syllables beneath the hissing in his ears. "I thought she'd come back. Instead, she whispers. All the time, whispers—"

Why wasn't Alice looking at him? Why was she looking past him? Something had drawn her attention, despite the pain, despite her terror. Fear was still etched in her features, though he sensed at that moment that the nature of it had changed. No longer focussed on him, it was instead a larger, more numinous emotion. Stefan followed her gaze.

A human form had materialised out of the wavering shadows. It moved without motion, nearer each time he blinked. Illumination from the dull lighting of the basement was unable to find a surface to adhere to. Instead it slipped aside, disappearing into a twilight so profound it made his eyes ache.

But Stefan knew who this was. She'd come back after all. He'd known that she couldn't stay away, but would return to seek forgiveness, to be reinstated into the weave of his life. She had no meaning without him. His was the defining passion. His was the power of life.

Yet something in him recoiled from this spectral delusion. Cancer cells in him screamed a warning. He pushed their noises away.

"Merrin—" he began.

She was directly in front of him, less than an arm's reach away. Her beauty trembled like a magician's glamour over cadaverous features. It might have been reassuring, but all he could sense was anger.

"My love," he moaned.

Her bony fingers snatched at him. The keys fell from his grip, clattering to the floor and skimming over the dust and blood. Stefan watched as they stopped right where Alice's trembling hand could reach out and take them.

"She'll ruin everything," he whispered to Merrin. "She doesn't understand what you are."

He tried to get to Alice, to stop her from using the keys, but Merrin cut him off. Once again her clawed hand swept toward him; this time he could feel it within his chest, a hard knot of alien presence that gathered his internal darkness to itself and fed on it. He collapsed to his knees. As Alice took the keys and staggered out of sight, he remained there, helpless to move, unable to intervene. Her irregular footsteps clumped up the stairs; keys rattled as she searched and found the correct one. Finally, the door squealed open, sending a momentary wave of light over the ceiling. "Bastard!" she shrieked. Then the door slammed shut and the light gave way to the basement's sick red glow.

The sound of the key turning in the lock, trapping him inside, drained Stefan of whatever optimism he might have had left. Alice would call the police, he knew that. How could they understand any better than she had?

But that wasn't the worst of it.

Merrin had retreated from him, disappearing into the gloom behind every box, into every shadow, yet all the while one step beyond the world itself. He saw her intermittently, like a trembling in his peripheral vision, and he could smell her — the barely familiar scent of her flesh, cold now and redolent of corruption.

Her voice whispered. The cancer groaned in response, moving further into his organs with each breath.

Stay here, Stefan. Or leave. The choice is yours.

He would decay in this basement, where Merrin and the others had decayed — and no matter how long it took the police to respond, a day or a month or forever, his life would dwindle slowly, painfully fading hour by hour, day by day, until he could stand it no longer.

Yet he would not be able to leave. There was nowhere for him to go, outside of himself.

"Don't do this, Merrin. Please."

The shadows were silent.

"Please, Merrin, don't leave me here like this."

If she watched him from the gloom, she gave no sign.

AFTERWORD

The inspiration for the story 'Ego' is straightforward enough. The God Machine's song of the same name is about egotistical obsession — that self-referential delusion by which we demand that reality conform to our own desires and in which others become objects defined solely by our own needs. In the normal course of events, we learn that such an ego-driven approach to life, within a pluralistic society that is an amalgamation of individuals, is neither realistic nor workable. So in creating the protagonist of my story, I found myself exploring how the delusion might become so all-consuming that it dominates not only the subjective life of an individual but also the objective realities of life and death. The story depicts an extreme instance, of course, but hopefully the narrative carries a metaphorical quality that makes it applicable to us all.

It was the line about an unknown someone calling the speaker's name at the back door and walking across the floor that suggested the supernatural element — a phantom that is both a subjective creation and an objective consequence. This is how I think of ghosts in my stories generally, so the notion of focusing on an individual's demented ego imaginatively conceived in these terms seemed like a good fit. For me, too, the combination of introversion and violence in the story's narrative approach resonates with The God Machine's music generally.

BIOGRAPHY

Robert Hood's horror-tinged science-fiction, crime and supernatural tales have appeared in many places over the years and recently in *Voices*, edited by Mark S. Deniz and Amanda Pillar (Morrigan Books, 2008), *Exotic Gothic 2*, edited by Danel Olson (Ash-Tree Press, 2008), *Dead Souls*, edited by Mark S. Deniz (Morrigan Books, 2009), and *Exotic Gothic 3*, edited by Danel Olson (Ash-Tree Press, 2009). Stories are due in *The Mammoth Book of Zombie Apocalypse!*, created by Stephen Jones (Robinson Publishing/Running Press, 2010) and in *In the Footsteps of Gilgamesh*, edited Mark S. Deniz (Gilgamesh Press, 2011). Hood's slipstream robot war novel *Robot War Espresso* is to be published by Twelfth Planet Press in 2010/2011.

SEVEN

STEPHANIE CAMPISI

With her forehead pressed to the frigid pane of her kitchen window, her breath blooming and fading on the glass, Elizaveta can trace the road that coils like an unravelling spool of thread from the town. It is a precarious road, thoughtless in its unmotivated twists that send it sprawling across the hill.

It is nearing ten o'clock, and the town is starting to fade beneath the heavy pillow of fog that sweeps in from the higher regions before rolling down to the cemetery, where Elizaveta's beloved Mikhail, her Misha, lies.

There are lights: the urine-yellow bulbs from the pub on the corner of the street; the soft pools of lamppost glow skating on the snow; and the hundreds of tiny pinpricks from the sky, shy and obscured: the type of light that you see when you become ensnared in a woollen jumper. There is a cool, damp smell in the air that is slightly offset by the freshly cut loaf of rye bread sitting on the narrow wooden table where Elizaveta is working. She almost expects Pavel Ivanovich, the baker's son, to knock on her window and invite himself in, but it has been years now since she left her home for a new life in this country.

She presses play on her battered cassette player, and Kino's *Igra* splutters on, Viktor Tsoi's vocals and soft guitar slightly deadened and marred with static fuzz from overplay. It is part of a mixtape that Misha had given her to play while she was studying for her final examinations at

MGU, and she still smiles each time she hears the sharp click of stop-start between each song. She thinks of the university often, of her Misha, and of the future that is no longer hers, or theirs. Here, in this country, she is the Russian woman with the downturned mouth who jabs at the sloping glass windows of the deli counter in the local supermarket, who hands over a hopeful jumble of mismatched coins when the price is given to her. She had taken years of English classes with her friends, but all of that is gone now.

She butters a fat chunk of bread and tries to unscrew the cheap jar of *ogurtsy*, a veritable prize found tucked away on the supermarket shelves bloated with tinned meals and invented flavours. She holds it against her stomach for leverage, and the lid of the jar pops up, like it is gasping for air, and for a moment it feels more like she, not the jar, who is desperately fighting for breath.

X

The first thing Elizaveta noticed was that his clothes were too bright, even for central Moscow, and she imagined for a moment that there was a flower within him, curling up and lurking brightly beneath the pale honey of his skin. His eyes were a forget-me-not blue, hooded beneath a concerned brow; his lips were chapped and red from the butterflies of snow flitting all around.

He carried a guitar case, flat and broad and of cracking leather, studded at the sides and scuffed at the edges. His knuckles were pale from the pressure of carrying the instrument, and Elizaveta found herself staring at his impossibly elegant fingers as he approached her, his boots, square-toed and black, kicking up the new layer of snow coating the street. He was slender, so slender, all beautiful lines that she never wanted to end, and she memorised them, the gentle flow of his body, and the weather-worn skin of the case that he carried, his hip butting against it with each step.

Her breath crystallised in front of her and she realised that perhaps she was trying to speak. She clutched her small bag of wrapped, hand-dyed *pysanki*, vivid and glossy and alive with colour. In this setting of overcast sky, muted clothing, age-distraught buildings, they were the only point of brightness.

He walked past her, beneath the slanting archway of a building scabrous with shedding plaster and eyeless with the always-drawn mould-patterned blinds.

Mesmerised, Elizaveta tilted her bag of *pysanki* and they rolled out of its thick hessian sides and onto the snow, like the drops of dye a child spatters into the soapy bubbles created in the hook of a clothes hanger. They nestled there for a moment, and Elizaveta fancied that they sighed before being immersed.

X

It is heavily overcast tonight, something for which Elizaveta is thankful. There are too many days in this country where the sky is blue and endless, held up in a way that she cannot fathom, but when the sky rolls with a fur of soft grey clouds, everything feels smaller, and she feels less alone.

It starts to rain, and the falling sheets interrupt the faint glow of the street lamps so that they flicker, like the flame of the broad candle Elizaveta uses to melt the wax onto her eggs. The water sketches a crosshatch across the kitchen window. Even the rain is wrong here, she reflects: it falls, instead of walking like it does at home. She smiles faintly as she remembers her friend Vera joking about this very thing so many years ago.

She sits down, *kistka* in hand, the back of her cracked red vinyl chair knocking up against the frog-green laminate of the kitchen cabinets. Her soft thighs scrape against the rough underside of the kitchen table.

The table is a strange, narrow thing with spindly legs like a foal, and is divided into three sections, two of which fold down like curved wooden flanks. It is spattered with fingerprints of wax and with dark furry blots, some caused long ago by Misha's dark, filterless cigarettes and others from a candle swept over during the involved hours of *pysanki*-dyeing. She runs her fingers over these marks, like they are poorly-aligned keys on a disrupted piano.

Each blotch comes with a memory, and as she caresses the dark pits and bumps, they come bubbling up...

Misha's fingers peck currants, like a bird, out of the sweet buns from the Asian bakery. The way he put the currants to his lips, sucked them in, his eyes calmly on her, watching her go through the familiar motions of heating a pot of tea—

His sitting at this very table, his acoustic guitar tilted up, his hands clutching its neck like it's a rifle, setting to music Elizaveta's favourite Pushkin poem, *Ja Vas Ljubil*—

The fresh, leafy smell of the tobacco as he arranged it over pale white rectangles, which he rolled up and smoked—

Then, Elizaveta recalls, suddenly, coldly, the time when he did so while cradling the earpiece of the telephone, thick and plastic and curved at the ends, like a detached handlebar, or a length of plumbing, and whispers, *'ona umerla...'*

She is dead.

His fingers instinctively pinching and rolling, the movements familiar and precise. His eyes, those eyes that sit so strangely between the different colours of blue, not quite meeting Elizaveta's.

He would ask, she knew.

X

The alleyway was a roaming mass of newly mewling kittens;

a soft clump of zigzagging coats of black and white and grey. Four of them lay dead, as the others — those now stumbling in the wadding of the snow — had been earlier, their tongues lolling out in impolite smiles, their legs and claws outstretched and stiff from a combination of rigor mortis and the freezing air. There were stains in the snow from where Elizaveta's eggs had cleansed themselves of dye. This was Elizaveta's talent, and her mother's before her.

An old woman, hunched and shrunken and bitter behind a floral headscarf, swept at the kittens with a straw-bristled broom. Her eyes were watery and pale, and the surrounding flesh seemed to be repelled from them, collecting in bags and folds so deep that she looked as though she had drawn a semi-circle beneath each eye in thick, dark kohl. She was probably beautiful once, and Elizaveta stared for a moment, trying to see herself in that pleated face, before trying not to. The woman met her eyes, gestured at the kittens, casting aspersions.

But then he appeared from around the corner, his guitar case knocking against his right knee with every step, as though part of some slightly deranged waltz. He met her nervous gaze for a second that was almost painful, and her cheeks bloomed the red of yesterday's *pysanki*, the colour of which had now bled across the snow.

He paused, resting the corner of the faded case on the top of his shoe so that it reminded her of an awkward harp, and placed hands, mottled from the teeth of the cold, together on the top corner of the case. He regarded her.

X

When Mikhail slept, his face yielded to a youth that swept over him like the smoothing touch of the ocean over marked sand. Elizaveta, propping her chin on the fragile ridge of his shoulder, tried to keep her breath silent so that she would not wake him. His eyelids were closed so gently over his eyes, so smoothly that the line of skin was broken only by the dark curl of his eyelashes.

Elizaveta had imagined that he would be taciturn, his words measured and considered, delivered with gravity. She had been surprised by his voice, which had fallen from his lips like a ribbon, quietly and quickly enough that it almost disguised his *okanye*, his O-saying, and the manner in which he stressed plural words at their ends. But not entirely: her friend Vera, upon meeting him, had raised a sharp eyebrow and had pursed lips outlined in cruel pencil and smothered with waxy lipstick. In the bathroom, stickily dabbing her lips with a folded square of toilet paper, she had dismissed his accent as Gorbachevian.

Mikhail shifted beneath the blankets, and she folded into herself as he curled about her like a comma. His breath dressed her neck with a warmth that curled over the gentle fuzz that marked the boundaries of her hairline. Elizaveta shifted her legs slightly, and she caught a musty note of sex as it mingled sweetly with the huff of ash that lay in blooms in the glass by the bed.

X

Elizaveta creaks out of her chair, her knees stiff and complaining like the swollen hinges that make it so difficult to close the bedroom door. The door has a split the size of a thumbnail in one of its decorated panels, from the impact of the jar Misha had thrown when he had asked, as she knew he would, to use her gifts to bring *her*, that other *her*, back. She had told him no.

It had surprised her as much as it had surprised him.

And then, after that, the accident, for which Elizaveta has spent seven years trying to atone.

Elizaveta slides the kettle onto the heat-burnished bracelet of a burner and traces her fingers down the stain that divides the spout in two. Her eyes are dry from the close-work with the *pysanki*, and her vision smears at the edges like watercolour paint on thin paper. She massages their inner corners. During the years she had worn makeup, the same action would have resulted in her fingernails collecting a polluted sediment.

The cassette tape has frozen at the end of its spool. Elizaveta does not know how long ago it lapsed, or if it ever really will: for her, the gentle bars of *Igra* hang in the air, the softly fingered chords reminding her, for reasons she has never been able to describe, of the sound of falling plums.

She absently fills the tea strainer that hangs from a noose inside the pot. Her thoughts are half a world, and a similar amount of time, away from the coloured eggs she has snarled with rhythms of wax that blot and weave over each other, in turn obscuring and revealing. Her fingers, mottled with dye and lachrymal nodes of soot-stained wax, press together the edges of the tea strainer, fumbling the worn clasp into place.

X

She finds herself in the past once more, gazing at Mikhail's long, thin hands, numbed from the cold he pretended not to feel, fumbling and squeaking over the stretched coils of his strings. Watching him pause, his knuckles white and flexing, to pinch a pickled onion between thumb and forefinger, following it with the lightning acridity of homebrewed vodka.

Elizaveta sat on a crate upholstered with an abandoned overcoat. The dust-hardened folds where the arms had been knotted together were pale and permanent, ridged like the neck of a vacuum cleaner. Her jaw ached from forcing her teeth together in an unwilling jigsaw. She feared that her chin might betray her by wrinkling into a peach-stone form of despair.

Your Mikhail, he is smooth, Vera had said earlier, after thinking for a moment, collecting her words and organising them so that they were viciously euphemistic. Oh, Liza, she had added sadly, knowingly.

Elizaveta had cupped her narrow mug of tea until it scalded her fingertips, and she was struck wonderingly with the thought that she had somehow dragged the warmth and life from it. She thought of the staggering kittens in the snow, their ice-teased fur and their scraping, blood-coloured tongues. Vera was right, Elizaveta knew, but her Misha loved her.

She thought, perhaps desperately, of the time when he had awoken to find her staring down at the gentle breadth of his face, studying him with compulsive intensity. His lips had bowed up at their corners, just slightly, but enough that they fought to cover his teeth.

If we're not careful, we'll fall for each other, he had said.

Elizaveta's foot had been tingling from a pinched nerve, and she ducked her head slightly as she massaged her heel, hoping that he would not see the way she was crumbling, the way her feelings, so bright and deep, were turning on her.

She had wanted to tell him how she already had, how even since before he had met her gaze that very first time, she had given herself to him. But instead, she had feigned slipping beneath the heavy, disquieting blanket of sleep, frozen and purposeless in the understanding that she was not the only one.

X

Elizaveta's tea has steeped to the point of bitterness, and she dilutes it with an uncertain trickle of water from the tap. Her mug leaves a sloppy ring of damp on the kitchen bench, which is the glossy, hyper-real green of a cartoon frog blocked out in thick black lines and drowned in the ersatzness of Technicolour. Sometimes in this country, she feels as though she is drowning beneath its assuredness. She thinks of the muted, hazy characters in *Yozhik v tumane*, an animated film she holds dear from childhood, and wonders how such a thing could ever survive here.

Her shoulders are curved and hunched from the night's work, and she worries at them with a thumb that aches from the memory of innumerable endless winters. She lifts the basket of *pysanki* from the table and skates it over the surface of the kitchen bench, where she will finish the last of the dyeing and the removal of the ink-smudged wax.

She pulls back her shoulder blades until they click proudly. Her head angles upwards into the profile that her mother's friends had once called beautiful, and which she had known to be true because no other girl had ever mentioned it. Not even Vera, who tried so hard to draw out her own beauty that it slipped from her grasp instead, lost beneath layers of cosmetics and self-consciousness, like the smallest *matryoshka* within its concealing nest of reproductions.

She scours with a dye-stained fingernail at the wax ringing one of the *pysanki*, watching it flake away in oily, hardened curls.

Mikhail, on their first night together, had told her that he could drown in her eyes. Secretly, she had wanted him to, and even now she wishes that he had.

X

Ona umerla, he had said as his fingers stuttered over his inchoate cigarette. The telephone in his lap was a heart of plastic, spewing knotted, confused arteries.

She is dead.

Nadia is dead.

Nadia. The woman about whom Vera had suspected, and about whom Elizaveta had known but had denied, had been named at last.

Nadia, a word, a name meaning *hope.*

Elizaveta's bowels had roiled like treacherous snakes. Like the way she unravelled the last flecks of wax on a *pysanka* to find its final form, she worked backwards through her time with Misha, retrospectively connecting all manner of comments and absences to a single, common theme. The confused way in which Misha's mother had first greeted her, turning to him for confirmation, her cigarette-wrinkled lips pursing; the way Misha's best friend's girlfriend had stared thoughtfully into her *shchi* when Elizaveta had mentioned offhandedly that their anniversary was approaching; the Chekhovian nicknames Misha had given her sometimes, spontaneously, but had never repeated, as they seemed not to fit, sliding off her pale skin with curious impermanence.

Liza, he had whispered, clenching the telephone receiver the way he clawed at his guitar some nights, lost in the depths of the consequences of her ultimatum. His eyes were like bleached lavender, and they caught at her, burring at her conscience, but she shook her head. Liza, he had said, for me, will you bring her back?

When they had left behind their life in Russia, Elizaveta had left behind her gift, a gift that terrified most but that tempted so many others, and Mikhail had left behind this woman that they had never spoken about, but who was all too often in Elizaveta's thoughts.

No, she said. No, I will not bring her back.

X

Elizaveta often wonders sometimes whether she was born haunted, or whether something settled into her one day, spilling through her bones and tormenting her with possibilities both good and bad. As a child, she would spend hours tracing and designing patterns to be eventually transferred to the quiet, speckled fragility of an egg. She remembers the first time she hefted one of them in her hand, her fingers curling nervously away from where it lolled in her palm, as though she were cautiously pressing it to the soft, whiskered lips of a horse. She would watch as her mother blew them empty of their fatty, drooling innards; their whites stretched like threads of saliva.

Elizaveta remembers other, more startling things that she slowly learnt to connect with her practice, with the quietly murmured requests of the women. Some young, with cold-flushed cheeks and forget-me-not eyes, others older, mottled with creeping bitterness, but still, seeking a panacea for the wounds that, like keloid scars, surfaced without warning after years of careful excuses and justification. Everyone wanted their loved ones brought back to them, a sin of which Elizaveta was capable.

Before they had left for this new place, Elizaveta trying so hard to dismiss both the accusations about her work and her suspicions about her beloved Misha, Vera had warned her that it was a land that was broad but shallow, its history scattered upon it like seeds rolling with the enticements of the wind but yet to take on any meaningful form. To remind herself of Russia, and of the gift she would leave behind, Elizaveta had packed her mother's old leather trunk, the one with the worn fabric lining that hung with the heavy memory of pot pourri, with a bristling wedge of furry-edged photographs, and typewritten letters with ink hazy from tears and the damp pressure of fingertips. Around these mementos she had packed a tiny box containing her amber earrings, and a few items of clothing, which, when the sun of this new country first caught them, seemed to fade almost to nothing. Elizaveta herself followed suit as she slowly acclimatised, shedding her *otchestvo* in favour of a surname, and her low-heeled short boots for a pair of cheap, disposable canvas shoes.

No one sought her out here, although occasionally she found herself hoping that they would. There were evenings where Mikhail would find her squinting through the faint perimeter of light where the curtain did not quite meet the windowsill, conjuring up a nudging cluster of women with their pleas and their faded photographs cut by bisecting white lines from where they had been folded to purse size.

No one here had asked her to bring back their loved ones. No one, at least, until Mikhail.

X

It has been seven years since Mikhail — his eyes the colour of tonight's dark, massing sky, his lips faded and etched with thin, splitting lines — had asked her to bring back the woman so cruelly known as Nadia.

It is seven years since Elizaveta, strengthened by the poisoned, dormant schadenfreude she felt towards this woman whom he had loved more than she, had challenged him for the first time. Seven years since, on a night of churning rain and bleak light and vodka untempered by *zakuska*, Mischa had climbed into the car and never climbed back out.

It has taken her seven years to complete these *pysanki*, layering the traits and memories she could adequately muster and transcribe. For Misha, of Misha, they are her most elaborate designs yet, the cumulative result of seven years of work; but simultaneously, she scarcely recognises them.

The front door, woozy from the cold, pulls out of its frame with the sound of smacking lips. Stippled light from the stooping street lamp seeps into the hallway, touching

Elizaveta's skin gently, knowingly.

Elizaveta stares, tracing the rhythm of the lolling, ambiguous road that stretches to the black metal wings of the cemetery gates. She pauses, suddenly shy, her fingers caressing the stippled surfaces of her *pysanki*, but she collects herself, stepping over the threshold.

These will work, she thinks, they must, and at last, like the other women whose loved ones she returned, she will have her Mikhail.

And inside her, so quietly tentative, so timid that it might not be there at all, is the tiny seed of hope that, at last, he will truly love her as she had once loved him.

AFTERWORD

The song 'Seven', to which this story was written, is an intensely alienating piece. It seems inevitable now that it was the catalyst for such a bleak and lonely a story as this one, which follows a lover who has always been on the periphery of a romantic relationship, despite losing herself so deeply within it. Even long after his death, Mikhail continues to haunt Elizaveta, manipulating her in death as he has done since their first meeting. This tragedy is compounded by the ease, both emotional and physical, with which Elizaveta can so easily change the lives of others and their loved ones to more closely resemble the things that ought to have been.

BIOGRAPHY

Stephanie Campisi is an Australian writer whose work has been published in magazines and anthologies worldwide, including in the US, the UK, the Czech Republic, Singapore, and Argentina. Notable publications include stories in *Fantasy Magazine*, *Shimmer*, *Sybil's Garage*, *Voiceworks*, the forthcoming *Polyphony 7*, and the World Fantasy Award-winning *Paper Cities*. She can be found online at www.stephaniecampisi.com

PURITY

KAARON WARREN

Therese was clean on the inside, but her mud-slapped, filthy, stinking home — with its stacks of newspapers going back as far as she was born, spoons bent and burnt, food for rats grown hard and crusty — kept her skin dirty. The floor all shit and mud and dropped rags.

Her mother was blind to it all, only seeing the bottle, and if Therese was living a cliché, she didn't notice. Her mother ate nothing but potato chips. She liked the ones with chicken flavour, so that's what she stank of. Not of chicken but of that yellow, chemical, thirsty smell of artificial chicken.

She knew her mother loved her. Hadn't she dumped Therese but changed her mind? Baby Therese was found abandoned at the hospital, covered with dirt, a thick, sludgy layer of it. They'd never seen a young baby so filthy. A nurse scraped it off, put it into a blood vial. Therese still has this vial of dirt. The nurse wrote, "Dirt from Baby Therese". The handwriting was neat, the 'i' dotted with a flower.

Her mother came to get her a week later when the love affair failed. The nurse gave her the vial of dirt, saying, "You need to keep your baby clean." Therese's mother puts on a voice when she tells this story, a low, scratchy voice, making the woman sound evil. Therese wondered how many children that nurse had and what her house looked like.

This was the last boyfriend her mother ever had. It was food from then on. Food in packets she'd eat without touching, tipping it into her mouth straight from the packet.

Therese never found out what happened to her mother to make her want to be fat and why she was always filthy.

"I don't want you to know," her mother would say, though not knowing was worse, especially as Therese got older and realised some of the crap that could happen.

She was loved, though. She knew she was loved, and she was never hurt, always fed. Her mother was fine but dirty.

She did her homework at school because if she did it at home, greasy fingerprints would appear, a dark smear, a drop of something viscous. Her desk was neat, clean, her handwriting perfect, her work pristine.

She wasn't good at schoolwork but she persisted. Wanted to be the first in her family to finish high school and she would do it, next year. She wasn't smart with the school stuff. She worked hard at it but the letters mixed themselves up in her head and the teachers dismissed her because of how she looked. She didn't blame them for this; there were too many children. Too many problems. They'd dealt with her older brother and knew what a hopeless case he was, and they didn't even know how he lived now. Down there in the basement, pale from the lack of sun, and he blinked when he came up to the kitchen, blinked and snuffled at the garbage until she wanted to push him back down the stairs.

There were layers of shit down there. He didn't care. He was strong and when he was clean he was good-looking. He could be funny when he wanted to; the funniest person Therese knew. She copied his style, when she made people laugh. Took his wink, his timing, took the way he flapped his hands, held his head when he was telling a joke.

The joke was him, though. That was the stuff which made people laugh. Laughing at where she came from before they did gave her the power of it.

She knew she would escape. Get where it's clean.

"There's nowhere cleaner," her mother told her. "The world is a filthy place." She said this as she ate her chips. Sometimes she ate them sitting on the toilet.

X

Therese worked at the supermarket after school and on the weekends, saving her money.

Most people were clean there but one young customer, he came in every week, she could smell the soap on him from three registers away. He was lovely. He started to come through her register every time and they talked. Up close the soap smell was good and his fingernails were white with cleanliness. He was a laugher. After every sentence, funny or not. Sometimes he brought his grandfather, a nice, white-haired old man, bent at the shoulders, clean, neat. Therese wondered what it would be like to have a neat old man like that in your life.

One Thursday afternoon, they came through her register with grapes, cherries, lychees and apricots. The old man was dressed neatly in beige pants and a collared T-shirt, the uniform of the old man everywhere. He wore a white baseball cap with a logo of the local bowling club.

"That's a lot of fruit," she said.

"Purification," the old man said. "Nothing like fruit for purification. Skin keeps it clean inside, and you know if it's rotting because it'll be soft and bruised. You can tell if it's no good to eat. And when it does rot, it leaves behind pure seed."

He and the boy laughed. Therese smiled and laughed, too, although there was nothing funny. The old man laughed harder, threw his head back, roared with it until his eyes watered. The boy gently placed his hand on the man's shoulder, calming him. The old man bent to pick up the next bag of fruit from the trolley and she saw that at the back of his cap, at the buckle, there was a red, creeping stain. It looked like blood but it could have been rust. It looked like he was leaking fluid from a small hole in his skull. She saw it everywhere, all over the shop; seeping wounds, pus, fat rotten flesh pushing at skin to get out. The boy slipped a packet of gum into his pocket; the old man took a chocolate bar.

He stood and caught her staring. Smiled. "These things happen slowly," he said. "Impurities begin to leak out. Better out than in, I say." He and the boy laughed again, so loudly people turned to look, but she didn't care. She wanted to laugh with them, laugh like that.

Therese's mother laughed a lot. Mid-sentence, she'd chuckle. If the milk was sour, she'd laugh. If kids threw eggs at the house, she'd laugh. When Therese was 14, her first period came, messy and painful. Her mother laughed. "It happens to all of us," she said, and directed Therese to scrabble in this cupboard and that, looking for sanitary napkins. She found a sticky, dusty packet behind some rusty tins of peas and she had to use them until she got to a shop.

"I stopped long ago, darling, when they took my insides out. You know what you did to my insides, don't you? Tore them up like a tiny Jack the Ripper." Her mother laughed at this.

There are times when the whole family fell into fits of hysterical laughter. Sugar-high laughter. This was when her aunties came over with cakes and lollies, lemonade, "Gotta feed you up", no intention of teaching good eating habits because as long as their sister was fat and dirty, they were better. Other times, the neighbourhood mothers took pity on her and invited her over for meals. They'd trick out ways to get her clean, they'd give her their kids' clothes and she loved the smell of them, the soap she could smell in there, the starch from the iron.

The old man and his grandson paid for their fruit. "You should join us, Therese," the old man said. "Come and share the fruit with us." He trembled and she wondered if he was nervous.

His grandson nodded. "There'll be lots of people there tonight. We have a lot of friends."

Therese looked around, not sure if they were talking to her.

The old man wrote down the address on the back of his receipt. "You'll have a laugh, Therese. Life is always better with laughter."

She stopped at a clothing shop on the way home, wanting brand-new things which hadn't been touched by her mother, by her house. She chose badly, though, and regretted it once she'd showered and dressed. A pink, fluffy skirt and a tight shiny red singlet top. Brand-new, unwashed, as clean as she could want. But it all itched and the skirt was too short.

She caught two buses to a large house in the suburbs. Three storeys, it seemed to extend out the back a long way. There were lights all around it and the lawns were lush and neat.

The grandson was waiting on the front door step. His name was Daniel. "We're always adding to it," he said. "I think the original house was a tin shack."

"Bit like my mother," she said, getting in early with the jokes. "She's been expanding since she was fifteen."

He laughed, really laughed, and she was glad he got her humour.

Inside, the place was surprisingly coherent. The entrance had three or four doors off it and a large staircase rising upstairs. Four people chattered against the walls, one nibbling a crumbly pastry, making Therese feel suddenly hungry.

"Through here. We're just in time to hear him speak."

"Who?" They hadn't warned her about any speaker. Therese pushed open the heavy door and stepped inside. It was the size of a small hall and full of people. It was cold; goosebumps formed and she felt her hair prickle.

She bent to scrabble a jumper from her backpack but a hand on her shoulder stopped her.

Daniel said. "Cold is purifying."

The gaps around them filled and she couldn't move.

They sat on hard chairs and on a tall stool at the front of the room sat the grandfather. He looked different; bigger, broader. Silvery grey hair, face barely lined, clear blue eyes.

"I am Calum," he said. He smiled, broad white teeth slightly sharp. "I am the Jester. I sit before you a humble man." There was laughter. A chuckle or two. Therese was surprised but waited for more before reacting. She shivered; it was freezing in the room. Around her, others shivered, too. Even the mass of bodies didn't help, though she thought it would eventually.

He spoke on. Nonsense in a deep voice. About football and fame and pressure and what he had for lunch. Music played beneath his voice and that explained why people swayed, butt cheek to butt cheek.

They laughed. It began quietly, but when he started talking about his pyjamas, they were hysterical. They wept, they sweated, clear fluids leaking.

Therese felt embarrassed for them. A woman three rows down wet her pants and no one seemed to notice. They laughed as if they'd forgotten how and were copying what they'd seen on television. Wide mouths, noise pouring out with no mirth in it.

Someone heehawed like a donkey.

She watched them. The dirtiness of their sweat. It came out clean but dust, there was always dust, clung to them, muddying their skin. She squeezed her eyes tight.

"Don't worry," Daniel whispered. "They will bathe and be clean for the afternoon meal."

At the thought of food, her stomach growled.

"Lunch?"

"We don't have the standard three meals. We have breakfast at dawn and then one meal between when you would normally have lunch and dinner. He says it's better to go to sleep with digested food in your stomach."

"That makes sense, it really does," Therese said. She hated the late-night, thrown-together meals at home. Leftovers of a week ago tossed with cheese, covered with melted butter and crushed potato chips and baked, all bad news and toilet stink.

She felt a hand poke in her ribs and turned, holding her side.

A middle-aged man glared at her. His face was runnelled with tear tracks; was he the donkey laugher?

"How dare you not laugh? Who do you think you are?"

"You're not laughing right now," she said.

He poked her again with his long, hairy forefinger, opened his mouth and brayed.

The woman next to her pinched her. "If you don't laugh, you don't belong."

Daniel poked her too, but sexy, sexy. He moved up the front, tugging her hand to take her with him and soon he was rolling in the aisle, hysterical.

Calum spoke, his voice loud over the laughter, but no one cared what he said. Therese listened as he talked about his childhood.

"Shivering is another hysteria," he said. "One year, when I was at high school, there was a heat wave. We stood in the courtyard, lined up, listening to speeches. We were not being respectful, we did not listen, we would fail and we would all have to work in petrol stations for life, be fat, pimply, greasy adults. We were too hot to listen.

"It was so hot the children were panting, and one girl fainted, then another. I looked at this and I felt something sharp, I smelled orange peel, but I didn't faint. I began to shiver uncontrollably.

"A friend touched me and he began to shiver as well, calling to his girlfriend, "Cold! It's cold!" and there was no sense to it but soon every child was fainted or shivering and the Principal lost his job over it and ended up tutoring maths to bored children. He no longer had parents sucking up to him, wanting favours. He had people crossing the street to avoid him.

"I did my final-year assignment on the hysteria. I took the girl who'd first fainted out a few times, seeing if there was something in both of us which made it happen. She looked close to fainting most of the time. I wondered if it was a scent, something to set people off. Was that it?

"I tried to make her faint, just by talking to her. But it made her so nervous that she giggled and couldn't stop. She couldn't even eat her chocolate mousse, kept spluttering it out. The waiter started laughing, and others. I watched it move like a wave.

"I spent years trying to find the source. The cause of it. But there is none. Not even love of God."

Therese walked close to him, until she stood at his feet, staring at him. Listening.

"Are you ready to laugh?" he said.

She nodded.

He opened his mouth so wide she could see down his throat, and he began to laugh. He took her face in his hands, made her look him in the eyes, and he laughed until she started and she knew this was it; she would not be able to stop.

A chuckle at first; sardonic, she thought, a sardonic chuckle. She thought she'd fake it but she didn't have to. It was like she'd lost control of her body; she shivered, her limbs weak, her gut filled with butterflies and she laughed so hard her muscles ached.

She took to laughing at a speed which was frightening. And she laughed so hard old wounds opened, and she bled, her arms, her legs, slick with blood and she made patterns on the lino with it, dark red finger painting. Therese laughed so hard a blood vessel popped in her eyes. And that became the goal. Even the Jester took to it, bleeding quietly. He'd score his thighs with a sharp knife and the others did it, too.

X

Therese tried to watch it dispassionately, tried to understand it, and looked for physical causes for the hysteria; incense, heavy breathing, drugs, alcohol, hypnosis. She saw none of this.

She saw things she didn't believe possible. She saw people collapse, not breathing, then wake with their fillings turned to gold. She saw this; mouths full of gold.

"People will do anything for money," Calum said as the numbers grew, as word got out. Only Therese listened to the words; the others laughed.

"Laugh until you sweat. Until you bleed. That is how you are purified." Daniel rolled at Calum's feet and he did bleed, from the eyes and the ears. Therese bent and gently wiped the blood away.

After each session, sometimes days-long, a cleaning crew would go through. Therese loved the meeting hall after this cleaning. Her eyes would sting from the bleach, but the smell and the shine were all she'd ever wanted.

X

Calum did not remind her of her grandfather, although they were of an age.

Her grandfather had walked the streets in rags held together by bodily secretions. They drove past him every day on the school bus. He knew she was aboard, could raise his hand in greeting. His teeth were rotted in his head, his gums swollen, and he no longer called out loud.

That was where she came from, that empty poverty. He was jailed 35 years for spitting at a cop, because he had HIV AIDS.

Calum trembled and sat stiffly. Only Therese noticed this.

"Are you all right, Jester?" she said.

"I embrace the symptoms. They will make me pure." But his stiffness and tremors lasted into meals, in the evenings, in quiet times when there was no laughter.

Therese went to a doctor and, while she was being examined, asked about her grandfather and his tremors.

"It sounds like it could be Parkinson's. You need to get him to come in for tests. There are drugs to control it. We need to be careful, though. Some of the drugs can lead to compulsive, self-rewarding behaviour. Gambling, sex, shopping."

"Laughter?" she asked.

"Yeah, I'd say. Laughter releases the pleasure chemical, too."

X

Calum did not deny it. "It's my family's impure blood."

"And you use your drug on them?"

"Sometimes, to help things along. Not always, though. It's themselves."

X

Those who laughed themselves close to death, they awakened with no memory. Every moment was their first.

Calum said, "This is a good thing. Clearing your mind of the past, cleaning out bad memories, will make you happy. We are safe here from the cruelties of the world."

They laughed. Therese watched the fluids leaking from them, the clear fluids. When people first arrived they leaked cloudy stuff, muddy stuff, but soon the liquids flowed clear, like from a well-done roast chicken.

The Jester sat in a large armchair. He was a big man but he looked small in its cushions.

"You seem happy, Therese."

Fresh from the shower, her skin still felt clean. Her clothes clean. It would be an hour or more before the dirt started to cling.

She turned around for him, her arms spread wide.

"Do you like me happy?"

He smiled. "Clean and happy, you are at your most beautiful."

He leapt about like a jester, jumping foolishly to make people laugh.

"I come from a long line of jesters. Not all of them funny like me. One dear man so upset his crowd they kicked him down the stairs. Broke his neck as if he were a chicken. My mum used to say I had the spirit of him in me. His essence."

The audience laughed, laughed louder.

"She said that as the jester died, he laughed once, a bitter choke full of hate and regret. The basement servant stood by, and he had a small pot he'd emptied of beer that very moment. He captured that laugh which came out brown and oozy. Kept it for good, a time of need. But while there were many times of need, there never was one strong enough for the essence. This is how time passes. We wait and wait for a moment that never comes. We should make the moment, take it. That's what we should do."

The infection was full in them now, and they were out of their seats, roaring with laughter. Children, too, filled with pure hysteria.

"My mother came into the essence when she was born. Her father told her, save it for the end of the world.

"But along the way I was born. Born sad, I was, full of misery and despair. Do you see?"

They saw, a hundred of them screaming his name.

"I didn't feel right in the world. It seemed so dirty and cruel. So I tried to take myself out of it."

Screams of laughter, louder from those who'd tried themselves.

"My mother found me with the gun all ready. I wanted to be sure. She told me to wait, she was very calm, and she brought me the essence of that old jester. It was a bitter liquid, thick like cough syrup, but it filled me with a good humour which has not left me yet. Who else puts any faith in purity? Who else cares? Drinkers like their vodka pure. Holistic people like their food pure. Is food ever pure? There is damage along the way, I think." This is what he told them. "Truth is confession. You must tell me all."

And they did. All their secrets.

"Pain is truth, beauty and purity. Scars are pain and they tell the story of an impure life. Beauty is without scarring. Do you understand that you are not beautiful? You think you are but not at all."

They gave him their bank details because he said that only truth, beauty and purity will give them wealth. They had mouths full of gold fillings and they had no memory.

"It's the same everywhere," he told them. "You are not alone, or special. Once you're gone it's like you were never there. All you can do is lead a pure life, worship the life you are given."

"I was threatened with a year of ugliness if I didn't pass on a breast cancer chain letter," Therese said.

He laughed. "All your ugliness is on your skin and your own actions didn't cause that. There is clear blood running in your veins. We are merely animals in the Purity Zoo. We follow our nature. But all animals can be pure. To purify something you need to corrupt it first. Fruit rots, leaving behind a beautiful seed." It seemed so long ago, that time in the supermarket. A lifetime ago.

She still worked there, though she brought the groceries to the Jester now. He no longer needed to shop. Sometimes Daniel would meet her, help her take the things home, and she liked those times. They would drive in the car, the groceries rattling in the back seat, and it was normal. Average. The sort of thing people did.

Then he would laugh, and she would, and they were back in that again. Daniel always slipped something into his pocket; homage to the Jester. Therese would smile, look away. It didn't bother her.

Until the day he was caught.

He'd taken a pen, a good heavy one for the Jester. Therese didn't see him do it, which should have helped when she was questioned later, but didn't.

He was caught as they walked out the door. The fact he laughed at them...no security man likes being laughed at. They wouldn't be in the job if they could deal with people laughing at them. So he was taken to the police station. He said to Therese, "Don't let them laugh without me. Okay? Don't let him lead a meeting."

The Jester was furious. "How dare they take our people? How is he to laugh in there? We must laugh as we have never laughed before." He was quiet for a moment. "Therese, this town is so dirty. So full of pus it's coming through the seams."

This seemed an exaggeration to her, and she wondered if perhaps the scales were lifting from her eyes.

"Daniel will be home soon. They'll only keep him a couple of hours. He said we should wait for him. That we should not have a meeting without him."

"This town is filthy, Therese. We must laugh, laugh. This is for Daniel's sake, Therese."

"We can't have a meeting without him."

"We can, you know."

That afternoon, as the meeting began, he said, "We have no control over how it will affect people. That is not our business. Our business is purity, our business is to take what has been cleansed and work with it. You must break something down before you can cleanse it. At least this way there is only one emotion out of control. Can you imagine Hatred? Or Lust? Or Anger? These things will cause damage to all around them. I have never done anything wrong. Even as a child my inner voice was very loud.

"Laugh, my friends, laugh as you have never laughed before. Let them hear your spirit, let them join us." Pachelbel's *Canon* played, soft, gentle, rhythmic.

People began to laugh. Laughed so hard their eyeballs were bloody, their bones cracked, and they couldn't breathe.

"It's the same everywhere. No one will behave differently. You all laugh. Laugh to purify this city, laugh for Daniel, laugh as if you have nothing to live for."

Laughter became pain. Therese's guts were dagger-struck, her bones mallet-shattered, her tongue split in two, her teeth cracked, her eyes swelled out of her head, but she could not stop. She felt her breath leaving, the oxygen out of her body, as blackness filled her eyes and she knew nothing more.

X

Hot dragon's breath on her face. She opened her eyes. Daniel bent over her, smiling.

"Welcome back from the dead, Therese."

She sat up. Around her, bodies lay; bloodied, emptied, pure. She pulled herself tall and didn't scream, though she took Daniel's hand. She turned her head, looking for the Jester.

"I'm here, Therese." He sat on his stool. He looked exhausted, almost bored.

"Did you die also?"

"Not this time." He slid off the stool, leaning heavily on Daniel's shoulder.

Daniel helped them both limp forward. His face was drawn, tears on his cheeks. "I told you not to run the meeting." He wept as they picked their way through the dead. Sirens in the distance.

"It's so terrible."

"It is. He can't control them like I do. But it is good. We have purified them all. Pain, beauty, purity. They are happy. It's all over. It's the same everywhere."

She bent down to look at a beautiful eagle necklace around the neck of a young girl.

"Take it," he said, spittle-voiced. "Take whatever you want. But we'll need to hurry."

They picked like vultures off the laughing dead; money, jewellery, iPods, Blackberries; picked and stashed the goods into four green shopping bags.

"How do you feel?" Daniel said once they were out of the house and travelling in their air-conditioned, perfumed sedan.

"I feel dirty on the surface but within I feel cleansed."

"Pure?"

"Pure."

She had a gash on her forehead from falling.

"That will heal to a beautiful scar," he said. "What does it feel like to think you are dead? To wake up among the dead?"

"I can see more sharply. Edges are clearer. I see bruises I couldn't see before."

"That's emotional bruising. What you see is heartbreak, or guilt, or fear."

"It really was like sleep. But it was much darker. Blanker. And re-birthing was like waking from a sleep supposed to last five days but you wake up after two."

The Jester shook. He tried to sip a soft drink, chinotto, bitter, but he could not lift it to his mouth.

He took Therese's hand. "My dear daughter."

The comfort those words gave her were beyond anything she had known. Her own father said fuck, fuck off, fuck you, and she'd watch him bleed to death in a pub brawl. Hiding under the table with her Barbie dolls.

X

"I think another town beckons," Daniel said.

She was quiet.

"A problem?"

"My mother. I hate to leave her alone in her filth. And my brother."

"We can bring them or we can purify them where they sit."

Could she do it? Burn the filthy house down, burn the clothes, the papers, the rotting carpet, the decades of boxes? The chocolate wrappers?

Daniel said, "It's up to you to decide. Then we'll spend some money. We'll hire a cleaner to scrub as we walk, scrabble on the ground before us to make sure we step clean. We'll buy a comedy club for you to star in."

Therese smiled. She still hadn't figured out what it was

she would have to do for him to thank him for giving her her life back. She saw through the Jester at least, overblown, arrogant man. He was kind, though, and she admired that. And the way he could draw an audience, that was something she wanted to learn. She would walk on with him, bringing people to laughter.

"How will we find another town like that one?"

"It's the same everywhere."

X

At the side of the road there were dead cows, burnt, hit by lightning perhaps, direct hit. Therese thought, *Perhaps we are like a bushfire, coming suddenly and burning a place to the ground. Bushfires clear the land to make it ready for new growth. That is what we are doing.*

There was a smell in the air, a sweet smell which made them smile. Each smelled something different.

In the back seat, her mother hummed softly. They'd paid a nurse to clean her up and now, covered with perfume and creams, her white hair soft around her face, Therese felt like hugging her. Her brother had refused to leave, although the Jester had made him laugh.

"It's the same everywhere," Calum said again, and they drove on to select the next town to be gifted with purity.

AFTERWORD

I started in the obvious way; listening to the song. I sat with pen and paper and wrote whatever came into my head. Automatic writing. A certain mood came out of this, of mindless crowds, and the image of a preacher in a stadium.

I sat down again the next day, after watching a documentary about the Jonestown massacre which coincidentally showed on TV.

The idea of a purity cult began to form, and my thoughts took a religious angle. I thought of laughter as purification, which led me to research laughter clubs and cults. From there, I listened to the whole album and wrote my first draft.

BIOGRAPHY

Award-winning writer Kaaron Warren's first novel, *Slights,* was launched by Angry Robot Books at WorldCon in Montreal. Two more novels will be published by Angry Robot in the next year. Her short fiction has appeared in *Year's Best Horror and Fantasy, Fantasy Magazine, Paper Cities* and many other places in Australia, Europe and the US. She is currently based in Canberra, Australia.

Her short story *A Positive* has been made into a short film by Bearcage Productions which will launch in Australia early 2010.

She is currently working on a novella about the goddess Ishtar, and a novel about the washerwoman in history. She has stories upcoming in *Exotic Gothic 3, Baggage* and *Haunted Legends.*

kaaronwarren.livejournal.com
kaaronwarren.wordpress.com

THE PIANO SONG

CAT SPARKS

The door was harmless looking enough, its texture fabricated
to resemble rustic wood. The window frame matched, flecks
of curling paint repeating at regular intervals. The sort of
detail you'd only notice if you'd been locked in the room for
hours.

Charise felt the tears start up but she wasn't giving in to
them, no way, not ever, so she focused her attention on the
frame and the bright blue sky beyond. Pretty blue, pretty
clouds. Children's laughter wafted from the playground
below.

"Y'hear that?" said the counsellor. "That's children
playing. Lil' Andre's first day at school. I can't believe you
wouldn't rather be down there enjoying the shoot."

Charise pressed her lips together, determined not to
speak. *All the lights in place, are they? All the little children
learnt their lines?*

The counsellor got up from behind her desk and moved to
perch alongside Charise on the lounge. "You could be in Lil'
Andre's clip if you want. There's roles for older students, not
just the little ones." She gestured, as if movement helped her
conjure inspiration from the air.

I'll bet there are, thought Charise. Everything was scripted
in this place. Every role pre-designated and defined.

"Something could easily be written in for you: Lil' Andre
trips and falls. A kindly student helps him up, brushes the
gravel from his knee. That sort of thing. The clip's not set in

stone, Charise, that's all I'm saying. Work with me and I can help you. Who knows what might happen down the track?"

Charise considered. "If you listen to my song I'll be in your stupid Lil' Andre clip or whatever. *If* you listen to my song."

The counsellor shook her head sadly, beginning a smile that didn't quite make it. "Girl, you know how Assignment works. Aces are aces. Spades are spades. You were screened for Talent and you don't have it — nothing anyone can do about that. I'm offering you a cutaway close-up and maybe even a minor speaking part, but you don't wanna play ball. I don't even understand what it is you *do* want! Nobody can change the way things're meant to be."

The counsellor's hands were still now, her eyes staring Charise down in a way that made her skin crawl. She wanted to look back to the window, but she couldn't. She didn't dare.

"You have any idea how many kids are busting to get into Hi-school?" said the counsellor, all attempts at a pleasantly modulated voice abandoned. "How many would take your place in a heartbeat if they could only get a break?"

Charise stared down at the desktop and tried to take her air in long, slow breaths.

"They're out there on the streets, fighting tooth and claw for crowd-scene positioning, and then here's you, a *scholarship kid*, handed it all on a plate. Only you don't want it. You believe highly trained specialists like me gotta listen to your stupid piano song when you know there ain't no point. It's all about infrastructure, honey. Everything happens for a reason. Why can't you see reason, huh? Why can't you play nice with all the other boys and girls?"

In the playground below, the two-minute siren blared and everything fell quiet while the scene got filmed. Charise had a sudden urge to run to the window and hurl herself through it. Land in a bloody screaming heap on the bitumen, ruining the shoot, scaring Lil' Andre out of his tiny wits. Only there'd be no point. They'd just mop up the blood and do another take, replace the kids that couldn't hold themselves together for the filming. Find themselves another Lil' Andre if she'd been lucky enough to crush him to death with her fall.

Charise pictured the scene unfolding in the playground below. Lil' Andre meeting his pre-selected brand-new friends. Special moments rehearsed to run like clockwork. Afterwards there'd be T-shirts, commemorative mugs and framed autographed photographs to coincide with the moment Lil' Andre's first single hit the charts. The counsellors were right. Her bloodwork was Mundane. She was fated for the chorus or the background at best. No one gave a shit about her song.

After her counselling session, a nurse led her away to Deportment, followed by an hour of Bollywood routines, then Psych. Archive and Marketing were the only classes she was missing while under Reprimand.

The beat don't stop just 'cos you're falling behind with it. Yeah, the beat didn't ever stop in this place.

They passed a room in which some of the older starlets were being drilled in running-from-camera routines.

"Steady, steady...three, four and twist from the waist. One arm back now, fingers splayed. What you doing with that other arm out, Kay-t? Other hand goes to your lips. How they s'posed to film your face if you're blocking it with your arm?"

From where Charise was standing, all the starlets looked identical, distinguishable only by sculptural aspects of their 'dos. Each head was a mass of braids, curls and beads, locks cascading over sweaty brows before springing into fluid motion.

The counsellor waited for Charise in the doorway of the
Psych ward, arms folded across her chest. "Your budget is all
blown, honey. I was getting all ready to expel you,
scholarship or no scholarship, but then the damnedest thing
happened." She double-checked her clipboard just to make
sure there had been no mistake. "2TrU himself has taken an
interest in your case! Yeah, I know, I can hardly believe it
myself because you sure don't deserve *nothing* for all the
trouble you've caused. But, see, that's how it is. It's all part of
how come the man's such a star. 2TrU truly cares for his
people. He wants you to see reason, Charise. Give you a
chance to straighten out your life."

"I don't need my life straightened."

The counsellor raised her hands as if Charise had been
pointing a gun. "Whatever you say, hon, whatever you say.
I've done my job. I'm betting you'll change your tune when
you've spent some time with 2TrU. 2TrU's gonna sort you
out. 2TrU's gonna show you what from what."

2TrU. Charise swallowed the lump in her throat as she felt
her resolve evaporate. He was just about the biggest Hi-
School star there'd ever been. Some said he even owned
shares in the place, which Charise found hard to believe —
why would anyone *that* rich bother owning a dump like this?

"He's on tour, but he'll be here for you, hon. Don't you go
letting the rest of us down."

X

The cell was small and sparse, but Charise had it all to
herself and that made it wonderful, even if the door didn't
lock. She hated the studio dorms, all the bullying and the
bitching and the noise, with every little detail filmed, cut and
recut until it slotted into scripts.

She didn't have much stuff, but what she did have could
be spread across every surface rather than stashed away in

secret places. There were no cameras. That was supposed to be a punishment, along with the silence. No soundtrack, no inspiration, no theme music.

Solitary suited her just fine. Alone in silence, she could begin to hear her own music seeping through to the surface. Faint, but persistent tunes leaving a trail to mark their presence. She had no means of recording them, but she didn't need to. So long as she didn't forget she had them, that was all that mattered.

But she couldn't sleep. Her songs ran rampant through her headspace, playing tag with all the legitimate, authorised imprinted material. Lyrics smashed head-to-head with product endorsements, biopics and silhouettes. Shadows she couldn't put a face to, or a name, yet were nonetheless as familiar as her own reflection in the mildew-encrusted mirror that hung above the corner washbasin.

Morning light streaming through the high-set window slit brought with it a different counsellor. The other one (Charise had forgotten her name) had apparently been summoned to higher duties at *Madonna-Vogue*. The new one was young, surely not much older than Charise herself, but as soon as she opened her mouth, Charise could tell that she was just the same as all of the others.

"Your case is very interesting," the new counsellor lied, "but you know, I have a feeling about you, girl. A good feeling, like all you need is for the time and place to be right. We can set that up for you. We can make it happen. Dreams come true in Hi-School, that's what it's all about."

"I hear music in my head that nobody else has written. Then I make up songs," explained Charise plainly. She'd used to say more, but she'd learned that the more words she uttered, the more they all thought they could get her to back down. Straight and simple was best. *I make up songs.* Not much room for misinterpretation.

"You know," said the new counsellor, nodding, "I was just like you. I was. It's so confusing being young. The world's so big and you don't know where you fit in."

Charise watched the woman's hands flutter and curl expressively, adding emphasis to her words. *So* confusing. *So* big.

"And my posse leader, she used to say, Janis, girl, where's your head at? Whatcha think you're trying to prove?"

"Janis?" The sound of the name cut through the autopilot bullshit, snapping Charise to wakefulness. "As in *Janis Joplin*, the Archive star? Were you named for her?"

Janis paused. "Yeah, well, maybe. It's an Archive name for sure, but I don't identify with the past as a form of personal self-expression. *Janis* is all about living in the moment. *Janis* says I'm free to be whoever I want to be, free to create my own blend of styles and —"

"Janis Joplin was a legend!" said Charise. "Nobody *made* her a star, she made herself. Nobody designed her a posse, people hung with her because she was so damn cool. She didn't sound or dress like anybody else. She left a legacy, *Janis*, and you don't even know what that is."

Janis stared at Charise for a moment, her mouth open. She closed it. "You know, they warned me you were *Archive* smart. Smart is good, Charise, smart can take you a long way. But you gotta know how to *apply* your smarts or it's all gonna count for zip. Archive is worthy, but living in the Now is worthy, too — more worthy, 'cos Now is where all the future grows from."

Crisp and clean, thought Charise, eyeballing the counsellor's outfit from top to bottom. Manicured, practised, rehearsed. Black, thigh-high leather boots with solid heels to reinforce an impression of sturdiness and reliability. Who could ever trust a counsellor sporting flimsy, open-toed footwear?

Janice's bling hung loosely from her wrists, fluorescent light refracting from her affiliation charms. Charise wasn't close enough to read their endorsements, but the sheer weight of them was impressive. Perhaps she was older than she looked.

"You got an audience with 2TrU today, that right?"

Charise nodded.

Janis smiled, a real smile this time. "Girl, you don't know how lucky you are. He is the *nicest* man. Absolutely the kindest, most talented, most warm-hearted star I have ever met — cross my heart."

Janis touched one of her blood-red enamelled fingernails to her bling as she spoke. An involuntary action, but Charise caught it, concluding that 2TrU had given this woman more than a gold trinket for her charm collection.

"Whatever's going wrong in your head, girl, 2TrU's gonna put it right. Trust him, Charise. That man truly cares for his people."

I am not his people! She wanted to scream the words at the top of her lungs, but she shushed herself. All that would get her was another round of celebrotherapy, derm patches and ice baths.

"Looking forward to it," she said.

"That's my girl!" said Janis, her impossibly wide smile creeping wider still. She winked and moved on to her next appointment, her sturdy footsteps echoing solidly on the linoleum floor.

X

Charise didn't have to sit through a preparatory dance routine — at least that was something. 2TrU's posse were short on time, she supposed. Probably had filming to get to. Everybody was always filming something.

A crew was already in place opposite the doorway

through which the great man was scheduled to make his entrance. Her heart fell when she saw it. She'd expected a webcast, naturally, but this looked like a full doco crew, and that would mean takes and retakes and close-ups, noddy shots — the works. Charise didn't want to end up part of somebody else's counselling program. *Well, what is it you do want, girl, can you answer me that?* No, she couldn't answer it. Not in any words that others could understand. They were right about one thing: she was privileged to be here. Hi-School beat the hell out of a manufacturing line, or packaging or programming, which is where she would have ended up were it not for random scholarship selection. The counsellors kept on asking her what she was holding out for. Truth was, she didn't know.

And then all of a sudden the crowd shushed and there he was, black fedora, cape and silver spats. He nodded recognition to his posse then singled Charise out for attention, directing her to the two chairs positioned for their meeting, cutting straight to the chase.

"They tell me Janis Joplin is a great inspiration of yours, Baby Girl."

Charise nodded meekly. 2TrU nodded back.

"When Joplin passed at 27 years, there was almost nothing to show for her. A few recordings, little bits of footage here and there. They say she did Woodstock, but where's the evidence? Stars can't run their lives like that. We got dues to pay. We owe the fans who worship us. Everything I own's enmeshed in the collaboratory input of others. When I pass, I'm leaving artefacts. Solid objects you can hold in your hands."

Charise found herself nodding in sympatico. "2TrU, I respect the truth of what you say, but why is it nobody will even *listen* to my song? What if I'm good? What if my music's better than Janis Joplin's? What if it's even better than yours?"

The subtle background murmuring shushed as the words left her mouth. 2TrU leaned forward in his seat, rested his chin on his curled fist, just like the silhouette in his *Big Bank Theory* album cover. 2TrU was a hefty man. Bigger than she'd realised from his clips.

"So. What if? You write some song and it happens to be awesome. Suddenly the world's gotta stop for that? The whole system breaks down, everything spins on its head just because some girl writes one good song, or maybe two or three? It's not as if the planet's running short of songs, Charise. We got rhythm enough to keep the whole globe swinging!" He laughed, the sound of a profoundly certain man.

"What about the merch? Who's entitled to residuals? Hell, forget the legals, what they gonna put on the T-shirts? The cover? Who gets rights? There hasn't been a bidding war in this town for twenty years, but some folks still remember the bad old days. Blood on the sidewalks. Shoot-ups every place you went. Star against star — now there was an ugly piece of Archive. It wasn't just the legal posses, either. Innocent people got gunned down all the time, and why? Infrastructure breakdown. Lawless running rampant, then cast gutterwards, gone to seed. You trying to tell me you want blood on your hands?"

"I—"

"Back in the old days, every star ran a seventy per cent chance of a violent demise. Choking on their own vomit, fried food, cirrhosis of the liver, bullets to the head — shot, more often than not, by members of their very own posse. Seventy per cent, Charise. That's no way to run an industry."

Charise opened her mouth but no sound came out.

"No one's saying you ain't special and that you can't make a valuable contribution, but you gotta go about your contributions in the right and proper way. It's all about supporting the system, Baby Girl, otherwise somebody gonna get hurt — and I know you don't want that."

No. She didn't want that.

2TrU raised a meaty hand and removed his shades. Behind them, his eyes were deep brown pools. They stared into her soul and she knew he had her. She'd forget about her stupid song. The man was a genius, a legend and a saviour. She loved him. She had always loved him.

She felt herself blushing so she looked away. The weight of his gaze pressed hot against her skin. Embarrassed, she looked to his posse for distraction. Buff men in dark shades, lean, large-breasted women in short, tight skirts. A fat guy. A cute kid with Mopsy curls and a backwards-on baseball cap. A plain-looking girl with glasses (no, she wasn't plain at all, she just dressed down for the role). A geeky guy with a bag full of hi-tech gadgets thrown over his left shoulder. All of them staring up at 2TrU in a wall of friendship and support, buffering the big man should he ever fall out of step, which he wouldn't.

Charise took a deep breath. This was hard. Really hard. "Let me sing just one song? If it's crap..." She shrugged. "I won't say anything again if you reckon my song's no good."

It was the wrong thing to say and she knew it, even as the words left her lips. She could feel the anger, the indignation like the heat coming off a burning car. When 2TrU spoke, his voice was different. Deeper, throatier, dangerous.

"I ain't got time for this," was all he said.

She couldn't bear to look as he stood up suddenly and turned his back on her. They exited together, him and his posse, tsking and shushing like a swarm of insects.

Charise clutched her hand to her chest. It hurt there, deep below the bone and if she'd had to speak at that point, she knew she couldn't have managed it. Her words were buried under an unseen, immeasurable weight. She'd let him down. She was letting them all down with her selfish, ridiculous fantasy.

Tears flooded out of her, cascading down her cheeks to soak the front of her blouse. Nobody offered her a tissue. Nobody paid her any attention at all.

It was time to go. Her shoes slapped rhythmically against the linoleum, the only thing to be heard in the soundproofed corridors.

Charise knew her future was bleak. At best she'd be designated a back-row extra for life. At worst, banished forever to the desolate wastelands of freelance fandom.

"I'm sorry," she said to herself, over and over and over. "I'm sorry, I'm sorry, I'm sorry," not knowing if she was apologising to herself or to the system she'd let down.

The susurrus of sorrys and the rhythm of her footsteps resonated a beat inside her head. She added a jump every second bar without even thinking. It just happened, as did the hopping and the tapping and the skipping and the clapping that followed.

A song bubbled up inside her, no song she'd ever heard before. She was sure of that. It was *hers*, a new one despite everything 2TrU and the counsellors had said, pulsing through her veins, slapping her round like a catfight.

> There's words in my head and they wanna get out
> Nothing I can do 'cept scream and shout
> Everybody tells me I don't got rhythm
> Can't stop the lyrics gotta make something with 'em!

She tried to hold still, hugging her arms for comfort. Were there cameras in the corridors? Of course there were. Everywhere had a live feed 24/7, even the bathrooms. Was anybody watching when nobody trod their linoleum floors?

Soon she'd be outside again, where snippets of soundtrack scented the breeze and sunlight drowned under halogen floods. Outside would bring her back to normal. This corridor was creeping her out. Quiet did things to her that quiet oughtn't do. There it was again. That infectious rhythm. Charise started skipping again, then broke into a run towards the double swing doors at the far end, clapping her hands over her ears for extra protection.

"It's not my fault!" she shouted.

She burst through the doors into fresh air and distant lullaby. Charise felt her heartbeat even out, her gunfire pulse sliding back into the green.

She'd come out the back of the therapy wing. A wide flow of cement steps led down onto the grass. Nobody used them — all filming was done out front where the steps were made of polished marble and the hydraulic eyes were poised to shoot from above.

She stood tentatively in the centre of the steps, tapping her toe as her own personal songtide began to rise. Soon, her shoulders were swaying. The rhythm. The beat inside her head. Infesting her blood. Embedded in her pulse. Her ribs vibrated with electric bass. Charise placed her hands on her hips and cast a glance back over her shoulder. Children! A daisy chain of multi-racial urchins spilled out of the doorway, their eyes glassy with wonder. She didn't have to say a thing. They all knew what to do.

As she took each step, they fanned out around her in precision accompaniment. She stepped, they stepped. She paused, they paused. When she clicked her fingers, they clapped an echo in response.

"Can you hear it, too?" she asked, amazed.

Of course they could hear it. Doves could hear it, and butterflies. The air was suddenly streaked with the lurid rainbow blurring of their wings.

Charise giggled. Her voice sounded cherubic, filtered, Altered. De-essed, autotuned, flanged, delayed then repeated over and over until it meshed like the bubbling of water trickling over moss-slicked pebbles.

A crowd began to gather on the lawn at the foot of the cement staircase. Charise was sure they hadn't been there a moment ago but they were now, plain as light. A nurse in whites pushing an old woman in a wheelchair; a man in a crumpled suit clutching a bottle, down on his luck; a little girl in pigtails holding a doe-eyed puppy dog; a skinny youth with a soccer ball tucked under one arm. Others, too, but she didn't have time for details. It was getting closer and closer to the moment where she was supposed to sing. She could feel her song pulsating, struggling to burst free. *Not yet...Not yet...wait 'til the dancers are all in place and we're all moving as one.*

When she could hold it in no longer, her voice exploded in a rainbow of glittering crystals: a song about all the sadness in the world and why can't we all just learn to love each other and be friends? Another voice accompanied her own: raspy, bluesy and wild. She looked around but couldn't see the other singer anywhere.

The sky began to peel, each cloud-encrusted sheet dangling in great curlicues, bouncing gently, buffeted by whispers of breeze. Behind the sky, velvet charcoal, where showers of blazing comets rained.

On the grass, the old woman sprung from her wheelchair to hug the little pigtailed girl. The drunkard cast aside his bottle and leapt, clicking heels from side to side. The soccer boy spun the ball on his finger and the little girl's dog yipped and yapped, walking on hind legs. Fireworks blazed across cerulean skies, and although she couldn't see much further than the grass, Charise knew the whole world was finally dancing to her song.

CAT SPARKS

AFTERWORD

To me, 'The Piano Song' is so terribly sad. The first images it brought to mind were of desolate urban wastelands; post-apocalyptic vistas devoid of life. But when I sat at my keyboard and began to write, a very different kind of story emerged. I imagined a society where all roles were predestined. Stardom and fandom were arbitrarily assigned, a bit like kings and serfs of old. When I think of incarceration, I picture prisoners trying to get out. What of a prisoner who's desperate to get in? Fighting the system, only to discover reality adjusting to render her incarceration seamless?

BIOGRAPHY

Cat Sparks managed Agog! Press, an Australian independent press that produced ten anthologies of new speculative fiction from 2002-2008. She's known for her award-winning editing, writing, graphic design and photography.

A graduate of the inaugural Clarion South Writers' Workshop, she was a Writers of the Future prize-winner in 2004. She has edited five anthologies of speculative fiction and fifty of her stories have been published since the turn of the Millennium. Cat has received ten Australian SF awards for writing, editing and art, including the Peter McNamara Aurealis Conveners Award 2004, for services to Australia's speculative fiction industry. She was the convenor of the Aurealis Awards horror division in 2006 and a judge in the anthologies and collected work category in 2009.

She is currently working on a trilogy and a handful of complicated short stories.

ABOUT THE EDITORS

AMANDA PILLAR is a speculative fiction author and editor who lives in Victoria, Australia, with her partner and two children, Saxon and Lilith, Burmese cats.

Amanda has had numerous short stories in print and is also the co-editor of the anthologies, *Voices* (2008), the award winning *Grants Pass* (2009), and *The Phantom Queen Awakes* (2010), published by Morrígan Books. She is currently editing *Scenes from the Second Storey*, due out at WorldCon 2010.

Visit Amanda's website at www.amandapillar.com or read about her adventures at:

http://amandapillar.livejournal.com

PETE KEMPSHALL has edited a range of writing, from *Judge Dredd* and *Winnie the Pooh* comics through to celebrity gossip magazines. The Australian edition of *Scenes From The Second Storey* means he can finally cross short stories off the list. He has also written a number of tales for Apex Publications, Twelfth Planet Press, Big Finish and Morrigan Books, one of which got to be dissected by editors for publication in *Scenes From The Second Storey*'s international edition. Got to love that karma...

Pete lives in Western Australia with his wife, two children and an ageing Labrador, and maintains a sporadic record of his publishing activities at:

www.tyrannyoftheblankpage.blogspot.com

ABOUT THE COVER ARTIST

REECE NOTLEY was born and raised in Hawai'i then, in her late teens, her feet grew itchy and she wandered off to see the world. After chewing through a pile of books, a lot of odd food and a stray boyfriend or two she eventually landed in San Diego, which she believes to be a very nice place but seriously needs more rain.

She currently has a day job that she mostly enjoys, herding pixels for the marketing department of a nice company with a fantastic view of the seashore from many floors up. As of this moment, she admits to sharing the house with three cats, a black Pomeranian puffball, a bonsai wolfhound and a ginger cairn terrorist.

Reece is also enslaved to the upkeep of a 1969 Ford Mustang Grand Coupe, a 1979 Pontiac Firebird and a Toshiba laptop. Her next published piece of writing will be in *Dead Souls* in 2009. She also rides herd on *Three Crow Press*, a horror, fantasy, sci-fi and speculative fiction e-zine (www.threecrowpress.com).

AVAILABLE NOW:

DEAD SOULS
edited by MARK S. DENIZ

Before God created light, there was darkness. Even after He illuminated the world, there were shadows — shadows that allowed the darkness to fester and infect the unwary.

The tales found within *Dead Souls* explore the recesses of the soul; those people and creatures that could not escape the shadows. From the inherent cruelness of humanity to malevolent forces, *Dead Souls* explores the depths of humanity as a lesson to the ignorant, the naive and the unsuspecting.

God created light, but it is a temporary grace that will ultimately fail us, for the darkness is stronger and our souls...are truly dead.

AVAILABLE NOW:

THE PHANTOM QUEEN AWAKES
edited by Mark S. Deniz & Amanda Pillar

The Phantom Queen, goddess of death, love and war, returns to strike fear into the hearts of mortals in the anthology, *The Phantom Queen Awakes*.

Meet a washerwoman on the shores of the river; cleaning the clothes of the soon-to-be-dead; try to bargain with the capricious goddess of war; hear the songs of the dead as they cry for justice; walk with heroes of the past

Revisit the world of the Celts; a land of mystical beauty, avarice, lust and war through stories told by Katharine Kerr, C.E. Murphy, Elaine Cunningham and Anya Bast, among many other talented authors.

AVAILABLE NOW:

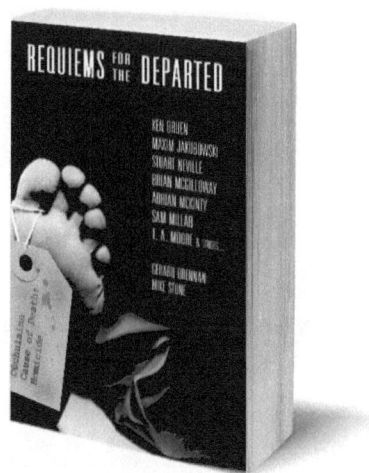

REQUIEMS FOR THE DEPARTED
edited by Gerard Brennan & Mike Stone

Requiems for the Departed contains seventeen short stories, inspired by Irish mythology, from some of the finest contemporary writers in the business.

Watch the children of Conchobar return to their mischievous ways, meet ancient Celtic royalty, and follow druids and banshees as they are set loose in the new Irish underbelly, murder and mayhem on their minds.

Featuring top shelf tales by Ken Bruen, Maxim Jakubowski, Stuart Neville, Brian McGilloway, Adrian McKinty, Sam Millar, John Grant, Garry Kilworth, T.A. Moore and many more.

THREE CROW PRESS
MORRIGAN BOOKS' E-ZINE

Editors
J. LEE. MOFFATT, T.A. MOORE &
REECE NOTLEY

Three Crow Press is an online magazine specializing in quality speculative fiction, fantasy (urban, dark and gothic), horror and steampunk as well as non-fiction pieces and articles.

Well written young adult will be considered if the piece is within the 16+ market.

We are prepared to consider all forms of dark fiction works and are looking for stories that capture the imagination of the Three Crow staff. Please check submissions guides prior to submitting.

www.threecrowpress.com
www.morriganezine.com

www.ingramcontent.com/pod-product-compliance
Lightning Source LLC
Chambersburg PA
CBHW030246200626
46816CB00002BA/533